An emotion fla... hot and hard.

Not recognizing it as jealousy, she called it anger and tried to twist her hands out of Theo's grasp, but his grip only tightened.

"I ask you again, Julie." He felt a quick, sharp jolt of panic and had to dig inside himself for the strength to push it away. "Do you want to go back?"

"No!" The denial rose to her lips without a thought. "No," she repeated. "But I will not be your mistress."

"No, you will not be my mistress," Theo agreed softly. "My lover perhaps, but never my mistress."

"You would seduce me?"

"Seduce? No." He smiled slowly, first with his mouth, then with his eyes. "Mistresses are seduced. Lovers come of their own free will."

Dear Reader,

Nina Beaumont is no stranger to her European settings; in fact, she has lived in Austria since 1970. So it comes as no surprise that she has set her fifth historical, *Tapestry of Dreams,* against the rich backdrop of nineteenth-century Europe. In this dramatic sequel to her previous work, a gifted nurse joins a former soldier on a dangerous journey to right the wrongs of his past. Don't miss this passionate tale of danger and desire.

And be sure to keep an eye out for *Addie's Lament,* by DeLoras Scott, this month's Women of the West title that tells the heartwarming love story of a young woman determined to make a better life for herself, and the man who seems to be always getting in her way.

Also this month are *Once a Maverick,* the first in an exciting Western trilogy from Theresa Michaels featuring the Kincaid brothers, and a Medieval tale from Merline Lovelace, *His Lady's Ransom,* the story of a nobleman who tries to discourage his brother's infatuation with a notorious widow. And don't miss either Theresa Michaels or Merline Lovelace in our August short-story collection, RENEGADES, featuring *New York Times* bestselling author Heather Graham Pozzessere.

Whatever your taste in historical reading, we hope you'll enjoy all four titles, available wherever Harlequin Historicals are sold.

Sincerely,

Tracy Farrell
Senior Editor

Please address questions and book requests to:
Harlequin Reader Service
U.S.: 3010 Walden Ave., P.O. Box 1325, Buffalo, NY 14269
Canadian: P.O. Box 609, Fort Erie, Ont. L2A 5X3

NINA BEAUMONT

TAPESTRY OF DREAMS

Harlequin Books

TORONTO • NEW YORK • LONDON
AMSTERDAM • PARIS • SYDNEY • HAMBURG
STOCKHOLM • ATHENS • TOKYO • MILAN
MADRID • WARSAW • BUDAPEST • AUCKLAND

ISBN 0-373-28878-6

TAPESTRY OF DREAMS

Books by Nina Beaumont

Harlequin Historicals

Sapphire Magic #101
Promises To Keep #153
Across Time #203
Tapestry of Fate #246
Tapestry of Dreams #278

NINA BEAUMONT

is of Russian parentage and has a family tree that includes the Counts Stroganoff and a Mongolian Khan. Born in Salzburg, she grew up in Massachusetts. In 1970 she moved to Austria, where she lives in the country with her husband and an overly friendly schnauzer.

An avid history buff, she enjoys traveling, which gives her the opportunity to use the five languages she speaks. She also loves music, books and the French Impressionists.

Her writing keeps her more than busy, but she also finds time to work as a translator and teach adult English classes.

To my Austrian friends who have helped me keep my sanity during a difficult period of my life.

My dear friend, Anneliese Notter, who has saved me a midsized fortune in counseling fees.

My oldest friends, Karin and Günther Steffen, and their children, children-in-law and grandchildren, Christoph and Uli, Bettina and Michael with Matthias and Alexander and Dieter and Elke.

My young friends from my Italian class, Barbara, Eva, Ilse, Michaela, Mojza, Robert and, last but not least, Horsti.

Chapter One

He was floating. Was it air? Water? He could not tell. Theo tried to move, but his limbs felt as if they were caught in quicksand. Where was he? He concentrated on remembering, but somehow the memory would not come. Deciding that the pain had probably driven him to empty yet another bottle of French brandy, he yielded to the numbness. He would wake up soon enough with the pain in his head a close second to the pain in his legs—and his heart. He never could decide which one was worse. It was then that he heard the voice.

"Can you hear me?"

The voice was soft and as sweet as honey, like one of the waltzes his mother and his sister liked to play on the pianoforte. He wanted to answer, but his tongue was thick and just as disinclined to move as his limbs.

He was coming awake already, Julie thought as she bent over him. She had seen the telltale twitch of his hands, the quiver of his eyelids. Her teeth worried her lip as she thought of the pain he would be waking up to. Gently she opened his mouth and placed the medicine Dr. von Berg had given her on his tongue, catching the faint scent of ether that still clung to him.

Forgetting that her feet hurt after the long day, she ignored the straight-backed chair that stood next to the bed. With a light hand, she brushed back the tawny hair that had stuck to his forehead in damp curls. Almost as pale as the white linen he lay on, he looked very young despite the white hair that peppered his temples and the lines that pain had carved around his mouth.

Strange that he and Dr. von Berg were brothers, she mused. There seemed to be no physical similarity between them beyond the fact that both were tall and lean. Her fingers stroked over the fine lines that fanned out from the outer corners of his eyes. Were they the same gentle smoky gray as his brother's eyes? she wondered. As her hands drifted further to rub his temples, Julie lost herself in a fantasy of Maximilian von Berg's gray eyes looking at her with the same love that lived in her heart.

Theo felt a cool, soft hand on his forehead. Maryka, he thought, and wanted to smile. It gave him so much pleasure when sweet, young Maryka with the tiny, delicate features of a porcelain doll touched him. Then, like poison seeping into the bloodstream, the memory filtered in that Maryka was gone, stolen by the Russians he himself had led to her doorstep. As the grief and the guilt and the hatred wound through him, his dry lips formed her name.

A ghost of a sound jolted her out of her reverie and Julie looked down, thinking that he had awoken. But he still lay motionless. As her hand continued to stroke his forehead, she felt a wave of sadness and need well out of him, as palpable to her as if it were something physical.

Her compassionate, young heart went out to him and she covered his hand with her small one. It was a long-jointed, slender hand. The hand of a poet or painter, she decided. Or a dreamer. She curved her fingers around his and settled down to wait and dream her own dreams.

When Theo opened his eyes, the world around him was blurred. The only things he could distinguish were the vague contours of a woman's face floating above him and the lemony scent of verbena.

"Maryka?" The sound of his own rusty voice pushed him a step further into consciousness and he remembered again that Maryka had been taken from him.

Theo heard the honey-sweet sound of the woman's voice as she spoke, but the meaning of the words did not reach him. As he closed his eyes again the memories came trickling back. The pain. Days and weeks and months of pain that stretched into years. Max. The hospital. The operation. Strange, he thought. There was no pain now, even though Max had said the pain would still be there before it began to get better. If it began to get better.

When he opened his eyes again, the woman's face was a little clearer. He saw eyes tilted upward at the outer edges, their color the golden brown of Hungarian Tokay wine. And a wide mouth that was gently curved and moving in words he could not understand.

His eyes were slightly more focused the next time he opened them, Julie thought. And they were not gray, she saw. Nor were they blue, but an odd combination of the two colors. A little like a bright sky emerging in patches from the morning mist.

Theo frowned. It puzzled him that he could see only her face as if it were a disembodied image drifting above him, surrounded by white clouds. Then the understanding flashed through him like a solution to a complicated chess problem. Suddenly everything was so clear that he almost smiled.

He had died. That was why he felt no pain. Relief that the pain was gone forever wound through him before it clashed with bitter anger that he had been cheated of his revenge.

The disembodied face must be an angel then, he deduced. But then he remembered that he did not believe in angels. Nor in heaven. And hell, if it existed, existed on earth.

The face leaned closer. The scent of verbena that teased his nostrils again was so real that the puzzlement returned.

"Who are you?" he managed to say.

"My name is Julie. Sister Julie." Julie felt his pain fighting to surface. Wanting to give him some respite, at least for a little while longer, she placed one light hand on his chest while she stroked her fingers over his forehead with the other. Focusing her concentration on him fully, she let the light and the power pour through her.

Already she could feel him calm and she smiled. "Close your eyes," she whispered. "Sleep now."

Did angels speak French? The absurd question nudged the edges of his consciousness. Before he could brush it aside, he felt her cool, soft hands on his chest, on his face. A calm stole through him and, although he was not aware of it, hope.

As he slipped into a healing sleep, Theo was truly at peace for the first time in four years.

When Theo next awoke, his eyes were clear and the pain that tore at him told him that he was very much alive.

"Well, Max—" he fought a losing battle for the flippant tone they had always affected with each other "—how well did you wield your knife?"

"As soon as I can tell, you will be the first to know." Max curved his hand over his younger brother's shoulder, the gesture belying his seemingly insouciant words.

Guilt weighed heavy on him as he studied Theo. The lines that bracketed his mouth, the bitterness in his blue gray eyes made him look older than his twenty-nine years. He remembered too well the carefree, dreamy, artless young man his brother had been a scant five years ago. He remembered that it was his fault that Theo had been pulled into the inferno of the revolution from which he had emerged an angry man, wounded in spirit and body, his only goal revenge—a very personal revenge.

"How do you feel?" Max asked, and suppressed the desire to take Theo into his arms as he would one of his own children.

"Like a Christmas goose that has just been carved with a dull knife." Theo's breath caught at the pain that was shooting through his back.

"Can you be a little more specific?"

A muscle in his cheek jumped furiously as he gritted his teeth against the pain. "No." Even as he pressed the single word out, the realization registered that somehow the pain was different than it had been before.

Max nodded to Julie, who stood at the foot of the narrow iron bed. She folded back the blanket and held her breath as she pricked first one big toe then the other with a needle.

Swearing, Theo tried to raise his head. "The devil—what are you doing?"

The relief that Max felt was so great that he felt his knees go weak. "Just checking, little brother."

Theo remembered what Max had explained before the operation. That he could not be sure that he would be able to remove the shell fragments from his back without damaging his spine and sentencing him to permanent loss of the use of his legs. He swallowed as he fought to tamp down the hope that welled up in him. "Does that mean—"

Max squeezed his brother's shoulder. "I do not know if I got everything out. I do not know if you will be free of pain." He let out a long breath. "But it looks like you have a chance—a chance," he repeated when he saw the desperate hope shoot into his brother's eyes, "of walking again."

Theo acknowledged Max's words with a brusque nod. The two men exchanged a long look where thanks were silently given and silently accepted. Then Max gestured to Julie to approach.

"This is Sister Julie, Theo." He touched her arm briefly, unaware of the quiver that went through her. "She will be taking care of you."

Stunned, Theo stared at the face he remembered from his vision. She was dressed in a simple gray gown covered by a white, bibbed apron and a white coif around her face that exposed only a narrow band of dark hair above her forehead. That was why he'd seen only her face surrounded by white. That was why his half-conscious mind had taken her for an angel. For some reason, the logical explanation annoyed him, as if she had purposely misled him.

Julie took stock of the frown and the chiseled mouth that had turned sulky. He would not be an easy patient, she thought with a small sigh. But she would give him her best care because she would do the same for anyone—and because she worshiped his brother.

Theo remembered her cool, soft hands touching him. Remembered thinking for a moment that it was Maryka. He took a long look at her. Unadorned by paints or jewels or fancy coiffures, the serene beauty of her face struck him all the more strongly. "Are you some kind of a nun?" he snapped, unsure of why the thought bothered him.

"No. I am not any kind of a nun." She spoke in the perfectly accented French she had learned from her parents. "I am a nurse." She had become used to the different ways men looked at her—with yearning, reverence, curiosity, even the very occasional lasciviousness. But for some reason, his rude, speculative gaze made her feel uncomfortable. She lowered her eyes and began to fold the blanket into pleats.

"I do not need a nurse." Theo gave Max a surly look. "Send me Fritz. He has been taking care of me long enough to care for me now."

"I am afraid I have to disagree with you. I've put too much effort into you, Theo, to have it ruined by improper care." Max smiled. "I suggest you be properly grateful. Sister Julie is the best nurse I have. But there is no reason why Fritz cannot attend you part of the time if you want."

Julie felt a jolt of pleasure at his praise. As she looked up at Max, her eyes solemn and reverent, her hands tensed on Theo's blanket, pulling it tight over his shoulders.

"What are you doing?"

Julie started at his growl, her fingers tightening further on the blanket for a moment before she released it.

"I'm sorry." As she smoothed the blanket, she saw the belligerent look in his eye. Wanting to forestall further conflict, she covered his hand with hers, instinctively opening herself to the power that always seemed to hover above her, like a ray of sunlight.

"You should rest now. The faster you recover—" the corners of her mouth tipped upward in a quick, mischievous smile "—the faster you will be rid of me."

The metamorphosis from serene Madonna to saucy minx puzzled him, but Theo felt himself settle. The tension seeped out of him and, with it, some of the pain receded. Although he would have denied it, he did not look away from her smile, nor retreat from her touch.

Max observed the exchange between his brother and Julie. Saw how she defused his anger. Saw how her touch eased him. He had done the right thing, he assured himself. Theo needed a miracle and this girl with her gentle soul and healing hands was the only one who could give it to him.

He had done his best to put Theo's body back together, but unless his spirit, his heart healed, everything would be for naught. His gaze wandered over to where Julie bent over his brother and he felt a ray of hope.

Theo was drifting along the edge of sleep when the scent of verbena insinuated itself into his consciousness. He opened his eyes, but the dim room was empty. He told himself that it was not disappointment he felt, but relief. He wanted to be alone. He wanted to be left in peace. He did not want anyone. He repeated the words to himself like a litany until his mind began to blur.

The drug Max had given him to take the edge off the pain took him under again and he did not feel the light touch of Julie's hands.

Why had she felt compelled to stop in Count Berg's room when she should have been on her way home long ago? Julie wondered. For the most part she had learned not to question her intuition, but simply to follow it, but this time the compulsion to ask questions had been as strong as the compulsion to look in on him one more time.

Leaning back against the door, she studied the man who lay on the narrow bed. The shadows softened the imperious planes and angles of his face. There was something about him that drew her. Something more than her compassion for the physical pain he was suffering. Something more than the fact that he shared bloodlines and childhood memories with the man she was so hopelessly in love with.

She moved closer to the bed. She knew almost nothing about him beyond the few facts his brother had shared with her. But somehow she knew that pain lived in his heart. Was that where the pull lay? she wondered. Did she recognize his pain because she had so much of her own pain to live with?

Moving up to the bed, she put her hands on his chest as if her touch could lift the pain out and away from him the way a magnet lifts a handful of scattered pins.

Theo could feel the dream coming and tensed against it. In the beginning it had come every night, turning sleep into a living hell until he had been afraid to close his eyes. Until he had been grateful for the pain in his back, in his legs, which kept him awake until he was too exhausted to dream.

He was slumped over his mount's neck, just barely able to keep himself in the saddle. The sickly sweet scent of his own blood was in his nostrils. The pain had faded to a dull throb. Only an occasional flash of agony had him gasping for breath.

He had to get to Maryka. He had to warn her. To help her get away. To hide. The final battle was lost and soon the Russian and Austrian troops would be swarming the flat Hungarian countryside, drunk on blood and victory.

He was within sight of the cabin when he felt his muscles give way, sending him tumbling to the ground. Raising himself on his elbows, he crawled forward. The effort and the heat of the August day had sweat pouring down his face, blurring his vision.

His blood was thundering in his head as the cabin door opened and Maryka came running out, crying his name. It was not until he saw the horses that he realized the thunder had not been his blood but the sound of hooves on the sun-baked ground.

The soldiers reined to a halt in a half circle around them. The sudden stillness was broken by a single man who urged his horse a few steps forward, then dismounted. He looked at Maryka for a long moment, then said something over his shoulder in a language Theo did not understand.

A grimy soldier cantered up to Maryka and plucked her from where she stood with the same carelessness with which he would have broken off a flower. She screamed only once before he silenced her, pulling up her skirt to stuff the fabric in her mouth and clamping his meaty hand over it.

Horrified, Theo pushed himself up from the ground. He had managed to maneuver himself onto his knees when a shadow fell over him. It took no longer than a breath for him to recognize the uniform of a Russian colonel, to take stock of the man's face, which looked like a sculpture that had been broken and badly repaired—the nose flattened and bent to one side, one cheekbone higher than the other, the skin scarred. It took no longer than a breath for the Russian to plant his boot on Theo's chest with such force that he heard his ribs crack.

Tipping over like a felled tree, Theo lay on his back, unable to move, barely able to breathe. As he stared up at the Russian's face, the curses formed on his lips, but no sound came. The man laughed sharply and walked away.

The ground shuddered as the soldiers rode away. Helpless, Theo lay there under the brutal August sun and swore that he would never forget that face. He swore that he would live to free Maryka. He swore that he would live to kill.

"Shh. It is all right. You were only dreaming."

Theo woke to the sound of the honey-sweet voice and the scent of verbena. He could feel his body quivering in the aftermath of the dream, but he was too weak to stop the trembling. Ashamed of his own weakness, he kept his eyes closed.

This time he knew exactly who was touching him. Even without opening his eyes, he could see her serene features. Her mouth would be curved with that gentle smile. And there would be a touch of sadness in her topaz eyes. Or would there be derision there instead?

The horrible pictures of the dream returned, so real that he could smell the dust, the blood, and a new wave of shudders went through his body. The pictures would go away, he knew, if he opened his eyes, but he stubbornly kept them closed, afraid that he would see mockery in the young nurse's eyes.

"Open your eyes," Julie coaxed. "You are in Turin, in your brother's hospital. You are safe." Cupping his cheek in one hand, she stroked his damp forehead with the other.

He did not want her here, Theo told himself. He wanted to be alone with his shameful memories. He wanted to push the cool, soft hands away, but he could not. He needed their touch, their solace, too badly.

When he finally lifted his eyelids, the pain she saw there made Julie gasp. She had learned to deal with the physical pain of her patients, but she was completely unprepared for the mental anguish she saw in Theo's eyes. Needing to do something, anything, to ease it, and yet afraid that what her gift could give him would not be enough, she lowered her head and brushed her mouth against his hollow cheek.

Theo felt her lips on his skin and the needs that had been buried for years had him turning his head, as a desert plant turns toward a spring rain, so they were mouth to mouth.

For a long moment they remained still, their lips chaste, unaware of the currents that had begun to course beneath the surface.

When he moved beneath her, Julie instinctively retreated. Stunned, her pulse unsteady, she sat up as embarrassment and guilt surged through her, obliterating the feeling that something momentous had happened to her.

There was confusion in her eyes and he closed his eyes against it. But her image stayed with him, a bulwark against a return of the dream. And against the darkness.

Julie felt her tension ease as his eyes closed. The drug and his pain had drawn them together for a moment out of time. Tomorrow, in the light, she told herself, they would not even remember it.

For the second time in as many days, she took his hand. But this time, as she waited for him to sleep, she did not dream of Maximilian von Berg.

Chapter Two

Julie finished putting the fresh dressings on Theo's back, and together with Max von Berg's assistant, she began to wrap the bandages around him.

"Are you almost through here?"

"In a few minutes." Julie smiled at the young doctor. "Did you need something else, Dr. Schalk?"

Coloring slightly, the young man shook his head. "I just thought to accompany you home," he said softly. "If I may."

Before Julie could reply, Theo snapped, "I suggest you make your assignations elsewhere."

Her patience with Count Theodore Berg was wearing more than a little thin, Julie decided as she bit her lip to suppress the sharp retort that came to her mind. Ever since that evening when she had soothed him after his nightmare, he had not missed a single opportunity to take his ill temper out on her, but this was the first time she had seen him take it out on anyone else.

Seeing the young doctor's discomfort, she nodded to him. "I can finish up here."

Deciding that, in this case, discretion was the better part of valor, Dr. Schalk picked up the suit coat he had discarded earlier. Sending Julie a shy smile, he left the room.

"Was it necessary to snap at him like that?" Julie demanded, when the door had closed behind him.

"Him?" Theo raised his head. "I was snapping at you."

"How comforting. I should thank you for that, I suppose."

Her tart tone had him raising his head further. "Ah, she bites back after all." His eyebrows rose in a sardonic curve. "And here I thought that you were a model of Christian forbearance."

Julie pulled the bandage taut and tied its ends before she looked at him. With his tawny hair tumbling over his forehead, he looked like a small, naughty boy and she forgot that his tone was caustic and his eyes bitter. "I am." Her lips quirked in a smile, belying the cool, haughty look in her eyes. "I just decided to make an exception in your case."

He stared at her for a moment, then he laughed, surprising both of them.

When had he last laughed? he asked himself, and found that he could not remember.

When had he last laughed? she asked herself, and found that suddenly all his faultfinding, his testiness of the past days were forgotten.

Max paused in the doorway, his heart stumbling at the sound of Theo's laugh. The only sound to compare with it had been the first time he had heard Felicity laugh and truly mean it.

"Well," he said, swallowing past the lump in his throat, "are you going to let me in the joke?"

"Your brother was being difficult."

"Your nurse," Theo mimicked, "was being impudent."

"No less than you deserved," Julie murmured as she skillfully turned Theo onto his back even before Max could reach out to help her.

"She is vexed because I reprimanded her for making assignations with her sweetheart at my bedside." The caustic tone was back.

"Sweetheart?"

Julie raised her eyes to Max's face. His eyebrows had risen in question like raven's wings and his eyes mirrored astonishment. Suddenly it was clear, so very clear to her that he had never seen her as a woman before, let alone a desirable one, and her heart broke.

"Ah, I see. So that is why my friend, Horst Schalk, has been mooning about like a lost soul."

The gentle smile he sent her did nothing to help the pain that was twisting her heart.

"Unless you have another task for me, I would like to go now." Pride kept her chin up and her eyes steady.

"Go ahead. I—" The joking comment Max had been about to make faded at the lost, reproachful look in her eyes. Of course, he thought, for once his intuitiveness deserting him, she was embarrassed. He had become so accustomed to her quiet efficiency, he tended to forget that she was young and pretty. But then, he had never really *looked* at a woman since Felicity had come into his life six years ago.

Both men stared at the door after it had closed behind her, both moved, both uncomfortable without quite knowing why.

"Where did you find her?" Theo asked with the cynicism that was his refuge from any unwelcome emotion. "In some orphanage? On the street?"

Max shook his head. "It was the other way around. She found me."

"Whatever. She is another addition to your lifelong collection of strays." He frowned, not quite certain why he felt such a need to debase her.

If it had been anyone else but Theo, Max would have taken exception to his contemptuous tone. "Julie is no more a stray than you or I, Theo."

"Do tell."

"Does it signify?" Max shrugged with as much nonchalance as he could muster. "She is an excellent nurse and I would say that is all that matters." He sent him the same smile he used when he tried to cajole his four-year-old daughter Genny into eating her carrots. "It would seem that you are feeling your oats today." His tone was hearty. Too hearty. "They tell me you refused to take any more of the poppy syrup."

"You know, Max, considering that you led a clandestine life for years, you can be a very poor dissembler. And that charming smile of yours may work on Genny, but not on me." Theo narrowed his eyes. "What is it that you are trying so hard not to tell me?"

"It does not signify, Theo. Why don't you just leave it alone?"

It was not like Max to be so evasive, Theo thought as he watched his brother stuff his hands into his pockets and pace to the window. Suddenly it was of paramount importance to know just who the girl who nursed him was, and his mind raced as he examined the possibilities. When he reached what seemed the only logical conclusion, he laughed aloud.

"Tell me, Max, is she my niece or our half sister?"

Max turned and met his brother's eyes. For a moment he was tempted to let him believe either one of the possibilities.

"No, Theo." He shook his head. "She is neither one."

"Damn it—" Theo winced as he propped himself up on an elbow "—who is she, then? And why are you bending over backward to keep it from me?"

Max capitulated. He had known that the moment would come when he would have to tell Theo the truth. "Because she is Russian."

Hatred and a cold fury flashed into Theo's eyes, turning them the color of steel. When he remembered that moment days ago when their lips had briefly met, the fury became colder still. Then he saw the edginess in his brother's eyes. "That is not all, is it?"

Max drew in a deep breath. "Her name is Princess Julie Muromsky."

"And—" Theo called on every bit of his strength to say aloud the name of the man who had taken Maryka and left him to die "—Boris Muromsky is...?"

"Her uncle."

"How could you? How could you let her touch me?" The words spilled out of him like poison from a lanced wound. "Or did you have a little homeopathic theory of having a Russian cure me of my hatred for the Russians?" His chiseled mouth curled in a sneer.

"I gave it a great deal of thought before I made the decision. You can believe that."

Theo snorted derisively and Max felt his own temper erupt. "Damn you, Theo, I wanted the best care for you and she was the one who could give it to you." He began to pace. How could he explain that she was a healer beyond her competence as a nurse? How could he explain the feeling he had had—that he still had—that she was the only one who could really help him?

"Besides, she has nothing to do with what happened to you." He whirled to face Theo. "Nothing. Her parents had to leave Russia after the 1825 rebellion. They are exiles just like you and me because they fought for freedom and lost."

"Get out of here, Max. And do not ever send her here again."

"Theo—"

Theo met his brother's eyes and held them. "Get out of here." Deliberately he turned his head aside to stare at the white wall. "Leave me alone."

He would not think of her, he told himself. He would not. He would think of Maryka. He closed his eyes and tried to call up his young lover's image, but, no matter how hard he tried, all he could see were separate features that would not merge into a face.

Four years of constant pain and disability had taught him to discipline his thoughts, to channel them. Controlling his mind had been his way out of the depths of despair where pain and guilt and his own helplessness had plunged him. Why then were his thoughts evading his grasp now, becoming even more wayward, more willful? They seemed to have taken on a life of their own, taunting him, provoking him.

He fought back. But even as he did, he knew that the weapons at his disposal were paltry.

Had he not hated her from the beginning? You are lying, the voice in his head said. But he pushed it away.

Had he not known that she was vile and base even before he had known that she was related by blood to a man who was vile and base and worse? You are unjust, his conscience said. But he ignored it.

The room grew dim, then dark. Night came. And with it came those hours that make the strongest man weak. Those hours that bring doubts to the most confident of men. Theo clung to his lies, his injustice, his contrived hatred with a desperate grip, because on some unconscious level he knew that if he did not, the thought that he would not see her ever again would be unbearable.

When he finally fell into a restless sleep, he dreamed of Julie.

* * *

Julie saw Dr. von Berg at the top of the stairs that led to the hospital from half a block away. She ducked her head and her steps slowed. For the first time since she had been working at the hospital, she was not in a hurry to arrive. Nor was she in a hurry to face Maximilian von Berg.

She was a silly little fool, she told herself. How many times had she berated herself for falling so desperately in love with Dr. von Berg? How many times had she tried to talk herself out of her feelings? But nothing had worked. But then how could it, when every day she toiled at the side of the most wonderful man in the whole world? A man who was kind and capable. A man who healed.

Risking a look from beneath her lashes, she saw that he was still standing where she had first seen him. He was looking straight at her, but he was not smiling that gentle smile of his. Instead his eyebrows were knit in a frown and his eyes were worried. Pushing her embarrassment and the ache in her heart aside, Julie speeded her steps.

"Will you come to my office before you start, Sister Julie?"

"Is something wrong?" She had reached out to touch his arm before she remembered that it was not her place to do so. "Your brother has not taken a turn for the worse, has he?"

Max shrugged. "In a manner of speaking." He saw the distress come into her eyes. He saw them grow warm with emotion. He saw the compassion there, but not the adoration. If he felt uneasy, he ascribed it to what he had to say to her. "I will be in my office," he said, and hurried off.

Dr. von Berg was standing at the single window of his cubicle of an office when Julie entered. The moment she closed the door, he began to speak.

"Do you remember how I asked you not to speak of your Russian background to my brother?"

"Of course. You said that he had been mistreated by my countrymen during the Hungarian uprising. I never said anything to him." Julie took a step backward when he turned around, his face grim. "I swear I did not."

"I know you did not." His mien softened at the distress and the earnest innocence in her eyes. "But I did."

"But—"

"He questioned me about you. When I evaded, he—" Max broke off, unwilling, unable to voice what Theo had suspected. "Suffice it to say that I told him who you were." He ignored the stab of guilt that accompanied his decision not to elaborate and tell her that the man who had abused Theo was the uncle she had never seen. It would only be a useless piece of information that would upset her further. "And now—"

"Now he does not want me to care for him any longer," she finished.

He nodded.

"And you? What do you want?" Julie's breath caught in her throat as she realized that she was talking about Theo von Berg and yet she was not.

Max closed the distance between them. Smiling, he took her hands in his, unaware of the undertones of her question. "I cannot explain it. Everything I have learned as a doctor, as a scientist, tells me that such things do not exist. But your hands work miracles." He squeezed her hands lightly. "And I want miracles for Theo."

Those were not the words she wanted to hear, but when he smiled at her like that, she would have willingly entered the jaws of hell for his sake.

"I will do what I can." She found she could do no more than whisper.

"He will make it difficult for you." He released her hands.

"Then everything will be as it was." Now that he was no longer touching her, her voice and her sense of humor returned. "Will it not?"

Max laughed ruefully. "Yes. He has not been exactly a model patient before this, has he?"

"He will get well with or without me," Julie said, remembering the dogged determination in Theo's eyes. "He wants it too badly not to."

Max nodded. But Theo wanted to get well for all the wrong reasons. Perhaps this young girl could give him the right ones. Still, as Julie left his office, he could not rid himself of the misgivings that crawled up his spine and he wondered, not for the first time, if his loyalty to family had gone too far.

Julie pressed her hand to her stomach to quiet the jitters there. He would do no more to her than he had done already, she told herself. He would snarl. He would complain. He would look at her in that surly way that she found so strangely attractive and that always made her want to ruffle his hair.

But when she entered the room, her chin was stubbornly tilted upward and there was fire in her eyes. She ignored the surly glance that Fritz sent her. When he left the room with a muttered imprecation, she moved forward.

Theo heard the soft click of the door and turned his face toward the wall. The restless sleep that had been fraught with dreams had left him listless and he had little interest in seeing who had come to change his dressings this morning.

The faint scent of verbena teased him and he felt a spurt of anger that she was not only haunting his dreams but his waking hours. When the scent intensified, he turned with an imprudent swiftness that had his breath catching at the fierceness of the pain.

Nothing had prepared him for the violence of the emotions that streaked through him. The anger was undiminished, like a solid fortress wall. But, at the same time, a vivid joy burst through it, dazzling him for one insane moment. And in tandem with it came the fear of loss of control.

The play of emotions in his eyes was so quick that Julie could not identify them, but they moved her in a strange way she could not have described. She set down the basin with dressings and bandages that she carried and moved to stand at the side of the bed.

"I told you once before that the quicker you recovered, the quicker you would be rid of me." She folded her arms under her breasts. "I can only repeat it."

"Damn it—" Theo struggled up onto his elbows. "I told Max—"

"I know what you told him." Gently but firmly she pushed him back down on the bed. Leaving her hand in the middle of his chest, she bent down toward him. "What kind of a man are you to blame me for what some faceless, nameless Russians did to you, just because I am of Russian blood?"

Theo stared at her. "Faceless? Nameless?" He opened his mouth to tell her what Max obviously had omitted, but he lost himself for a moment in her golden eyes, which were full of sparks. Then she was speaking again and it was somehow too late to say anything.

"Yes. Now you listen to me very carefully because I am only going to say this once."

She could feel his body warmth through the thin linen shirt he was wearing and her hand began to tingle, distracting her for a moment, but she forced her mind back to what she had to say.

"Your brother has done everything in his power to make you well again. Now it is your turn. And if that means that you need to suffer my presence, then you will suffer it." She pulled in a deep breath. "If you have no gratitude for him, then have at least some common courtesy."

Anger streaked through him again, but it was not the wretched, morbid anger he had felt before. Anger that had nothing to do with *her*. This anger was clean and sharp and hot—and it was for her only.

Theo gripped her wrist. "How dare you say that? You have no concept of what I feel."

His fingers circled her wrist painfully, but Julie smiled. "Be angry at me. Me." She tapped her breastbone with her free hand. "Not because I happen to be Russian, but because I have made you angry."

His grip on her wrist gentled and the anger in his eyes faded, giving way to puzzlement and a reluctant admiration.

"Why are you doing this?"

"This is what I do. I help people to heal," she said, deliberately misunderstanding him.

"No. Why are you doing this for me?"

Julie shrugged, reluctant to let him see her wounds.

"You are doing it because Max asked you." Again he felt a streak of anger, this time for his brother. "You are doing it for him, are you not?"

"Yes." Her eyes met his and held. Because his grip on her wrist had tightened again, she added defiantly, "For him I would stand up to anyone. Even you."

"Touché." His mouth tilted up in a lopsided smile. He had seen enough of the love and devotion his brother inspired not to be surprised, and yet he found himself resenting it.

As he released her wrist, he saw that his fingers had left marks. Frowning, he reached for her again, this time his fingers gentle.

"I am sorry." He rubbed his thumb over the reddened skin. There was a tracery of pale blue veins beneath the delicate skin and he wondered how such fragile hands could work so hard.

"It's all right." Julie pulled her hand away. Although she would not have admitted it, she had felt something when he had touched her. "I do not bruise easily."

Theo gave her a long look, surprised by the subtle warmth that wound through him. "I wonder."

"I need to get to work," she said briskly, refusing to acknowledge his last words. "You are not the only patient I have to care for."

Her hands quick and efficient, she began to unwrap his bandages. As always, Theo struggled against the tranquil contentment that stole over him when she touched him. As always, he lost the battle.

Chapter Three

They had settled on a kind of armed truce, Julie thought as she opened the window to let in the crisp air that seemed to carry the first hint of spring, although it was just after Christmas. Theo von Berg rarely let an opportunity go by without sniping at her, but that was purely personal, she mused. The fact that she was his enemy by the accident of her birth no longer seemed to matter. There were no more pitched battles.

But they certainly locked horns often enough, she mused, thinking of how he had cursed her when he had started walking—first with a chair to support him, then crutches, then two canes. And she teased and provoked and bullied him every time, knowing that if he was angry with her, he would feel his own pain less. She figured they were due for another battle today.

Yesterday she had watched him try to negotiate the staircase that led to the garden and fail. She had seen the fury, the self-disgust in his eyes. It was time to take the next step.

Turning around, she approached the chair where Theo was sitting.

He frowned suspiciously when he saw her mischievous smile. "Since you are grinning like that," he grumbled, "I can only assume that you've devised some new method of torture for me."

"Your abilities of deduction are truly excellent," she said dryly as she plucked the blanket from his lap and folded it away. "However, not quite precise today."

His eyes narrowed. "What do you mean?"

"I have devised *two* new methods of torture for you today." She kept her tone as light as she could. "That way I thought I would save myself one tongue-lashing."

"What—"

"Today, Count Berg, you will graduate to only one cane and—" she waved her hand in a little flourish "—that cane will support you down the steps for a little turn in the garden."

"I need both canes, damn it. You know that." Theo felt the sweat break out on his forehead at the thought of negotiating the stairs. She did not know it, he thought, but he had stood at the top of the steps just yesterday. One step, just one step had been all he had been able to manage before the ground had rushed up at him. Before his muscles had begun to tremble. Before his head had begun to spin. "I cannot—"

Julie shook her head. "There are three possibilities, my dear count." Her hands curled in the folds of her skirt as she braced herself to say the cruel words. "You are too lazy, too weak or too afraid. If you want to, you can do it."

The pain she felt at her own harsh words she goaded him with was offset by satisfaction at the anger that flashed into his eyes, turning them a steel blue. She handed him the cane and stepped back to allow him to rise.

"Good." She ignored the glare he sent her. "Now close your eyes and take a few deep breaths."

As he obeyed her, she moved so that she stood at right angles to him and placed one hand against the small of his back and one on the hands that were gripping the cane. Closing her eyes, as well, Julie pictured him strong and straight and without pain, enveloped in the light that poured through her.

Theo felt the calm steal through him even before he realized that some of the pain had ebbed. He would probably never be completely pain-free, Max had explained to him. Too many muscles and nerves had been irrevocably damaged for that. But someday he would walk again unaided. He held on to that.

Julie felt his grip on the cane ease a little. "We will walk now," she said softly, and moved to stand at his side.

She took a step. When he did not move, she looked up at him.

"How do you do it?"

His eyes no longer held anger and they had softened to the color of a misty morning. Dazed, Julie could only shake her head.

He lifted one hand toward her cheek before he remembered that he had no right to touch her. He loved Maryka, he reminded himself. He had no right to touch any other woman when he loved Maryka, whose fate lay heavy on his conscience. He had no right to touch another woman when he had vengeance to wreak. He let his hand fall to his side.

"I am furious at you. I hate you," he said without heat. "Then you put your hands on me and I feel—" Unable to find the right word, he shook his head. "It is like a drug, but instead of deadening the senses, it revives them."

She shrugged because mention of the gift she possessed disconcerted and troubled her. She did not understand it, she could not define it, and when she thought about it logically, it made her feel like a freak in a circus sideshow. Even her parents, who loved her deeply, were confused and alarmed by it.

"Come now," she urged. "If you need more support than the cane gives you, put your hand on my shoulder."

Side by side they slowly moved down the corridor.

Theo could feel the sweat trickling down his back as he lowered himself onto the garden bench. He had made it, he thought, feeling suddenly like a conqueror instead of a man who had taken the better part of a half hour to walk a stretch that would have taken a toddler a few minutes.

His breath caught as the spasms shot through his legs and back, but, for the first time, he did not curse the pain. No, he welcomed it. For the first time the pain was a badge of honor for a task well-done. For the first time he really believed that someday he would be well again.

Julie watched him. His nostrils fluttered from his uneven breathing and the lines around his mouth had whitened from the pain. Feeling instinctively that he did not want relief now, she did not touch him. But she wanted to touch him, she realized. To touch him and to share for a moment the happiness she knew he was feeling.

Slowly his breathing evened, the lines of his body relaxed as the pain eased a little. Soon he will be well, she thought, and then he will be gone. She pressed a hand against her chest where her heart had grown heavy. And with him that special link that connected her to Maximilian von Berg would be gone, as well.

Suddenly she saw the future stretched out in front of her like a barren, windswept landscape. The vision lasted only a moment before it disappeared, but it left her feeling off balance. There would be others to care for, she reminded herself. Others who would need her.

Theo turned toward Julie, wanting to share the moment of triumph with her. She was facing him, but the faraway look in her eyes told him that she did not see him. Where had she gone? he wondered. A sudden lightning bolt of emotion blazed through him. It dissipated before he could identify it as jealousy, leaving him perplexed.

He had no business feeling any kind of emotion where she was concerned, he reminded himself. His obligations lay elsewhere. Besides, he would do well to remember just who she was. The old images of loss and helplessness rose, bringing bitterness with them.

Julie surfaced from her reverie, chiding herself for neglecting her patient. Whatever words she was going to say died on her lips as she saw some violent emotion flash in Theo's eyes. It reached out to touch her as if it had been meant for her. Before she could grasp what she had seen, his eyes went steely with bitterness.

"Is something wrong?"

He laughed a bark of a laugh. The feeling of triumph had fled and he was a cripple again. "Only that I feel like I just ran from Marathon to Athens." He laughed again sharply. "On all fours."

"Don't you dare make fun of yourself," she flared. Catching the lapel of his jacket in one hand, she shook him.

Again Theo laughed, but this time the sound held humor. "What a strange mixture you are." His gaze warmed as his eyes leisurely scanned her face. "One moment you are an angel of mercy caring for the sick and infirm of this world and performing small miracles, and the next moment you are a firecracker with a very short fuse."

"Your cynicism and mockery would make a firecracker of a saint," she grumbled, only marginally aware that her heart echoed the warmth she had seen in his eyes. "You should be glad and proud."

He opened his mouth to say that he *had* been glad and proud and he had wanted to share it with her. But she had not been there in all the ways that counted. Suddenly he saw her eyes light up so that they gleamed like burnished gold. But only for a heartbeat. Then they went dull and lifeless.

Looking over Theo's shoulder, Julie caught sight of Maximilian von Berg beyond the garden's wrought-iron grate and her heart gave a little joyful skip. Then she saw that he was looking down at a tiny blond woman at his side. She could not see his face, but she saw him lift his hand and brush his fingers along the side of the woman's face. The love, the tenderness in that gesture leaped across the distance between them and struck her like a fist to her middle.

Theo turned to follow her gaze and saw Max and Felicity. The warmth he always felt when he looked at his brother and his wife somehow would not materialize. Shifting to look at Julie again, he saw that she was still staring beyond the garden.

He felt something strong and sharp, but without being aware of what the emotion was, he translated it into motion. Gripping her shoulders, he shook her until she lifted her gaze to his face.

"It is pitiful," he jeered, not certain why he suddenly felt the need to hurt her. "You were looking at him as if you were a starving child and he a plate of gingerbread." He gave her another shake. "He is married to a woman he loves above all else. He can never be yours."

"Do you think I do not know that?"

The sound of her soft, bleak voice had the anger leaching out of him. Deliberately, he summoned it back. "And does my brother know that he is the object of all this calf-eyed adoration?" he demanded.

Her eyes widened, and before she realized what she was doing, her fingers curled into the front of his jacket. "No. Promise me that you will say nothing to him." Her voice rose. "Promise me, Theo."

Something touched him. The panic in her voice? The hint of tears that shimmered in her eyes? The urgent pressure of her fingers? The fact that she had called him by his given name for the first time?

Who was he to judge her? Theo asked himself. Had she ever judged him? Who was he to withhold comfort? Had she ever withheld comfort when he had been in pain? His hands traveled upward from her shoulders and he cupped her face.

Julie stared, fascinated by the change in his eyes. Suddenly she was reminded of meadow flowers and misty skies instead of ice and steel. Then she became aware that he was touching her and the calm eddied through her. It soothed like the gentle waves of a warm river.

Then it changed. Quickened. Heated. Grew intimate as if they were the only two people in the whole world. Her eyes drifted half-closed.

Her skin, which was as cool and soft as rainwater, warmed beneath his touch. Theo's fingertips began to tingle in time with the pulse beneath her ear. He found his gaze drawn irresistibly to her mouth. He bent toward her, wanting, needing a taste of that innocence.

Then another image began to superimpose itself on her face. Golden eyes became eyes of a clear water blue. The features shifted and changed. He jerked his hands back as if he had been burned and the moment was shattered.

"I don't think you can get Julie away from the hospital." Prince Alexei Muromsky brushed his hand over his wife's dark hair. "Not even with a trip to Paris. And I'm not sure we should." He was less than enthusiastic about his daughter's work at the hospital, but he knew how much it meant to her. And he knew what it was like to be dedicated to something.

"That hospital is depleting her, Alexei. Every evening when she comes home, the shadows under her eyes are darker and her eyes are sadder." Princess Irina Muromsky tossed her embroidery aside with an impatient sigh. "We have to get her away from there, at least for a little while."

"I know you are right, my love. But we do not always do what is objectively good for us, do we?" He raised one dark eyebrow and aimed a sharp look at his wife.

Princess Muromsky elegantly ignored her husband's sarcasm. "Once she gets something into that thick head of hers, it's impossible to get it out." She brought her fisted hands down on her knees. "She's as stubborn as a Caucasian mule."

"I do not really think that you can throw stones at anybody about being stubborn." Alexei Muromsky stroked thumb and forefinger up and down his cheeks to hide his smile. "Especially not your own daughter, who inherited it from you." He saw his wife open her mouth to speak and held up a hand.

"Correct me if I'm wrong, my love, but I seem to remember that you were rather insistent about accompanying a fleeing prisoner from the Peter-and-Paul Fortress across Russia in the dead of winter. And almost died in the process." He paused to draw a long breath. Even after almost thirty years, the enormity of what Irina had risked for him moved him unbearably.

"That was different— Oh, don't look at me like that," she said crossly when he arched an eyebrow at her again. "It *was* different. You were a bachelor. And Julie is in love with a married man."

"What?" Alexei Muromsky half rose, murder in the uptilted golden eyes above the Tartar cheekbones, before his wife's slender, elegant hand pushed him back into his chair.

"I didn't say that she is having an affair with him, Alexei. She's in love with him and he probably does not even know it."

"Who is he?" He rose and paced to the desk to rummage for his cigars. "Talk, for God's sake."

"The head of the hospital, Dr. von Berg. We saw him and his wife at the opera a few months ago, remember?"

"And why do you think he doesn't know that she is in love with him?"

"Because I saw the way he looks at his wife." She rose and went to him. "Not unlike the way you look at me." Smiling, she laid her head against his shoulder.

Prince Muromsky curved his arm around his wife's fragile shoulders. "We'll think of something."

Julie closed the door behind her as softly as she could. Now if she could only sneak upstairs before her mother could waylay her, she thought. She loved her dearly, but tonight she was so sapped of energy that she did not think she could bear her mother's gracious, subtle concern.

Slipping off her cape and bonnet, she laid both on a chair. The weakness stole through her and, impatient with it and herself, she leaned against the wall and closed her eyes, telling herself that it was only for a moment.

She'd been all right until that strange moment in the garden, she thought. She was wrong to fear the time when Theo would be well. It would be better then. Just being with him reminded her of his brother, she told herself. And yet she did not want to think about the time when he would be gone. In his own way, he had slipped into her life.

For the first time she wondered if she was unfit for the work she had chosen. Was she too weak? Too emotional? Was she unable to draw the boundary lines between herself and others? Would she give pieces of herself to her patients until she became an empty shell?

But then, had she ever done that before? Had she ever invested quite so much of herself in anyone she had nursed?

Irina Muromsky heard the soft click of the door with the sharp ears of a mother waiting for her child to come home.

"Alexei, she is here." Disengaging herself from her husband's arms, she went to the door of the library.

Her lips tightened as she examined her daughter from the doorway. There were lavender shadows under her eyes, which held no trace of their usual golden gleam.

"Julie, *ma petite*." She came forward with a lithe grace that belied her forty-eight years. Brushing her cheek against her daughter's, she allowed herself but a light touch of her fingers to the girl's face, although she would have wanted to embrace her and hold on tightly. Much too tightly.

"You look tired, *chérie*. You should rest for a little while before supper."

Julie sent her mother a decent imitation of a smile. "I am tired tonight, *maman*. Would you excuse me perhaps and have a tray sent up to my room?"

The princess hesitated for a moment, then relented. "But only if you promise me you'll eat what's on it."

Julie nodded, knowing that she could always count on her dog, Beppo. She had saved him years ago from drowning and he never refused her anything. "Tell *papa* good-night for me." Turning, she began to climb the stairs.

"Julie."

Turning back, she saw that although her mother was smiling, her pale green eyes were worried.

"Beppo is quite fat enough."

Julie returned the smile before she continued her way up. Apparently it was as difficult to outwit a mother at twenty as it had been at ten, she mused. Frowning, she wondered what else her mother knew.

The old dog thumped his tail in greeting as she closed her door behind her. She sat down on the rug next to him and buried her face in his white-and-brown checkered fur.

Beppo made the little singing noise that told her he was being affectionate and sympathetic and she burrowed her face deeper into his neck. Things were so simple with animals, she thought. They took whatever affection you had to give and gave you their own in return. No questions. No judgments.

For just a moment, it had been easy today with Theo. She paused and lifted her head so that only her chin was tucked into the dog's thick fur. When had she begun to think of him as Theo? she wondered. Somewhere between that first evening when their lips had just barely met and today when they had not.

She'd wanted him to kiss her today, she realized. Kiss her and make her forget the pain she'd felt when she'd seen Dr. von Berg touch his wife with the love and tenderness she so badly wanted for herself. And it had hurt that he had not.

Shifting, she lay down, half beside, half on top of the dog. How odd, she mused, that she never thought of Dr. von Berg by his given name. Not even when she spun the dreams she knew would never come true. On that thought she drifted off into sleep.

Chapter Four

Julie had found a dozen reasons to avoid Theo today and she detested herself for it. As she changed into her street clothes, she thought of the way her steps had slowed every time she had passed his room. She thought of the way she had not found the courage to go inside. Forgetting all the reasons she had given herself, she acknowledged that she had not wanted to see his mouth curve with that mocking smile of his. She had not wanted to see his eyes turn cynical and bitter the way they had yesterday when he had seen her looking at his brother.

She hung up the simple gray gown in the narrow cabinet and her hands stilled. Up until now, she had found his manner at best a challenge, at worst an annoyance. Since when did it disturb her? she asked herself. Ever since yesterday, she admitted. Ever since that odd moment in the garden when his eyes had grown soft and he had touched her face, making her feel as if they were the only two people in the entire world. Ever since that dreamy moment when she had almost been able to feel his lips against hers. Ever since he had released her with such insulting precipitousness, thrusting her away from him as if he suddenly found her somehow repugnant.

The memory was pulling at her and she stepped back from the cabinet, as if she could physically distance herself from the memory at the same time. But it remained with her.

She was almost at the main doors when she whirled around and retraced her steps. She would stand for such evasion and cowardice from no one. Least of all herself. Taking a deep breath, she pushed down the door handle. It was then that she heard Dr. von Berg's mellow voice as he said something and then laughed.

No, she thought. She couldn't do it. She couldn't face both of them together. What if Theo had said something? What if they were laughing at her?

Letting the door handle snap upward, she half ran down the white corridor while she tugged on her gloves with unsteady fingers.

Still fiddling with the closure of her gloves, Julie walked straight into Dr. Schalk.

"May I accompany you a little ways?"

"Of course." Because he was a sweet man, Julie gave him the best smile she could muster and laid her hand on the proffered arm.

They had only gone a little way down the sidewalk when Julie stopped and laced her fingers.

"I'm sorry. I'm not very good company today. Perhaps it would be better—"

"You don't have to make brilliant conversation. I'm quite happy just to walk with you."

"Dr. Schalk—Horst," she corrected herself, remembering belatedly that they had graduated to first names weeks ago. What would have been considered unorthodox at best in polite society was quite routine here in the hospital, whose staff offered a cross section of all the failed revolutions in

Europe. "I don't want to—" She looked down at her hands as she searched for the right words.

"Julie—" He tipped her face up with one finger. "You don't have to say anything. I know that you are not for me." He chuckled softly. "We may both work at the same hospital, but you are still Princess Julie Muromsky and I am the son of a merchant from the Austrian provinces. Besides—" his light eyes twinkled with humor "—I've seen how you look at him."

Julie's eyes widened with alarm before she whipped her head to the side and began to walk again, her steps quick and jerky. Oh God, she thought, if he has seen it, then everyone has. I can't stay here. I can't. I can't.

Horst matched his steps to hers and continued to talk ebulliently as if her world had not been suddenly knocked awry. "You're good for him. I haven't seen him smile so much in a long time. Even Max thinks so."

"What?" Julie stopped and stared at him. "What are you talking about?"

"Why, Theo, of course."

The relief that she had not been found out after all had her giggling. She opened her mouth to disabuse him of the idea that her interest in Theo went beyond that of a nurse for her patient, but she closed it immediately. Let him believe it, she thought. It was bad enough that Theo knew the truth.

She and Theo had lost something, Julie mused, her thoughts wandering away from what she was doing even as her hands worked gently and competently. They'd lost that sense of camaraderie, of closeness that had slowly developed in the weeks she had cared for him, badgered and bullied him into taking one more step than he thought himself capable of and taken some of his pain away. He did not let her do that anymore and she missed it.

She wasn't sure if he just did not want her hands on him or if he did not want to let go of the pain. It was as if he wanted, needed the physical pain to punish himself, or perhaps to counteract a pain of the mind, the heart. Did he, she wondered, perhaps have a guilty love for someone just as she did?

Somehow she could not get through to him any longer, she brooded. But she needed to—very badly. And it had nothing to do with Dr. von Berg and everything to do with Theo.

At the same time, she had lost something of her own, she realized. She had lost some of the joy in her work. Oh, she still did what she had to do. She could still help. She could still help heal. But suddenly everything had become an uphill battle that more and more often seemed to be defeating her.

Finishing her task, she sat down to soothe her restless patient. As her hands stroked, she spoke softly—words to ease and comfort. The woman quieted and grasped two fingers of Julie's hand much as a child would before she drifted off into a half-sleep.

Suddenly Julie felt a surge of energy, as if that little bit of comfort she had been able to give had renewed her faith and her confidence in herself. She rose to go find Theo. She was smiling as she walked down the corridor and, for the first time in days, she meant it.

Theo heard the door open and stiffened, knowing that it was Julie even before the scent of verbena had reached him. Annoyance thinned his mouth. Annoyance because she had come to disturb his brooding. Annoyance that his faithful, taciturn manservant Fritz jumped up and left the room as he could not. Annoyance because he remembered too well the look in her eyes when she'd watched Max and Felicity.

Annoyance, too, because his own fierce reaction still lived within him although he still had not been able to put a name to it.

"I did all my exercises, ate all my carrots and walked three times around the garden."

"Excellent." She ignored his surly, insolent tone. "Then you should be in just the mood for what I have planned for you." Her voice was brisk.

"I'm not in the mood for anything except to be left alone," he snapped.

"Isn't that just too bad." Pleased at the anger she heard in his voice, she goaded him further. Anything was better than the cool, cynical indifference he had been showing her.

He turned around, leaning heavily on his cane, furious words on the tip of his tongue.

Before he could speak, he saw that the subdued, almost defeated look she had had in her eyes for so long was gone. Instead they were lively with sparks, making them the color of golden flames. He felt a jolt of surprise at the pleasure that spread through him when he saw that her spirit had rekindled. He hadn't realized before just how much he had missed it.

"What do you want?" His words held far less heat than he had intended.

"This." With a quick movement, she maneuvered the cane from beneath his hands. Holding it tightly against her body, she stepped back.

Deprived of the support of the cane, he pitched forward briefly, then regained his balance and righted himself. He lunged after the cane, but she took another step backward so that she was just out of reach.

"Damn you, give it to me!" The breathless sound of his own voice infuriated him.

"You want it?" Julie took another step back. "Then come and take it back."

Theo stared at the cane. He needed it. He did not dare take a step without it. Or did he? He kept his eyes on it, as if the sight of it alone could keep him upright.

"Theo."

He forced himself to tear his gaze away from the cane and his eyes traveled upward.

Her eyes were still like golden flames, but there was no mockery, no provocation in them now. There was a softness there and more. He had no name for it, but whatever it was, he knew that he wanted it, no, needed it very badly.

"Please."

She'd never said that to him before, he realized. She had given orders. She had bullied him and taunted him. But she had never said "please" before. Holding on to that and the softness in her eyes, he dragged one foot forward. Then the other.

And so they moved. He one step forward, she one step back, not stopping until she felt her shoulder blades collide with the wall at the end of the long narrow room. They stilled, both breathing as hard as if they had run a mile.

She held out the cane. He took it and looked at it for a long moment before tossing it on the nearby bed. When he turned back to Julie, he saw that she was leaning back against the wall, her eyes closed.

"Look at me, Julie."

She raised her eyelids and the tears that had filled her eyes spilled down her cheeks.

Theo felt the answering sting in his own eyes. "Why are you crying?" he asked. "What do you see that you have to cry?"

"A man." Her whisper was barely audible. "I see a man."

He took one more step to close the distance between them and pulled her into his arms.

Julie turned her face into Theo's shoulder and slid her arms around him. For long minutes they remained like this—still, silent, each aware only of the other. Slowly, their breathing returned to normal and settled into a smooth cadence that had them breathing as one.

When they moved again, that, too, was in unison. Shifting so that each could look in the other's face, they kept their arms wrapped around each other.

"Thank you," he said softly.

Unbearably moved, Julie could only nod. He'd never said that before, she realized. Only now did she realize how much it meant to her to hear those simple words.

Theo looked down at her. Her eyes were huge and golden, tears still tipping her dark lashes like tiny diamonds. He raised his hand and traced it over her cheek. A stray tear fell and he wiped it away with his thumb.

The wetness of her tears on his skin had the emotion moving through him, hot and strong, and he jolted at the pain. It was not unlike the pain he had experienced the first time he had stood on his own two legs again.

His face came closer and Julie experienced the same feeling she had had in the garden those many days ago. It was as if they were the only two people in the entire world.

He was so close that she could feel the warmth radiating from his skin. His eyes had darkened to the color of the sea just before a storm. They were full of emotions she did not recognize, but she knew instinctively that they were dark and dangerous.

Theo cupped her head, his fingers slipping under her nurse's coif to touch her hair. As he lowered his head toward her, he saw her eyes begin to drift closed and a sudden, wild panic seized him.

"No." His hands tightened around her face. "Look at me," he demanded. "Open your eyes and look at me."

Julie's eyes flew open, less because of his words than because of the urgency of his tone.

"What is it, Theo? Is something wrong?" Already her hands were moving up and down his spine, seeking to soothe.

Theo let his forehead rest against hers as relief coursed through him, washing away the panic. She had said his name. She was looking at *him*. Him. No one else.

"Theo?"

Her breath—soft, sweet, inviting—trembled over his lips. His hands eased. Where they had gripped before, they now caressed. His fingers moved over her eyebrows, which rose like wings above her golden eyes, then down over her high cheekbones.

Soft. Had he ever touched anything quite so soft as her skin? His hands drifted down and hovered over her mouth for a moment before they alighted as delicately as a butterfly alights on a flower. Slowly he traced its outline, taking as much pleasure in that simple caress as he took in the first stirring of his blood.

Her lips parted beneath his fingers. Sighing, she shifted and tilted her head back ever so slightly in unconscious invitation.

He was holding her—as much with his stormy eyes as with the hands that framed her face—and Julie saw only him. Her hands had slipped down to lie loosely at his waist. When his fingers began to drift over her face, she wanted to close her eyes with the pleasure of it, yet she did not. Somehow she knew it was important that she keep her eyes open, although she could not remember why it was so.

When he reached her mouth, his fingertips lingered, as if he wanted to memorize the shape of her lips. But she needed more. She wanted to tell him, but her tongue would not form the words. Again his fingers slid over her mouth. She could feel her lips warm under them. The warmth seeped into her and spread, turning her bones to the consistency of warm honey. Giving in to the weakness, she tipped her head backward.

Theo angled his head and closed the space between them. Their lips met and clung for a moment. Slowly, carefully, his tongue began to retrace the path his fingers had taken moments before. Her lips parted and he sipped at the sweetness. Then she opened for him. He slipped inside and knew that he had come home.

His tongue teased the seam of her mouth. Julie parted her lips and offered him a taste. But when he dipped his tongue inside, she found that it was she who needed to taste. She opened for him and invited him in.

Even when he took her mouth fully, the kiss remained gentle, but desire simmered just under the surface, as red-hot lava flows beneath innocuous rock. Her taste went to his head like a sweet, heavy wine, and this time it was Theo's eyes that drifted closed.

Even as he fell deeper into the pleasure she was offering, the images that lived and festered within him were fighting their way upward. They clawed their way past the sensation, past the emotion, and suddenly the world turned gray and crumbled into ashes.

Theo ended the kiss and pulled back. The memories, the guilt were threatening to choke him, and yet, in some strange way, their power over him had diminished. Unable to bear letting Julie go completely, he kept his arms around her, holding her close as if just the press of her body against his could keep all the old nightmares at bay.

Julie surfaced from the pleasure as one surfaces from a dream of a warm fire to an icy reality. As the pleasure, the warmth leached out of her, the chill crept in and took their place.

How could she have done that? she asked herself, appalled. Yet even as the questions, the shame whirled through her, she found herself incapable of disengaging herself and stepping away. So she remained in the circle of Theo's arms, her body pressed against his as if they were lovers.

She made no excuses. She had known that it was Theo who held her. She had known that it was Theo who had kissed her. And she had wanted the pressure of his mouth on hers. She had wanted his taste. And while she had wanted, she had forgotten that anyone else existed. What kind of woman was she? How could she love one man and at the same time melt with pleasure at his brother's touch?

Theo released her, but unable to sever that last contact, he left his hands on her shoulders.

"I'm sorry. I got carried away and took advantage of you."

"No." Julie met his eyes. "You did not take, Theo. Or rather you took only what I gave you."

The gold of her eyes had dulled and he knew why. And the knowledge hurt, although he did not quite understand why it should.

Forgetting his own disgust with himself, Theo wanted to comfort, to ease her. "It was only the moment. You had given me something immense, something important, and it touched both of us."

Julie held his eyes as she fought through the thicket of her emotions. "Yes, Theo, it was the moment, but not the moment you mean. It may have started that way, but, in the end, it had nothing to do with it." She swallowed the tears that were rising to clog her throat. "In the end it was a moment between two people who wanted and needed each other, even though their hearts belong to others."

Shamed by her honesty, Theo dropped his hands from her shoulders. "There is nothing else I can say, is there?"

No, she thought, there isn't. And yet as she moved away from him, she was dimly aware of a voice in a faraway corner of her mind that whispered the contrary.

As she brushed past him, Theo reached out to hold her back, but the memories, the guilt stayed his hand. With a quiet despair, he watched her walk from the room.

Chapter Five

Exhausted, helpless, Julie watched as the life ebbed away from the young woman. The child she had spent herself to bear had been stillborn. And just as they had been powerless to save the child, they were powerless to save the mother. There was nothing left to do now but wait.

The young woman's breathing grew shallow and more shallow still. Then one last breath trembled out. And still Julie sat at the bedside, her fingers still stroking the woman's folded hands.

When she finally stood, her shoulders bowed with sorrow, she saw that Dr. von Berg was standing at the door watching her.

Forgetting her own exhaustion, she saw only that there were dark shadows under his eyes and that the lines life had dug on his handsome face had deepened.

"You should rest." She went to him and almost gave in to the need to touch him. "You've been on your feet for almost two days."

"And you haven't? Thank you for staying with her." Max touched her shoulder. "Are you all right?"

Julie managed to nod. "I'll be going home now."

Pushing past him, she fled down the corridor. She had

barely closed the door of the tiny nurses' room behind her before the tears came.

She lowered herself onto the hard, narrow cot and bent forward. As she buried her face in the curve of her arms, her hands dislodged her coif, but she did not notice. Giving way to the grief, the tears poured down her face and the sobs racked her frame. She did not hear the door open, nor the approaching footsteps.

When she felt the weight on the cot beside her, her head snapped upward. She raised the back of her hand to her mouth, but she was able to stop neither the tears nor the sobs.

Max slid an arm around her shoulders. She was slim and fragile, not unlike his own wife, and he knew that just like Felicity, Julie had a huge reservoir of strength beneath that fragility.

"It is terrible to lose a patient," he said softly. "You never get used to it, but if we want to do what we do, it is something we have to learn to deal with."

"But she was so young," Julie sobbed. "And she wanted to live so badly."

Max remembered another young woman who had died in childbirth and his eyes darkened to a slate gray. He sighed. His guilt had tormented him for years after his first wife's death, but he had come to terms with it long ago. But the memory still ached at odd moments, like an old wound aches when the weather turns.

"It is not only the old and tired that die, Julie. But we have to learn to let the young ones go, too." He cupped her tearstained face and lifted it up to his. "When their time comes, we have to let them go, too."

"You are so wise." Julie's eyes spilled over anew. "And so good."

"*Mon enfant,* child—" Max smiled sadly and shook his head "—I am neither."

"Oh, yes. You are wise and good." Sharpened still further by the physical exhaustion, by the tears just shed, the emotions in her heart overflowed into words. "And I love you."

Even as she heard herself say the words, she gave a little gasp and her eyes widened in realization of what she had said. What she had revealed.

"Oh, Julie." Max felt his heart fill with tenderness for the young woman who could have been his daughter. He stroked a hand over her dark hair. "You do not love me, child. You have made me into a hero that I am not and now you think yourself in love with this hero when in reality he does not even exist."

As horrified at his words as she had been at her own, Julie pulled away from him. "I am not some silly child."

"Julie—"

"You think you can pat me on the head as if I were a three-year-old." She straightened, pulling the remnants of her pride around her. "I am a grown-up woman who knows her own mind." Anger was rising now and she welcomed it, knowing that it could be a protective shield as well as a weapon.

Realizing too late that the words he had meant as comfort had been taken as an insult, Max reached out, not knowing what to say.

Julie stood up quickly and moved out of his reach. She could not bear it if he touched her now with pity. It crossed her mind that Theo had been right. It was pitiful. *She* was pitiful. She swiped at the tears that were still running down her face.

"Please, don't say anything." She dragged in a breath in an effort to steady her voice. "I beg you, forget my foolish words."

Max nodded, feeling helpless and hating it. He could feel the hurt radiating from her and he knew that he could do nothing, say nothing, without risking making it worse.

Her spine as straight as a ruler, Julie went to her cabinet. She put on her pelisse and bonnet with movements as careful and precise as if she were handling the most fragile glass. Then she pulled on her gloves as if she were putting on armor. When she turned back to face him, her eyes were dry.

"Why don't you rest for a few days." Max felt unreasonably touched by the tracks the tears had left on her face. "You have been working much too hard."

Julie forced herself to look him in the eye. A small sigh of relief whistled through her lips when she saw no pity there. "I will be here tomorrow."

Max lowered his head in assent and admiration. She would be all right, he thought. She might stumble, but someone with that much courage would not fall by the wayside.

Julie knocked on the door of the library, waiting for her father's invitation before she pressed down the door handle.

"*Chérie!*" Prince Muromsky stood and went toward his daughter. "What a pleasant surprise. Usually you steal away in the morning before I have a chance to see you." He kissed her on the forehead and then on both cheeks.

He felt a flash of alarm when he saw that she was so pale that even her lips were almost colorless. And he had seen enough female tears to recognize that she had been crying. Before she could turn away, he caught her chin between thumb and forefinger.

"What's wrong, Julie?" He remembered what his wife had told him and he felt the fury streak through him, followed by the fierce desire to protect what was his. "If someone has hurt you—"

"What will you do, *papa?*" Despite the heaviness in her heart, Julie smiled. "Behead them with your sword as you gallop by on your Tartar pony?"

The prince laughed and put his arm around his daughter. If she had the spirit to make clever, sharp-tongued remarks, he decided, it couldn't be that bad.

"You know what they say, my sweet. Scratch a Russian, prince or peasant, and you will find a barbarian underneath." He tapped her on the tip of her nose. "But before you agree with too much alacrity, just remember that the blood that runs in your own veins is just as Russian as mine.

"Now tell me what it is that has made you so pale," he demanded, his eyes narrowing to golden slits.

"We lost a patient yesterday and that—" She shrugged, unable to go on with what was both the truth and a lie.

Pacing away to her father's desk, she began lining up his writing utensils in a straight line with fingers that were not quite steady. Now that she was here, the words she had dissipated. How could she tell her father that she had to leave Turin? Now. Forever. What would she tell him when he demanded her reasons? She could not tell him the truth, she thought suddenly. What if he believed that it was Dr. von Berg's fault? What if he called him out?

"I just wanted..." she began. "I just wanted to see you for a few minutes," she finished lamely.

"Julie, is something wrong?" He heard the strain in her voice and remembered his wife's words. "You know there is nothing you cannot tell me." With difficulty, he reined in the urge to demand answers.

She jerked her head up, her eyes wide, the look there awakening all his paternal suspicions. He knew from personal experience how cavalierly men seduced young ladies of irreproachable reputation.

"I am just tired, *papa.*"

"Well then—" the prince cleared his throat "—perhaps you should think about a holiday." He touched her shoulder. "How does a trip to Paris sound? Or the Riviera?"

Julie looked up at her father, her eyes heavy with sadness. How could she tell him that a trip to Paris would not be enough? How could she tell him that she had to go away and never return?

"I need to go now, *papa.*"

"Julie—" He reached out to hold her back, but she was already at the door.

Alexei Muromsky stared after her, his golden Tartar eyes merciless. If that Berg blackguard had seduced his daughter, he swore silently, he would kill him.

Julie watched Theo come down the garden path toward her. He still carried his cane, and he would for a long time, but right now, it was tucked under his arm. His steps were slow and still uneven, but sure.

"You're almost as good as new," she said when he had stopped in front of her.

"Apparently." He smiled with only a trace of bitterness.

Moving to his side as they started up the steps, Julie automatically adjusted her steps to his.

"At any rate, Max tells me that he is turning me out of the hospital soon."

"I know." Julie caught her lower lip between her teeth. She clearly remembered the day when she had thought of the time when Theo would go and been afraid that he would take the link between her and his brother with him. Now she would perhaps be gone from here before he was.

She had ruined everything, she thought. If only she had kept her guilty secret, everything would have been all right. But even as she told herself that, she knew that she was lying. Sooner or later it would have become unbearable and she would have had to leave. So now it would just have to be sooner rather than later.

"But it is time for me to leave anyway."

Theo's words, which echoed her own thoughts so precisely, broke into her brooding like a whip crack.

There was something in his grim tone that had the questions spilling from her. "Leave? And go where? Do what?"

"There is something I have to do. Something I have to finish."

As he turned to look at her, Julie watched his eyes turn the color and hardness of gunmetal. His gaze drilled into her and she found her step faltering at the bizarre feeling that the savagery she saw there was somehow connected to her.

"You aren't planning to go back to Austria, are you?" She gripped his arm as she drew the logical conclusion from the fierceness in his eyes. "Oh, Theo, you mustn't. If you're caught—" She shook her head at the terrible picture that came into her mind. "No, please."

The murderous emotion drained out of him and Theo felt the same sense of relief as one feels when a poison is drained from the body. She had nothing to do with his demons, he reminded himself. She was innocent.

"Promise me you won't."

Something moved inside him as he looked into her golden eyes. They were filled with concern for him. For him. And he wanted— No, he rebuked himself. He could not afford to want. Or to need.

"I should think that you would be well pleased if my countrymen, or whoever, made mincemeat of me after all the trouble I've given you." He hid his feelings well beneath his caustic tone.

Already regretting her emotional outburst, Julie sniffed and swept past him into his room. "And have all my hard work ruined?" She sent him an oblique look over her shoulder. "Besides, if anyone is entitled to make mincemeat out of you, I would say it was me."

Theo laughed as he closed the door. Oh, he would miss her, he thought.

They turned simultaneously and found themselves face-to-face.

"I'm going to miss you." His thought tumbled into words, unplanned, unwanted.

The tears shot into her eyes too quickly for her to control them. Her mouth worked for a moment before she managed a crooked smile. "Miss Attila the Hun?" Her voice thickened despite her efforts to keep her tone light. "What appalling taste."

Her mouth was soft and tremulous. Her eyes were swimming with tears, yet, at the same time, they were vibrant and full of power. Theo took a step closer and then another. Unable to resist, he whispered her name as he raised a hand to touch her.

They jumped apart as the door swung open so violently that it bounced off the wall.

"What the devil is the meaning of this?" Max shouted, skidding to a stop a handsbreadth in front of his brother. Between his office and Theo's room his rage had reached the boiling point and he was barely aware that his brother was not alone. Max thrust a sheaf of papers at Theo, crumpling them against his chest.

Theo took the papers with no outward sign of agitation, although he felt his heart begin to pound. As he thumbed through them, his mouth curved in a soulless smile.

When he raised his gaze to Max's face, his eyes were the color of an Arctic wasteland. "Since when do you amuse yourself by reading my mail?"

Theo's cool voice raised the temperature of Max's anger by a few more degrees. "It was among my letters, damn it, and I opened it by mistake."

"And you were so fascinated," Theo drawled, his tawny eyebrows curving upward mockingly, "that you read the whole thing, I wager." His own anger heated. "The devil take you, Max. You're not my keeper."

"Well, you need a keeper," Max exploded as he gripped Theo's jacket. "Have the past years warped you so badly that all you can think of is your revenge? And—" he rapped his fingers sharply against the papers in Theo's hand "—would you really think nothing of involving an inno-cent person in your accursed plan?"

Julie stared at the two men, buffeted by the powerful emotions that bounced off them—so much so that the meaning of their words passed by her as if they were speak-ing a language she did not understand. They had both for-gotten her existence and she was eavesdropping on what was obviously a most private conversation, but she found her-self incapable of moving. She stood rooted to the floor, both horrified and fascinated by the temper, the passion, the heat that she had never seen either one of them display before.

"Stay out of it, Max. It's my life." Theo started to turn away.

"Theo—" Max rubbed his hands over his face. "Theo, please don't do this." The heat had gone out of his voice, leaving only a deep weariness. He put a hand on his broth-er's shoulder.

Feeling the pull of a lifetime of closeness and affection, Theo jerked away from Max's touch. "Leave me alone, Max, I'm warning you."

"Theo, think—"

"Listen to me and listen well." Theo rounded on Max, brandishing the papers in his face. "I am going to Russia and I am taking a woman with me to make my masquerade complete. And the swine who made a cripple out of me is going to pay. Do you understand? He is going to pay."

His breath was coming in jerks now. "I will find out what he did with Maryka and if she is still alive—" He broke off, his mind suddenly completely blank. He had absolutely no conception of what he would do if he found her. The thought terrified him, especially since Maryka's image had been immediately obscured by Julie's face.

"If anybody's made a cripple out of you, Theo, it's you yourself. You've crippled your mind and your soul with your hatred, your need for revenge."

The word *cripple* broke through to her awareness as Julie saw Theo pale and take a step back, as if he had been physically struck. Pain tore through her heart, stealing her breath. It took a moment for her to realize that the pain she was feeling was his. She moved forward as if she were in a dream state, unaware that she did so until she stood between the two men.

"He is not a cripple." Her gaze moved from Theo to his brother. The anger that stirred her blood lent heat to her words. "He is not *any* kind of a cripple."

Both men stared at her, aware of her presence for the first time since Max had stormed into the room. Then they looked at each other, both remembering a similar scene when another woman had stood between them.

"Saved again from my brother's wrath by a woman." A cynical amusement filtered into Theo's eyes. Then it had been Max's woman. And now— His mouth curved into a bitter smile. Was Julie any less Max's woman just because he did not want her?

"I'm sorry, Theo. We all have to do what we have to." Max acknowledged defeat with a sigh. "But I would give a great deal if you did not have to do this."

Theo nodded grimly. "So would I, Max. Believe me, so would I."

Julie looked from one man to the other. They had both forgotten her again, she thought. The pain, this time her very own pain, flared up and spread through her. Whirling, she ran out of the room and down the corridor, oblivious to Theo's voice calling her name.

Chapter Six

Julie leaned back against the door of her room. Beppo was looking at her, his brown eyes liquid and sad, as if he already knew that she was leaving. Lowering herself to the floor to sit next to him, she rested her chin on his head.

Her mind wandered back to the scene that afternoon. Her memory of it was blurred, like a watercolor that had been left out in the rain. Only an occasional line, a random contour, remained clear.

The need to defend Theo against his brother had been so strong and sharp that its echo still sounded within her. But they had laughed at her. Julie buried her face in Beppo's fur as the hurt returned in waves. Oh, she had made such a fool of herself. They were probably laughing by now, already in full agreement about whatever it had been that they had been quarreling about.

Somehow, in the heat of the moment, the whole issue of the argument had slipped past her, but now the angry words that had passed between the two men began to filter back to her.

Revenge. Maryka. Russia. Suddenly her head snapped upward. Russia! Theo had said that he was going to Russia! Her mind began to race through what she knew of his past. Suddenly everything fell into place as a puzzle falls into place when a key piece is fitted into it.

There is something I have to do. Something I have to finish. Now she understood what he had meant in the garden today! That was why she had known that the unrelenting ruthlessness in his eyes was somehow connected with her. He was going to Russia to find revenge for what he had suffered.

Danger. The word shivered over the surface of her skin, once and then again. This meant danger for him. As much danger as a return to Austria would have meant. How did she know this? she asked herself. It followed as a matter of course that there was danger in an oppressive Russia ruled by treacherous, iron-fisted Nicholas, her head answered. Her instincts told her that this had nothing to do with it.

And who was this Maryka he had spoken of? She had heard the name before. It had been the very first word she had heard Theo say. Who was she? Julie remembered the tortured way he had said the name when he had been in the throes of the nightmare that first night after the operation. Was she a relative? A lover?

War. Like the blast of a gale, the single word swept the crazy jumble of thoughts out of her mind away, leaving only that one. Russia was at war and soon the European powers would enter it, as well, her father had said, and Theo would be in the middle of it.

The germ of an idea took root in her brain. Within minutes, no, seconds, it sprouted, burgeoned, spurred by desperation and need. She recognized the first. Even if she had recognized the second, she would have denied it.

Shifting away from the dog, she sat up straight, her eyebrows drawn together in concentration. Generally she was a creature of instinct, but now her mind ran like clockwork as she began to plan. Beppo sent her an inquiring look and then with a resigned sigh put his head down on his paws.

The smudges beneath Julie's eyes that attested to a sleepless night were carefully concealed by paint and powder. The qualms, the embarrassment were concealed beneath a breezy smile. The fear was concealed beneath defiance. She entered the hospital as if she were going into battle. And she was.

When she walked into Theo's room, he was out of his chair before she had closed the door behind her.

"Where did you go yesterday, damn you? And why?" He signaled Fritz impatiently to leave them alone.

The vehemence with which they were spoken flustered her more than the words themselves, but only for a moment.

"And good morning to you, too." She returned his glare measure for measure before she turned away, needing a moment to quiet the edginess in the pit of her stomach that seeing him had brought.

He spun her around so fast that she almost lost her balance. "Answer my question."

She opened her mouth to demand that he take his hands off her. Then his touch gentled and she forgot what she had wanted to say.

"If you must know, I went home." She fought to keep her tone tart. "I am not in the habit of idling where I am *de trop*. And I was quite superfluous yesterday. Would you not agree?"

His hands moved up her arms until they curved over her shoulders. He felt her body turn pliant until it seemed to flow into his touch. Whatever still remained of her resistance softened, then melted away.

"Julie—"

His voice was soft and mellow, making just her name sound like an endearment.

"I'm sorry that you had to witness our argument. If we somehow offended you, I apologize."

"There is no need for that." She looked him straight in the eye. "I made a fool of myself and had no desire to linger to hear the applause."

Beneath his hands Theo felt the tension in her shoulders return. He heard the hurt that shimmered through the brusque words, and although he was unsure why she felt it, he knew that he had put it there. And he felt a need to ease it.

He lifted his hands away from her shoulders to raise them to her face. When she flinched away from him, he lowered both hands to his sides, surprised to find how much that one small movement hurt him.

His hands fell away from her. That was better, Julie told herself, even as she fought the feeling of loss. What she was about to suggest to him did not mix well with gentle touches. Turning away, she laced her fingers. She wished there was a more elegant way of saying this, but there was not. Or if there was, she had no talent for finding it.

She faced him again and met his blue gray gaze squarely before she spoke. "I have a business proposition for you."

Her words were so far away from anything he had expected that Theo stared at her in dull-witted surprise, unable to form the most elementary thought. "What?" he finally said, wondering if he had misheard her.

"You heard exactly what I said." She swallowed and hurried on. "I want you to hear me out before you say anything. Will you do that?"

Puzzled, he nodded his agreement. "All right." Because he saw the urgency in her eyes, he promised himself that he really would do as she asked.

"I heard you tell your brother yesterday that you were going to Russia and that you were taking a woman with you. I want that woman to be me." The words spilled out quickly on a single breath.

"You cannot be serious."

Julie gripped his arm. "You promised to hear me out." At his choppy nod she continued.

"I must leave Turin." She heard him draw breath to speak and her hands tightened on his arm to silence him. "If you take me with you—" she schooled her voice to a business-like tone "—it would be to our mutual advantage."

The insane desire to say yes almost had him agreeing. Almost. He drew in one long breath before he spoke and then another.

"Julie, you don't know what you are saying. You are a young lady of irreproachable reputation. What do you think would happen to your reputation if you traveled with me?" Because he wanted to shake her, Theo fisted his hands and turned away. "If anyone decided to travel with my sister, I would kill him."

"My reputation is not a consideration for me." She lifted one shoulder in a shrug. "And, fortunately, I do not have a brother who would seek your life."

"No, it's impossible." He shook his head. "Impossible."

"All right then." Leaving him no time to recover from the surprise of her unexpected capitulation, she went on quickly. "If I cannot leave Turin with your help, I will leave without it. Perhaps another man will be less choosy." Shock at her own words mingled with the certainty that she would do whatever she had to as she began to turn away.

The rush of panic had Theo gripping her shoulders. "Would you do that? Go away with another man?" Anger rushed in, mixing with the panic to form a volatile emotion that made him light-headed. "A stranger?"

"If I must." She tilted up her chin as she spoke.

"Julie, you do not know what I need to do in Russia." He gave her a shake before he let her go. "If you did, you would run from me as fast as you can."

This time it was he who turned away. This time it was she who stopped him.

"I know that you are looking for revenge."

"And knowing that you would still go with me?" He frowned.

"Yes."

"And all that just because you wish to leave Turin? What is so pressing about it?"

Her eyes went dull. "Do you really need to ask?"

"Ah, yes." His mouth took on a cynical curve. "I had almost forgotten your adoration of my sainted brother."

"Don't you dare patronize me," she flared.

"Careful, Julie. You are the one who wants something from me."

"Then you will take me with you?" Her breath caught in her throat.

He looked down at her. Her eyes were a vibrant gold again as if that one bleak moment had never been. The temptation was almost overwhelming.

"No, I cannot. You know I cannot." Because he felt himself weakening, he tunneled his fingers through his tawny hair and turned away. "Damn you, why do you resort to something like this?" he demanded. "Buy a railroad ticket and go somewhere, anywhere." He threw his hands up in an impatient gesture. "You have enough money. And if you do not, I will give it to you."

Julie stared at his back. He had cut to the chase. She certainly did not need to resort to this for material reasons.

Why was she so set on going with him? Why did she feel panic at the thought that he would not allow her to accompany him?

Suddenly a vista opened before her and she shook her head in surprise. It was as if she had been looking at a partially concealed stage and now, suddenly, the curtain had been jerked aside to reveal the whole tableau.

Understanding, though, that words would be too much or not enough, she closed the distance between them and touched him now as she had touched him so often in the past months, one hand at his waist, the other along his spine. She felt a tingle in her palms and knew that this time the contact was somehow different, although she could not have defined it.

For the first time, Theo did not feel the pain he lived with ease at her touch. Instead a heat seeped into his blood. Not a blaze that flames instantly and extinguishes just as swiftly, but a slow, strong heat that smolders on and on.

So they stood, both caught in the moment. He forgot that he had asked her a question. She forgot that she had not answered it.

Theo fought his way free first. "You haven't answered my question."

"Because I want to go with you. Because I need to go with you." Julie felt a little jolt of surprise at the ease with which the words slipped out.

A shaft of pure joy went through him like a bright beacon in the darkness. But it faded quickly as he remembered. Turning around, he broke the contact between them. Broke the spell. "How can you say that when you are in love with my brother?" he demanded.

She had lived with this emotion for a long time, but hearing Theo say it aloud left her with the jarring sensation of having jumped from a great height. Stunned, appalled at herself, she looked at him for a long moment before she spoke. "I don't know. But it is none the less true for that."

He could not do it, he told himself. It would be base and vile to drag an innocent like her on his mission of vengeance. And the fact that the man he planned to kill was her uncle only made it that much worse.

But she could be of use to him, an insidious voice whispered. Perhaps just the fact that she was related to his quarry would be what would tip the scales in his favor.

"I could be of use to you."

He stared at her as she echoed his thought aloud.

"I speak Russian. I could help you." She took a deep breath. "Think about it. Who knows how many people you will have to question to find this woman you are looking for? This Maryka."

He grabbed her wrist. "What do you know about Maryka?"

"I know that you spoke her name when you dreamed." She passed her tongue over lips that had suddenly gone dry. "Who is she?"

"She was my lover." His eyes unfocused as he stared back into the past. "After the last battle I rode to her to warn her. To tell her to flee. I was wounded and wasn't thinking straight. If I had been, I might have realized that I was being followed. I led them straight to her." The fingers around her wrist slackened and dropped away.

"They threw her over a saddle like a sack and rode away while I lay on the ground in a puddle of my own blood, unable to move."

Self-disgust rose hot and bitter in his throat. But for the first time Theo found the emotion had more than one facet. It was no longer merely rooted in the past, in his weakness, in his inability to protect what was his. The self-loathing, the guilt were just as strong for the man he was today. The man incapable of recalling the face of the woman he loved. Incapable of even remembering what his love for her had felt like.

Julie watched as the self-hatred distorted his beautiful mouth. For the second time in as many days she felt her heart contract with a pain she knew was his. She moved toward him, slowly, carefully, as one would approach a hurt animal in the wild, unsure if it would flee or lash out. When he did neither, she closed the space between them. With a soft sigh of relief, she slid her arms around him and laid her head on his shoulder.

"I will help you find her." Her hands ran over his back in a soothing rhythm. "Together we will find her and then everything will be all right."

For long moments they did not speak. Theo was the first to step back, but unable to let go of her completely, he took both her hands in his.

"Julie, are you sure you know what you are doing?" His thumbs rubbed back and forth over her knuckles.

"Do I look like a complete idiot?" she asked, bristling. Now that their bodies were no longer pressed together, everything within her seemed to level and cool and it was easier to recapture her flippant tone.

"I will travel in the guise of an arms merchant, prepared to sell to the highest bidder. You will travel as my wife." His fingers tightened briefly on hers.

Because her breath caught at his words, she lifted her chin still a notch higher. "So?"

"I don't think you look the role. What self-respecting arms merchant would take to wife a slip of a girl who looks like a nun?"

"You are baiting me and I will not be baited."

"All right." Theo released her hands. "Then let's see if you look like a nun under that coif, as well." He gave the starched white fabric a tug. "Take it off."

Julie started to protest, but she saw the stubborn set of his mouth. Reaching up, she unpinned the coif and pulled it off.

He'd known that she was pretty. But without the coif that had framed her face so severely, her loveliness took his breath away. Yet it was her hair that caught and held his attention.

It was the dark, rich brown of the finest Swiss chocolate. It was combed back severely, but as soon as the coif was gone, feathery curls sprang up to frame her face. A thick braid hung almost to her waist and, giving in to impulse, Theo reached out and pulled it forward over her shoulder. His fingers lingered and tightened as he felt the silky texture. He let his hand slide down the braid and even when he reached the end, he did not let go.

Julie felt the slight pull at the back of her head as he slid his hand down her braid. There was an answering pull in the pit of her belly. She could not have defined it, but she knew that it speeded her pulse.

"My father gave *maman* a fur cloak once."

Julie watched his eyes take on a faraway look again, but it was not the glassy look of moments ago that had made her blood run cold, but just the soft look of a long-ago beloved memory.

"I used to love to touch it. Once when I was sick, my mother put it on my bed so that I could put my hands on it all the time." His eyes focused on her again and his fingers tightened on the end of her braid. "Russian sable. You have hair like Russian sable."

He touched no more than her braid and yet she had the oddest sensation that he was touching her body. Her skin, her blood heated. Her breath grew as uneven and as quick as her heartbeat.

His fingers held no more than the tip of her braid and she told herself to move away, but his gaze held her. His blue gray eyes remained on hers, immovable, unyielding, as if he could see into her soul.

Theo looked into her exotic eyes. They were innocent and yet there was something untamed about them. The golden color alone was enough to conjure up visions both of a wild gallop across the steppes and of voluptuous Byzantine pleasure in perfumed chambers.

"I wonder what else is Russian about you."

His words sounded harmless enough, but she heard the grim, cynical undertone. Resenting the inference that lumped her together with the Russians who had mistreated him, Julie remembered her father's words about scratching a Russian and finding a barbarian, and a perverse sense of pique had her repeating them aloud.

His laugh was hollow. "That makes excellent sense. My family and I haven't exactly had the most harmonious of experiences with your countrymen."

She felt a flare of annoyance. "Well, I haven't exactly had the most harmonious of experiences with Austrians, either."

This time his laugh had more warmth. *"Touché."*

His mouth grew serious and he looked at her for a long time before he spoke. "There are more than enough reasons to deny myself your company on this journey. You have even given me some good ones yourself. Perhaps I should reconsider."

"No, please." She put her palms against his chest.

"Can you give me one good reason, Julie, why I should not reconsider? Just one."

"I already did. I told you—"

He shook his head. "Those were objective, logical reasons. I'd like—" he knew that he was playing with fire and yet something was driving him and he could not stop "—I'd like a purely subjective reason."

"I already gave you that, too." She did not repeat it, afraid that he would again throw it back into her face.

"So you did." Winding her braid around his hand, Theo pulled her toward him until their bodies were almost flush, one against the other. "Tell me again." One more gentle tug had them almost mouth to mouth.

"No." Julie pushed against his chest, but her hands were caught between them and had no leverage. "No! What kind of cruel game are you playing?" Her voice rose as she began to struggle in earnest, but he still held her captive, her braid wound around his hand. "What do you want from me?"

Her eyes were molten gold and full of fire and defiance. Her scent was in his nostrils. Her body, soft and warm, was pressed against his. Theo felt the heat of arousal move his blood. What kind of poor excuse for a man was he, he asked himself, that he desired a woman who worshiped the ground his brother walked on? That he desired one woman when he loved another?

He told himself to let her go. But he wanted to hold her just a little longer. Yes, he thought, if he were fair, if he were honest, he would tell her that he wanted her. Warn her. And watch her run.

Julie felt his body stir against hers. She saw the color of his eyes darken and deepen until they were more blue than gray and shimmered like precious stones. Although her mind called to her, warning her to push him away, she remained utterly still. Confusion, shock, alarm swept through her, leaving behind an ache she did not know how to deal with. And still she did not move.

Theo saw her eyes widen in recognition of desire. He saw the conflicting emotions race through their golden depths. Slowly he unwrapped her hair from around his hand and let the braid swing free, releasing her. "And now, Julie? Would you still accompany me now?"

She knew she could step away now, but she did not. "Yes." Her voice was soft but firm and she felt a certainty so strong that she almost smiled.

"Are you so brave or so foolish? Or so naive?"

"No, naive I am not, nor am I particularly brave. Foolish?" She shrugged. "Perhaps."

"Don't you understand?" His fingers dug into her upper arms as he shook her. "Don't you understand that I want you?" He shook her again. "And we will be traveling together as man and wife. Do you understand how easy that will make it for me?"

"I'm not afraid of you, Theo."

"You should be."

She smiled now. "No, Theo. You will not take what I do not choose to give and we both know it."

His hands fell away from her as he recognized the truth of her words.

"Your hand then to seal our agreement." Julie held out her hand.

As Theo clasped it, his gaze drifted over her mouth.

She felt his gaze brush over her lips as surely as if it had been his mouth. The answering heat wound through her and for a moment she wondered if she was making a mistake. But the moment passed and she assured herself that she was safe. Her heart was elsewhere and she was safe.

As she left the room Theo frowned, wondering if he was making a mistake. But the moment passed and he assured himself that they were both safe. Their hearts were elsewhere and they were both safe.

Chapter Seven

Theo stood in the shadow of a doorway across the avenue from the hospital. He told himself that the impatience he felt was only for the journey he was about to take, but he waited for Julie's appearance as if weeks had passed since he had seen her, instead of a few hours.

When he saw her emerge from the building, he moved forward. When he saw that she was not alone, he stopped at the curb and cursed under his breath.

"Long day?"

Julie's head whipped upward to find Dr. Schalk smiling at her.

"Yes." She forced her mouth into a smile. She had no idea how she had managed to get through today. Theo had left the hospital immediately after their conversation and she had spent the day half expecting Dr. von Berg to confront her.

"No brilliant conversation, then." Horst placed her hand on his arm and patted it. "I promise."

As they fell into step, Julie began to relax. The sidewalk was crowded with strollers eager for the pleasantly warm air of a spring afternoon, their gliding movement almost like a ballet. The women in their pastel-colored gowns, their wide skirts swaying gracefully. The men in their uniforms or pale suits bending to whisper compliments in their ladies' ears.

Her gaze wandered across the wide avenue and stumbled over the tall, lean figure standing at the edge of the sidewalk. His absolute stillness halted the continuity of the movement and the harmonious moment shattered.

Julie stopped so suddenly that Horst gripped her elbow to steady her. "Is something wrong, Julie?"

"No." She shook her head a little wildly as a fleeting uncertainty raced through her. Had he come to tell her that he had changed his mind? She saw Theo turn away from the curb and her heart started pounding. "Will you excuse me?"

She had already stepped down onto the cobblestones when she was struck with the sudden conviction that she would not return to the hospital again. Theo was moving into the crowd on the sidewalk and for a moment she was torn, but then she turned back and retraced her steps. She took both of Horst's hands in hers and the sadness coiled through her as she looked into his mild, puzzled eyes. Her own gaze clouded as the image of other eyes rose. Kind, patient gray eyes. Beloved eyes.

"Adieu," she whispered, knowing that she was saying goodbye to her girlhood, to her whole life as she had lived it up to today. Excitement twined with the sadness and, before he could say anything, she turned and darted across the avenue.

Julie was still in the middle of the street when she lost sight of Theo. A jolt of panic had her dashing forward, barely aware of the sudden whinny of horses and a stream of Italian curses behind her.

Caring nothing for the grumbling and nasty looks of the passersby whom she elbowed aside in her haste, she plowed into the crowd. Her skirt caught on something, then tore. The sidewalk widened, the crowd seemed to thicken, obstructing her path still further. When she caught sight of Theo's head and shoulders above the crowd just as he disappeared into a narrow alleyway, her breath whistled past her lips in a sigh of relief. She pushed on, and finally, her momentum propelled her headfirst into the alley. She slammed right into Theo's chest.

"Going somewhere in a hurry?"

His arrogant drawl and cool gaze had her pushing away from him. "Yes, although now that I've seen you, I can't imagine why."

Despite his annoyance, Theo's mouth curved into a grin as he looked into eyes that were glowing with temper. "The sharpness of your tongue bodes well for our journey."

"It's no more than you deserve. You saw me," she accused. "You looked straight at me. Why did you disappear like that?"

Her hands tightened on her reticule because she wanted badly to curl her fingers into his waistcoat of discreetly patterned brown-and-gold silk and shake him. Almost as badly as she wanted to slide her hand down his back and ease the pain she knew he was feeling.

"Was I supposed to stand there and watch you make calf's eyes at your beau?" he demanded, surprised and displeased at the violent emotion that had swept through him a moment ago. It could not possibly be jealousy, he told himself. It was nothing but irritation pure and simple.

Julie opened her mouth to protest, then closed it so abruptly that her teeth clicked. "I refuse to dignify that ridiculous statement with an answer." She twitched her skirts. "It does not bode well—" she purposely used his own words "—for our journey if you set out to annoy me every time you open your mouth."

Theo grinned again, feeling suddenly lighthearted. "Why should I change something that has worked so well up to now?"

"Indeed, why should you?" she asked, bristling.

"Truce?"

Julie sent him a suspicious look, but the smile that had softened the sharp angles of his face had her forgetting just how much he was able to annoy her.

As his gaze drifted over her, Theo realized that it was the first time he had seen her dressed in anything but the simple gray dress she wore at the hospital. The pale green of her gown and matching bonnet made her look soft and lovely. Suddenly he drew himself up short. He was mad, he told himself. He was thinking of her as a desirable woman again, even as she dreamed of his brother. He wanted her, even though he was about to use her to revenge the woman he loved. Unless he stopped, this would never work.

His smile faded and Julie found herself shivering as the warmth leached out of his eyes. After all these months she had thought to know him as well as she knew anyone. But would she be able to live day after day with this man who seemed to run hot and cold at will? Soon she would be cut off from everything and everyone familiar and he would be the only known quantity in her life. Would she be able to bear his moods, his coldness then, too? She shivered again.

"Is something wrong?"

"No." Her spine stiffened.

His tawny eyebrows arched. "Then why are you shivering as if you have the ague?"

Her spine stiffened still further. "It occurred to me that soon I will be tied to a man who has a smile as cold as the steel of a well-honed rapier."

"Afraid?" he challenged.

"No." She threw up her chin. "I told you before that I'm not afraid of you. But you will forgive me if the ease with which you run hot and cold gives me a moment of pause." She met his eyes. "And when you run cold, as you did a moment ago, anyone might be forgiven for cringing a bit."

"Then we will suit well enough, my dear, since you always seem to run hot."

Temper sprang into her eyes again, but his quick grin had her subsiding.

"You see what I mean?" He laughed softly. "Truce?" he repeated. "Truly this time?"

She nodded. Silence fell. The babble of the crowd seemed far away and its murmur only underlined the silence between them. Somewhere above her head a canary in its cage trilled.

Words had always come easily to him, Theo thought. Why was it that he could not find the right ones now to tell her that he had moved heaven and earth so that they could leave tonight, before she could change her mind? He would be uprooting her from her family, from everything she had ever known. He would be ruining her reputation and placing her life in danger for the sake of his revenge. All because he selfishly wanted to hold on to the simple joy she gave him for a little while longer.

Julie looked down at her laced fingers. "It would seem that we have something to say to each other only when we are sparring."

"Not only then." Theo paused. "It's time, Julie."

"Time?" Her eyes raced up to meet his. Understanding, she pressed her hands against her middle, where excitement warred with terror and heartache. "When?"

"Tonight."

"So soon?" The words slipped out. How many things had she left undone? How many words had she left unsaid? No, she thought as she remembered what she had said to Theo's brother. It was the other way around. She had said too many words.

Quickly she shook her head. "No, I'm glad." Her hand brushed over his arm. "Truly."

Even though the taste of guilt was sharp and bitter, he could feel his heart beat a quick tattoo of relief. Only now did he realize how afraid he had been that she had thought better of it. His guilt deepened as he admitted to himself that had she changed her mind, he would have done his best to persuade her.

"Would you rather wait?"

"No." She shook her head. "This way, at least, there are some goodbyes I will not have to struggle through. I am not very good at subterfuge."

Their eyes met and they both knew exactly which good-byes she meant.

"Then you will have to learn to use subterfuge quickly, Julie." Theo's mouth thinned. "That's something you will need for the role of loving wife."

She bristled, hearing the cynicism but not the heartache. How could she, when Theo did not hear it himself? "And your role as loving husband?" she demanded. "How do you plan to manage that?"

Reason, logic, discretion flew out of Theo's mind as if they had never been. His silver-topped cane clattered to the ground as he reached for her. His slender hands cupped her neck, holding her still for a kiss that punished more than it spoke of gentleness.

Julie lifted her hands to his to pull them away from her. Her fingers hooked around his—and clung. It was the taste she remembered from that one kiss they had shared so many weeks ago—coffee, tobacco and that flavor that was his very own. And it went straight to her head, like wine on an empty stomach.

And like wine, his taste provoked, heated, intoxicated until her mouth began to make demands of its own. Her hands slipped from his to tangle in his thick, tawny hair. Her tongue dueled with his as if she wished to punish him with her kiss as relentlessly as he wanted to punish her. Her body pressed against his, propriety, discretion forgotten in the flash and heat of the moment.

Instead of exhausting itself, their abandon escalated, spiraling upward. The need to punish had long since been consumed in the heat. Now there was only need, pure, simple need between them. His. And hers.

The kiss ended. Not because either one of them had even begun to have enough, but because they seemed to have depleted every bit of air in their systems. Now they breathed as if they had run a race, neither one of them quite sure if they had won or lost.

Sanity returned, but they found themselves so weak that they remained pressed against each other long after awareness had cleared their minds.

Julie marked Theo's withdrawal in his eyes, but he still held her. She could feel every single one of his fingers on her skin. Her nerves seemed to be concentrated on the skin of her neck where he was touching her, setting off pulses like small blazes. Even through her petticoats she could feel his arousal and her body answered with an ache she could not quite understand.

Theo watched the incandescence of passion drain out of her eyes, although the pupils remained dark and dilated with only a ring of molten gold around them. Her body was pliant as if it had melted against him. The skin of her neck where he still touched her was throbbing against his fingertips. My God, he thought, I have gone mad. Mad! And still he could not bear to stop touching her.

"Be sure, Julie. Be very sure that you still want to go with me." His hands slid down her back to press her more firmly against him. "Are you?"

It was madness, Julie thought as color crept across her cheekbones. How could she be so wanton with a man she did not love? And yet she did not fight him as he pressed her against his aroused body.

She released his hair, the joints of her fingers aching, so tightly had she gripped it. Her hands slid down over his neck and she felt his shudder. They were so close that they might have been two halves of one body and she could feel the quick beat of his heart as it raced against her own.

Her fingers rested against his face and she felt her fingertips begin to tingle. Warmth flooded through her. The heady, feverish excitement of a moment ago had subsided to an entrancement that was no less strong. Wanting to savor the magic a moment longer, she let her eyelids begin to drift closed.

Again Theo felt that surge of panic when her eyes began to close. It galvanized him into movement and his hands spanned her waist, pushing her away from him.

"Are you sure?" he demanded again, satisfied when her eyes flew open. "Look at me and tell me that you are willing to join the game with all the odds against you."

Julie could feel the magic of a moment ago filter out of her as if it were something physical. Yet something of it remained and settled within her like precious gold dust settles within clear water. His hands were at her waist, holding her away from him. Her own hands had dropped to her sides, but her fingertips were still tingling in that peculiar way.

Something moved within her and clicked into place, but she could not have defined or described it. But she felt an absolute certainty that what she was doing was right.

"It is not a game for me, Theo." She met his eyes and held them. "If it is a game for you, perhaps you had better make certain that *you* can live with the odds."

He frowned, not quite certain that he understood what she was saying, but she had already freed herself from his grasp.

"What time?"

It took him a moment to react to her question. "After midnight. I will come after midnight."

Julie nodded and then turned back to the street.

Chapter Eight

The clock had barely struck one when the sound of carriage wheels on the cobblestones had Julie jumping up, her heart pounding. Beppo raised his head and looked at her with mournful, liquid eyes. Crouching down, she pressed her cheek against his fur one last time. Then, her shoes in her hand, she flew down the stairs.

Moving past the valises she had carried down earlier, she opened the heavy entry door. Then she remembered. Carefully she closed it again and lowered herself to sit on one of her valises. She decided that it was a good omen in itself that she remembered to observe this custom that no true Russian goes on a journey without.

The thought brushed her mind that, yes, she was running from the bittersweet love for Maximilian von Berg that she carried in her heart, but even more, she was running toward Theo. And, although she was unable to fully understand, she accepted that this was so.

As she put her hand on the door again, grief blocked her throat as she thought of the letter that lay upstairs. Her father would not understand her, she mused. He had always had the freedom to do as he pleased. But her mother might. She had had to fight for the freedom she had taken. And she had paid for it.

Her heart lightened. *Maman* would explain it to *papa* and they would have each other.

As she picked up her valises, the grief still lingered, but, her chin high, she walked quickly down the short path toward the street.

"Julie!" Theo struggled down the carriage steps. "Fritz was just coming to help you carry your things. He'll go for the rest."

She shook her head. "That is all there is. I took you at your word."

She heard Theo's manservant mumble something behind her as he picked up the valises to hand them up to the driver. Her lips thinned, but she said nothing.

Frowning, Theo stepped over to Fritz. Laying a hand on his shoulder, he spoke emphatically to the smaller man, temper coloring his tone. Patiently, Julie watched the two men, seeing both their annoyance with each other and their affection.

Theo turned back to her and they both stilled. Julie felt something stir within her as she looked into his face. Although she could not have named it, the emotion reverberated strong and clear within her like the silver sound of a bell. She held out her hand to him.

Theo felt something stir within him as he looked at Julie, her amber eyes wide, her mouth serious. When she held out her hand, palm upward, to him, something poured through him like sun-warmed honey. He could not have defined the feeling, but it rippled through him like a prayer, a promise. Closing the distance between them, he placed his hand against hers, palm against palm, and laced their fingers. Then he lifted their joined hands to his mouth and brushed his lips over her knuckles.

"I wish us *bon voyage*, Julie."

His lips were warm, in keen contrast to the chill rain on her face. "So do I, Theo." She smiled. "And it will be. I know it."

"So sure?" A raised eyebrow gave subtle emphasis to his cynical tone. "Do you have a crystal ball or do you have a special line of communication with the Almighty?"

She shook her head. "It's raining."

Staring, Theo repeated her words.

Julie nodded and turned her face up into the rain. "Rain blesses a journey." Even as she said the words, the memory of her mother's voice repeating the old Russian proverb had tears springing into her eyes.

"Julie—" The guilt was a knife being turned slowly and torturously in his belly.

Lowering her eyelids, she shook her head as she pulled in a long, deep breath. When she opened her eyes, they were still swimming with tears, but she was smiling.

"Come now," she said softly.

Their hands still linked, they turned toward the carriage.

They sat side by side in the carriage, their shoulders touching, but they did not speak until they had long passed the outskirts of Turin.

"Is Fritz going to make the journey with us?" Julie asked.

Theo nodded apologetically, knowing of the odd resentment his manservant bore Julie. "He would not have forgiven me had I left him behind. And I owe him my life." A shadow passed over his face as he remembered how he had lain in the dank, filthy prison, half out of his mind with pain and grief, helpless. Although he had been a stranger, Fritz had cared for him with a single-minded devotion that had saved his life.

"Yes, I know. But if we are to function as a unit, perhaps you should explain to him that I am after neither your money nor your virtue." She smiled to take the sting out of her words.

"You understood what he said?" Theo flushed. "I didn't know you spoke German." He covered her hand with his. "He didn't mean it."

"I appreciate your trying to smooth the waters, Theo, but he's always thought that I was a money-grubbing little whore who wanted to become a countess." Her tone was brisk. "He just said it out loud today for the first time, at least within my hearing."

Theo gave her a chagrined look. "I'd forgotten your ability to whittle things down to the core and to put them into a few succinct words."

Her eyes filled with mild amusement. "Yes, that's one of the things I have in common with Fritz."

"Julie—" Theo shifted and gripped her hands. "Julie, I know how much I owe you, but—" He broke off and took a deep breath. "Don't ask me to leave Fritz behind."

"You owe me nothing. And did you hear me ask you to leave him behind?" Exasperation warred with tenderness as she realized just how deep his loyalties ran. "Just explain why I am here. Time will take care of the rest."

But time did not take care of the rest. Fritz remained unimpressed and unappeased. Nothing—not Theo's explanation, not the fact that Julie slept alone at the inns where they stopped at night, nor her separate compartment in the train they boarded in Milan—changed his attitude. He was coldly polite, but the antagonism endured.

She was pounding on a door made of wood so heavy that her fists made only muffled thuds. Sharp metal studs that were randomly scattered over the surface had made her hands bleed, but still she kept pounding with a fierce desperation. She did not know what was behind the door, but she knew that she had to get inside. She had to reach—

Julie started out of the dream and jackknifed up in the narrow bunk. Her head was spinning and she rubbed her hands over her face, which was damp with cold sweat. Oh God, she thought, she could still hear the pounding. It was then that she heard the voice calling her name.

Rolling out of the bunk, she moved toward the door of the compartment. It was Fritz, she realized, as, still dizzy, she fumbled with the lock. The glass rattled as she finally managed to unlatch and open the door.

"What is it?"

For a moment Fritz stared at her, his mouth working soundlessly. Then the words flooded out of him in a jumble of broken French and German colored with the dialect of his native Vienna.

Understanding only half of what he was saying, but understanding that something was wrong with Theo, Julie pushed past Fritz's slight figure and moved swiftly down the narrow corridor. She sensed Theo's pain even before she stepped inside the compartment.

Theo lay on the lower of the two bunks, his arms thrown back over his head, his hands clutching a brass grip on the wooden panel with such violence that the veins stood out like cords. His eyes were closed and the tautness of his features left no doubt about the agony he was suffering.

Julie dropped down to the floor beside the bunk and laid her hands on his chest, willing them to ease his pain.

"Julie?" Theo opened eyes that were glassy with pain. "Fritz shouldn't have woken you." The words came out choppily as he pulled in a tortured breath between each one.

"Shh. You'll be all right in a little while." Her hands moved upward toward his shoulders, pressing lightly.

Leaving one hand on his shoulder, she curved the other around his hands. "Can you let go now?" Gently she worked his fingers free of the metal and drew his arms down to lie at his sides.

She brushed his tawny hair back from his forehead and cupped his face. "I have to turn you over now." Knowing that that would strain his spastic muscles still further, she made her tone apologetic.

Just her presence seemed to ease him. Theo felt his body relax marginally. The pain was still there, slashing through his back and legs like hot knives, but that sharpest edge had been taken off. He concentrated on the touch of her fingers on his face.

"Did you hear me?" Julie asked softly, needing to make certain that he would not tighten his muscles still further against an unexpected movement.

Theo opened his eyes and mouthed a silent yes.

She feathered her thumbs over his sharp cheekbones, wanting to give him another moment of respite before she caused him more pain.

The pain receded yet another step. He needed to somehow acknowledge the comfort just her presence gave him, but he had neither the words nor the strength to say them. His eyes still on hers, he moved his head to the side so that his mouth came to rest at the base of her palm.

Julie felt a rush of sensation as his breath rippled over her hand. This was not the time for this, she chided herself, appalled at her reaction. Still, she could not resist pressing her hand against his face for a moment longer. Even when she slid her hand back down to his shoulder and looked up at Fritz, the warmth remained.

"Can you help me turn him over?"

Fritz's eyes widened when she addressed him in German and, chagrined, he lowered his gaze before he moved forward.

Together, their hands as careful, as gentle as they could be, they moved Theo. The sharp hiss of his breath followed by a half-suppressed moan tore through Julie like an arrow. She felt her stomach turn over at the sound and she schooled herself to calm despite the heartbeat that seemed to race up to her throat.

"Bring the brown leather case from the smaller valise," she instructed Fritz, suddenly afraid that whatever she would be able to do for Theo would not be enough and she would have to use the laudanum. As she began to touch him, she could feel the knotted, cramped muscles, the convulsive trembling that came both from the pain and his need not to surrender to it.

Her mind still muddled from the dream, her only thought to give him comfort, she did not reach for the power and the light. Instead, she heedlessly concentrated every fragment of her essence on Theo as she inched her hands down his spine and legs, once, then again, then a third time. She did not notice that her breathing shuddered and took on a slow, drawn-out cadence. She did not notice that she grew pale and paler still. She drew her hands down Theo's body again and again, draining away his pain, pouring her own energy into him, unaware of the cost to herself.

Finally, her strength sapped, she slumped against the bunk. If Fritz had not reached out to support her, she would have toppled over. Not knowing what else to do, he shifted her so that she leaned against the bunk. Afraid that she would fall, he held on to her shoulders and felt her body tremble and then go completely lax.

Theo lay still, the lassitude that comes after acute pain fades making it impossible for him to move. Half-drugged with relief, he drifted for long minutes in that nebulous region that was almost sleep. When he finally emerged into awareness, he realized not only that the agonizing pain was completely gone, but that an unfamiliar energy, disquieting in its power, coursed through him like a quick-flowing stream. Almost simultaneously he realized that something was terribly wrong.

Shifting onto his side, he saw Fritz, his eyes wide and panicked, holding Julie by the shoulders. Her head lolled back against the bunk on which he lay, her skin as white as the nightgown she wore. He sat up with a reckless swiftness.

"What's wrong?" he demanded, fear making his voice harsh. "Lift her up here."

"Julie?" He slid an arm around her shoulders and tilted her face up to his. "Julie, can you hear me?"

Her stillness, her pallor, her shallow breathing sent his fear spiraling into panic. He drew her closer so that she lay pressed against him. Tracing his hand down her limp body, he willed the strength that coursed through him into her.

When she stirred and opened her eyes, relief had Theo's eyes stinging.

"What—what happened?" Her voice was slurred and thick as if she had slept for a long time.

"I don't know." Theo lifted a hand to brush his fingers over her face. "You tell me." Her eyes fell closed and he felt the panic swirl up again. "Julie—"

"I'm all right now." She passed her tongue over lips that were bone-dry. "You gave it back to me."

"What?"

"Could I have some water?"

Before Theo could say anything, Fritz produced a tumbler and Theo held it to her lips.

Julie drank greedily before letting her head fall back against Theo's shoulder.

He gathered her to him, close and closer still. His hand stroked over her sleep-tousled hair and he berated himself for wondering what it would feel like to unplait her thick braid and run his fingers through the softness.

When she began to speak, her voice was muted so that he had to lean close to hear her words.

"I was seven or eight when I found a young rabbit in our garden. It had been mauled by a cat and it just lay there, trembling from pain and fear but too weak to flee. I put it in a box in my bedroom and my parents warned me not to expect it to be alive in the morning."

She was silent for so long that Theo thought she had fallen asleep, but then she began to speak again.

"I lay in my bed and I could feel the rabbit's pain." Her brow knit and she shifted closer to Theo, seeking his warmth. "Not the pain itself, but it was a kind of pressure, an agitation inside me. I got out of bed, knelt next to the box and put my hands on the rabbit. The last thing I remember is that it stopped trembling."

"*Maman* found me on the floor next to the box the next morning. I was barely breathing." She paused. "The rabbit was fine."

She turned her gaze up to his. "That was my introduction to my...gift. I learned that I could help. It took a few more experiences for me to realize that I had to protect myself—" she smiled ruefully "—although none of them were quite as drastic as the first."

Theo felt the ice gather in the pit of his stomach. "And tonight you did not protect yourself," he said dully.

She moved a shoulder in a small shrug. "I was dreaming when Fritz woke me. I was still half-asleep when I came in here. And I could feel your pain."

"Oh God." Theo dropped his forehead onto her hair. "I'm sorry."

"It's not your fault." She lifted her hand to his chest. "Besides, you gave it back to me."

"I'm not sure I understand."

"You touched me and gave me my strength back."

"And what if I hadn't?" Theo's voice dropped to a whisper as the understanding sank in that a lucky instinct had caused him to set things right. "What if I hadn't?"

She shrugged. "I don't know."

He drew back and tilted her face up to his so that he could see her eyes. The answer he saw in the golden depths sent an icy streak of horror through him.

"Julie—"

"Please, Theo, don't belabor it. It's past. I am all right and so are you."

His guilt cried out for absolution. "But—"

"Let it go, Theo. Please." Julie shivered as reaction and the accompanying chill set in.

"Here."

She looked up at the sound of Fritz's voice. He stood there, his eyes cast down, his thin shoulders stooped, holding her robe out to her.

Theo took the robe and settled it around her.

"Thank you, Fritz."

Julie waited until the manservant raised his gaze to hers. Their eyes met and held. She moved her head in a small nod and he acknowledged it with one of his own. Then he bowed and slipped out into the corridor.

"I think you've just made a conquest," Theo said once the compartment door had closed behind Fritz.

"Mmm," she murmured, the exhaustion beginning to pull her under. "I'd rather think I've made a friend."

Theo felt her body relax into sleep. Taking her with him, he stretched out on the narrow bunk. He closed his eyes, but the thoughts roiled within him like the waves of a stormy sea, allowing him no rest. And the press of her soft curves against him robbed him of any peace of mind he might have had left.

He held her throughout the night, wondering how he would ever erase the debt and the guilt.

Chapter Nine

The trees, stunted by the winds that blew off the sea in the winter, told Julie that they were nearing Venice. The next stage of their journey had come. A dangerous stage. During the course of their journey, every time she had seen an Austrian uniform, every time their papers were examined, she had understood better just how dangerous. She felt the gathering tension in her shoulders and lifted her hand surreptitiously to rub the knotted muscles.

"It is not too late for you to turn back."

"What?" Her head whipped around to look at Theo.

"I'm not blind, Julie. I have seen you grow more tense and nervous every time our papers were checked."

"Stage fright." She tilted her chin up belligerently. "It will be better once we are in Venice."

Theo shook his head. "Venice is not going to be any better. The city is occupied by the Austrian army. You'll see plenty of uniforms there, too."

"Do you think I do not know that?"

"And the ship on which our passage is reserved sails under the Austrian flag."

"Are you mad—"

"There was no other way," he said, cutting her off. "The French ships that also ply this route are all engaged in carrying soldiers and supplies for the Crimea." He paused. "Or have you forgotten that we are on our way to a war zone?"

She welcomed the surge of annoyance as his eyebrows took on that mocking curve. "Are you trying to frighten me off?"

Theo inhaled, the facile words of denial already forming on his lips. But there was nothing facile, nothing casual about it. "Yes."

They stared at each other, his answer surprising both of them in equal measure.

"Listen to me." He leaned forward. "In Venice the possibility that I could be recognized is very real. The same goes for the ship."

"And is that not why you wanted a woman at your side?" she demanded. "So that you would appear innocuous? Less recognizable? So that if you are recognized, the chances of covering it up would be better?"

"If I am recognized, perhaps I can weather it alone better. I remember well that you said yourself that you are not good at subterfuge."

The memory of what else had been said—and done—that day sprang to life in their eyes.

"Do you have a quarrel with my skills? Have I done poorly up to now?" She leaned forward so that their faces were only inches apart. "Can you look me in the eye and tell me that I have not lived up to your expectations? If I have not, there is no need to frighten me off. All you have to do is tell the truth."

There was so much fire in her eyes. Fire enough to warm the coldness in his soul. Warmth that he wanted so badly. Warmth that he had no right to take.

"Julie, you have surpassed my expectations beyond all measure," he said, remembering the night before. Remembering that she had freed him from agonizing pain and placed herself in jeopardy.

"You feel gratitude and guilt for last night. That's why you are doing this." Her words were not a question.

"Yes, but that is only part of the reason." He rubbed his hands over his face and looked out of the window as if the fields of young corn that whisked by could give him the right words. "I was wrong to use you. I should never have allowed you to come with me."

He was going to send her back, she thought, and when she came right down to it, she was powerless to stop him. Julie felt the panic streak through her. Panic that had nothing to do with returning to Turin and everything to do with not continuing the journey with him. She would not let him do it. Anger swirled up inside her, and knowing what a good weapon it was, she grasped it. Because she wanted to storm at him, she sat quietly, schooling herself to stillness as she waited for him to turn back to her.

When Theo looked at her, she had her hands folded demurely in her lap, as if the firebrand of a few moments ago had never been. If he had looked carefully enough, he would have seen the temper in her eyes.

"How many women are you?"

"Perhaps, my dear Theo, I am better at subterfuge than you think. I look perfectly peaceful, do I not?" When his nod of confirmation came, she moved forward as quickly as a hawk striking its prey and curled her fingers in the front of his shirt. "I look peaceful even though I could strangle you with your own cravat." Now that the gate was opened, the words tore out like stampeding cattle.

"I chose to come with you. *I chose.* Besides, you have nothing to allow or disallow me. You are neither my father nor my husband—" she dragged in a breath "—nor my lover."

The relief of having spoken her mind and set the boundaries and Theo's look of a man suddenly confronted by something utterly bizarre had the laughter bubbling up within her so suddenly that she had no defense against it. She pressed her lips against it, but only succeeded in transforming it to a half-stifled giggle.

"Oh, the devil take it." She gave in to a full-bodied laugh. "Now I have completely spoiled the effect of my tirade."

Her laughter floated through him like the first breeze of spring after a long, cold winter. Theo stared at her as if he had never seen her before. Something within him softened, then shifted, and although he did not recognize it, he fell headfirst into love.

Julie told herself that everything would be easier now, but, as the train moved onto the two-and-a-half-mile bridge that separated Venice from the mainland, the tension returned, underscored by the whine of the metal construction outside. On either side of the train all she could see was the blue water of the lagoon, which shimmered through the hazy sunlight, heightening the feeling that she was now truly severed from everything that had gone before.

The jolt of the stopping train almost sent her crashing into the glass. Her hands released the reticule she had been clutching as she braced herself against the window frame of gleaming wood.

A cloud of steam rose in front of the window with a hiss, blocking her view. When it cleared she saw that Theo had been right. Well over half the men on the platform wore Austrian uniforms, the more ordinary green-and-red uniforms interspersed with flashy gold-trimmed white tunics coupled with scarlet trousers.

Even though the milling crowd on the platform looked innocuous, her stomach tightened and she pressed a hand against her middle. Was there someone out there who would have seen Theo before? Who would recognize him? Who would denounce him? She took a deep breath and tilted up her chin. And if there was, damn it, that was what she was here for.

Feeling Theo's eyes on her, she turned away from the window to meet his gaze.

He said nothing, but she could read the question in his eyes so precisely that she knew exactly what words he would have used.

Her dark eyebrows curved upward haughtily. "Don't even think it."

Theo felt himself relax muscles he had not known he had tensed. He rose and held out his hand, palm upward, much as she had done in front of the house where she had left her girlhood behind.

Julie slipped her hand into his and stood. The narrowness of the compartment and her voluminous skirts pushed them together so that their bodies were almost touching.

She needed him, she thought. She hadn't realized exactly how much until she had thought he was going to send her back. For months she had taken care of him with an intensity she had expended on no other patient, but she had not perceived until now just how much that had bound her to him. She understood that in many ways she was bound to Theo more strongly than to his brother. Her heart filled with love so sweet and melancholy that she was not aware that she had not thought of the man she loved by name for a long, long time.

He needed her, he thought. He hadn't realized exactly how much until he had given her the option of going back. It was not right, he told himself. It was not right to feel this overwhelming need for her when he was using her to obtain his revenge and find Maryka.

Maryka. Theo stilled. He had not thought, really thought about her for days. What kind of base creature was he to forget the woman he loved? The woman who was suffering only God knew what terrible fate because he had not been able to protect her?

Julie watched the color leach out of his face. "Theo? What is it? Are you in pain?"

Theo focused his eyes on Julie's face. Pain? Yes, he was in pain, but not the kind of pain she meant.

He shook his head. "No. I'm all right. Shall we go?" He pulled his mouth into a smile of sorts. "I believe that *madame*'s gondola is waiting."

Their hands were still linked as they moved out of the compartment.

The moment they stepped out onto the wide, flat steps that led from the railway station down to the water, a medley of scents and sounds surrounded them.

The voices raised in the singsong Venetian dialect were cheerful and stubbornly overlaid the German spoken by the men in the Austrian uniforms. The breeze blew the slightly brackish smell of the green water of the canal just below up the steps. A boy carrying a basket of bread whistled the Duke's insolent melody from Verdi's *Rigoletto*. The acrid smell of coal smoke drifted from the trains and mingled with the sweet, tangy fragrance of hyacinths that were already drooping in front of an old flower vendor who dozed in the spring sunshine. And above it all was the vivid scent of the sea.

A long row of gondolas bobbed lightly at the bottom of the steps. The gondolier in his black trousers and waist-length black jacket, which was buttoned against the fresh breeze, gave an extravagant bow and handed Julie into the gondola, steadying her until she settled herself and her wide skirts onto the bench with its ornately carved headrest.

Theo watched her as she ran her fingers over the ruby-colored velvet that covered the bench, then slid her hand over the carved side of the gondola with its rich coat of gleaming jet black paint. She touched the vessel as if it were a living, breathing being. What did she feel with those magic hands of hers? he wondered.

The gondolier pushed away from the dock, guiding the gondola with his single oar, and the gondola sliced through the green water, its black prow sharply silhouetted against the faded pastels of the buildings that lined the canal. If Theo had not been watching Julie so carefully, her quickly suppressed shiver would have gone unnoticed.

He said nothing, but he shifted so that he was closer to her.

"Do you feel it?" She brushed her hand over the carving again, her fingers lingering on a gilded ornament.

"What?"

"All the black and gold and red. It's beautiful, but there's an aura of menace about it. The perfect vehicle for voluptuous courtesans and spies in black capes and masks engaged in dire intrigue." She shook her head and laughed. "That must sound silly, but it feels so different than I imagined it."

"And how was that?"

"I used to dream about Venice when I was fifteen or so. The daughter of friends of my parents had gone to Venice on her wedding trip and I pretended for weeks that I was gliding through the canals in a gondola, lying in the arms of my beloved."

He twisted his head a little so that he could see her face, which was hidden behind the sides of her bonnet. She was smiling and for some reason he was reminded of this morning—had it only been this morning?—when she had laughed so irresistibly. When he had felt—something. Something he could neither define nor understand.

"You can still pretend." He touched her shoulder as the words slipped out before he could call them back.

Was he mad? Anger and pain intertwined, forming a new emotion. He was asking to be a proxy for his brother in her fantasies. And yet he knew that if he could unsay the words he had spoken, he would not.

For a fraction of a moment Julie reacted only to the murmur of his voice, which was so soothing, so inviting that she yielded to his light touch and relaxed against him. Even when his words sank in, she wanted to stay where she was and she did—for the space of one breath and then two. Only then did she follow the command of her mind. Slowly she stiffened and shifted away. What had possessed him to say something like that? she asked herself. And what had possessed her to want to give in to it? No, she corrected. She had given in to it. And she had not pretended that she was in anyone's arms but Theo's.

"*Signori.*" The gondolier's musical voice broke into the strained silence. "*Questo è il famoso mercato Veneziano. This is the famous market of Venice.*"

They turned to where he stood in the stern of the gondola, both equally relieved at the interruption, and followed the direction of his outstretched right hand. The space under the massive stone arches was crowded with tables piled with fish, seafood and whatever vegetables were available this early in the season. The smell of fish and the jumble of voices shouting, cursing, praising their wares drifted over the water.

"And this—" the gondolier pointed straight ahead "—is the Rialto Bridge."

For the next half hour they listened as the gondolier commented on every landmark, extolled every *palazzo,* told anecdotes that all celebrated the glory of Venice. Although neither one of them noticed, the tension between them began to ebb.

When the gondolier pointed out a sand-colored house that was only three windows wide, but whose stone balconies were carved as delicately as if they were made of fine lace, and explained that this was *"la casa di Desdemona,"* about whom *l'inglese* Shakespeare had written a play, Julie could not resist a giggle.

"He sounds rather piqued that a mere Englishman would dare to write about a Venetian woman." She looked up at Theo with a grin.

Theo looked down into her laughing eyes and felt relief ripple through him, closely followed by pure pleasure. It would be all right, he told himself. They would be all right.

He answered her grin with one of his own. "The height of presumption, you must admit."

The easy mood lasted as they glided past Saint Mark's Square and the Doge's Palace. It lasted as they disembarked on the broad quay. It lasted still as they entered the hotel hall with its red carpet and crystal chandeliers.

When the door of their suite closed behind the porter who had helped Fritz carry their luggage, Julie jolted at the sound. They were alone now in a way they had not been alone during their journey. In a way they had never been alone before.

Chapter Ten

Theo felt her edginess. Perhaps because it was a mirror image of his own.

"Julie—" he began, wanting to tell her that she had no reason to be afraid. Wanting to assure her that he would not touch her, not hurt her. But the words died on his lips. Anything he could say now would be a half-truth at best. "A maid will be up directly to attend you."

Julie felt the knot in her stomach begin to loosen as she realized that he was as uneasy as she. "That wasn't what you were going to say."

A room apart, they turned simultaneously to face each other.

"Does it matter?"

"I don't know." Her dark eyebrows rose in question like graceful wings. "Does it?"

"I was going to give you all kinds of assurances, but I am not sure that I wouldn't be lying." He looked down at his hands for a moment before he returned his gaze to her face. "There is so much that I want to promise you and I know in all honesty that I can promise you nothing."

Another woman might have been afraid, might have recoiled from the blunt words. To Julie they meant more than any evasion, any pretty pledge. She was not sure she was comfortable with just how much they meant to her.

She looked at him from across the room. His eyes were more gray than blue now, almost identical with his brother's eyes. She waited for the love and the sweet, sharp pain to fill her heart. The emotion flooded her, and because it was so familiar, she did not recognize that it was so new.

"It was so simple before." He drove his fingers through his tawny hair once and then again. "When did it become so complicated?"

She went to stand in front of him. "Was it ever simple, Theo?" No, she thought, it had stopped being simple the moment she had sat down at his bedside. She smiled because she wanted to give in to the tears that burned suddenly behind her eyelids. "In any case, we have to deal with it as best we can."

Theo nodded, a corner of his mouth lifting in a crooked smile. "My mother would say you have to play the best game you can with the hand you've been dealt."

"A laudable sentiment, although, to continue the metaphor, she would probably say I folded in Turin."

"No. I would say you picked another card. It's debatable though, whether you improved your hand with it or not."

"Are we back to the question of odds?" An ache moved through her. "But then I told you once before that it is not a game for me, Theo." Her dark eyebrows curved upward. "Or don't you remember?"

"Oh, I remember." He gave in to the temptation to touch her and feathered the backs of his fingers down her cheek. "I'm afraid I remember far too well."

His fingers slipped under her chin to tip her face upward and he lowered his head slowly enough to give her every chance to retreat. When she did not, he felt his heartbeat, and his blood, quicken. When he brushed his mouth over hers and felt her lips part beneath his, he almost moaned with the pleasure of it.

The knock on the door had them jumping apart like children caught at a guilty pastime. Disappointment and a feeling of loss wound through them in equal measure as a maid in a dark dress and white apron and cap entered and curtsied, closely followed by Fritz.

Blindly, Julie moved toward the bedroom. She knew that her jerky movements made it more a flight than a graceful withdrawal, but she could do nothing about it.

Behind her, neither one of the two men took their eyes off her.

"I insulted her," Fritz said softly. "So many times I insulted her 'cause I din't want to believe she could help you bettern' me. And she still looked at me kindly." He rubbed his thin, scrawny neck with a surprisingly large hand. "I saw what she did last night. The devil take it, I saw her perform a bloody miracle." His eyes were still on the door that had closed behind Julie. His voice lowered to a whisper. "Is she some kinda saint?"

Theo looked down at Fritz's earnest, homely face. He remembered all the times Julie had lit into him like a Fury. He remembered how a moment ago her mouth had parted against his and suddenly he felt his heart lift.

"No, old friend." He slapped his hand down on Fritz's shoulder. "Whatever she is, she is not a saint."

Theo stood and stretched his body, which was exhausted from the bumping and jolting of the journey. He could almost taste what it would feel like to stretch out in a clean, soft bed, but still he waited.

He opened the French doors and stepped out onto the stone balcony, which was just wide enough to open the doors fully. The wind had risen, rippling the black water below, intensifying the scent of the sea. Beneath the lamps that burned on the quay, the gray stones glistened from the spray the wind had swept over them.

He stared over the dark water of the lagoon. A few more days and the journey he had been waiting for so long would begin. No, he had not just been waiting for it, but living for it. At times perhaps it had been the only thing that had kept him alive.

He remembered well the day when Max had flung the papers at him. The papers that had contained the final details, the final plan for his revenge. The plan that had cost him a small fortune, which he had borrowed from his father against his inheritance. Theo smiled grimly. His father had understood his need for revenge as Max, who had inherited their mother's gentle, forgiving soul, had not.

He remembered, too, the fierce joy he had felt that day. The joy that soon the revenge that would balance the years of suffering, Maryka's and his, would be his. He still felt the need for revenge, because it burned under his skin like an unhealed wound, but that savage joy was gone.

Stepping back into the sitting room, he looked at the door behind which Julie lay. He should never have agreed to take her with him. It was she, he told himself, who had deprived him of that cruel joy of anticipation as surely as if she had cut it from his flesh. She had taken that from him and made him soft. Anger flared, and bitterness, fueled by the fear that the spark, the edge that had driven him were gone, as well.

Another kind of joy had slipped into the void and taken root, but he refused to see it. And yet it did its work within him no less steadily.

He splashed brandy into a glass and lifted it to his lips. But the smell reminded him of the time when he had used it too freely to dull the pain and he set it down untasted. His gaze went again to the bedroom door. Julie had retired more than an hour before. Surely she would be asleep by now.

Quietly he opened the door to the bedroom and slipped into the room.

Julie schooled her breathing to evenness as she heard the door open. Her body was crying out for sleep, yet she had lain in the dark room, waiting, wondering, made wakeful by the thud of her heart. Of course she had known that at some point of their journey they would be forced to share a bed-chamber, but now that the reality of it was here, she found herself unsettled.

The bed, with its canopy and velvet curtains, which were loosely tied to the posts with gold-tasseled ropes, was wide, but she felt it dip with the weight of Theo's body. Heard the rustle of bed linen as he lay down. Felt the tug on the blanket.

For the second time, laughter rose within her to dissolve tension as quickly, as surely as the sun dissolves an April snowfall.

Theo stiffened when he heard the gurgle of laughter.

"Theo, if you take the blanket all for yourself, I will nail it down. See if I don't."

The absurdity of the situation struck him and, helpless, he began to laugh.

"You know," he said when his laughter had quieted, "I'm quite sure that there's no one in the world even remotely like you."

Julie tipped her head toward him. All she could see was the dim outline of his straight profile and she wished suddenly that she could see his eyes.

"That could be the nicest thing you've ever said to me."

All the tension that had knotted her muscles had eased and her body fused with the soft mattress with the effort-lessness of a liquid fusing with a mold. She turned onto her side and burrowed her face into the feather pillow.

"I think I can sleep now," she murmured, her voice slurring.

Her breathing was already evening out into sleep when she started up, remembering how she had found him in pain the night before. "Theo? Will you promise me something?"

He frowned into the darkness. "If I can."

"If you are in pain in the night, wake me. Please."

"All right." She had surprised him again, he thought. He did not know what he had expected to hear, but it had not been that. But then when had she ever done anything ordinary?

"Promise?"

"Yes, Julie, I promise. Sleep now." He heard the bed-springs sigh as she shifted, and within moments her deep, even breathing told him that she slept.

His eyes were accustomed to the darkness now and, against his better judgment, he rose on an elbow and edged toward the center of the bed.

She lay on her side, her hand tucked against her cheek like a child. Her wrist-thick braid had fallen forward over her shoulder and lay like a dark rope on the white linen. Unable to resist, he reached out and touched the tip, which curled lightly below the pale ribbon.

Soft. So incredibly soft. His hand traveled upward, over the velvet ribbon, to curl around her hair. For a moment he lost himself in the erotic vision of unplaiting the braid and running his fingers through the silky strands. His blood began to heat, and yet, at the same time, the softness made him feel completely and utterly safe, as if it were a talisman that could protect him from evil, even the evil within himself.

Not wanting, not able to let go, he twined the braid between his fingers. He would hold on just for a moment longer, he thought. Just for a moment.

Minutes passed and, as the exhaustion began to take him under, he slid down to the sheets. His last conscious thought was that he could smell the scent of verbena, as if he were lying next to Julie and not half a bed away. His fingers still twined with her hair, he, too, slept.

Julie felt the pull on the back of her head as she began to surface from sleep. Wanting to ease it, she shifted, but her limbs were too heavy with sleep to take her far. Her face half-buried in the pillow, she groped her way down her braid. When her hand met Theo's, she stilled, first with sleepy pleasure as she brushed over his lean hand, then with anger that he would take advantage of her sleep to touch her.

All traces of sleep vanished, she gave her braid a little tug, but it did not budge.

"Theo?"

There was no answer except his deep, even breathing, which sounded as if he were asleep, although she was all but certain that he was merely pretending to be so.

Caught between irritation and amusement, she repeated his name. "Let me go."

When there was no answer again, she subsided for a moment with an exasperated huff. It was difficult to deliver a severe reprimand when you were fighting a feather pillow and laughter at the same time.

She inched a little closer to him to give her braid more slack and turned her head to face him.

He lay in the middle of the bed without the benefit of a pillow, and the boneless way his body merged with the mattress assured her that he really was asleep. It would have been a simple matter now just to tug her braid out of his grasp, but the thought never crossed her mind.

Shifting closer so that her braid lay loosely between them, Julie propped herself up on her elbow and looked down at Theo. She remembered well the first time she had seen him as he had been fighting his way out of the drug-induced sleep.

His face, its skin as white as the sheets he had lain on, had been all sharp angles, and the brackets that pain had dug around his mouth had been deep. His face was still lean now, but no longer so thin that the bones seemed about to pierce the skin, and the many hours he had spent walking in the park had put color back into it. He would carry the lines that pain had carved for the rest of his life, but they no longer seemed quite as deep.

How much had changed since that day? she mused. How much had stayed the same? Even as her mind put that question to her, her heart knew that nothing had stayed the same. Nothing at all.

The light was dim still, and deciding to let him sleep a while yet, she put her hand on his and began to work his fingers away from her hair. But instead of releasing it, he curled his fingers around it even more tightly, like a child who refuses to let go of a favorite toy.

She chuckled softly. Brushing his hair back from his forehead, she nestled her cheek into her palm and settled down to wait until he awoke.

He was floating in the midst of a vague dream. He was alone and the world around him was wrapped in a wispy fog, its tendrils reaching out to encircle him. He knew that

Julie was there somewhere, but the mist hid her from him, and no matter where he turned, his fingers grasped only yet another ribbon of fog. It was then that he heard her soft laugh.

Hope leaped up in his heart and he moved toward the sound, but found only fog. Undaunted, he pushed through it, although it swirled around him, ever thicker, until its very texture became more compact and it was as if he were fighting his way through a viscous vapor. He thought to catch a glimpse of her silhouette and he reached out for her, but when his fingers closed, they were empty.

The first thing Julie noticed was the change in his breathing. The smooth, even breaths quickened, became ragged as if he had been running. She saw his brows knit in a frown. He made a sound that was half murmur, half moan, and his hand tightened around her braid until the skin of the knuckles whitened.

Mindful of the other time she had seen him fighting a dream, she put a hand to his cheek, which was rough with a night's growth of beard. Wiping away a drop of sweat that trickled down from his temple, she rubbed her thumb over his cheekbone.

"It's all right," she whispered. Wanting to soothe, she ran her fingers through his thick, tawny hair, brushing it back from his face.

He could hear her voice. Surely if he could hear her voice she must be near. If she was near, then surely he would find her. He could all but feel her hands on him.

"Julie."

Her eyes flew to his face as she heard him murmur her name. Her name! Was he dreaming of her, then? And if he was, why was the dream making him sweat and moan?

There was no thought to propriety in her mind as she shifted closer. All she knew was that he suffered and needed and that she could perhaps ease both. Leaving her hand threaded in his hair, she tucked his head beneath her chin so that she could place her cheek against his crown. As her fingers stroked the back of his head, she spoke soft, soothing words, her breath ruffling his hair.

The dream began to fade and with it all that had troubled him. With a long, shuddering breath he fell back into a deep, dreamless sleep.

Julie felt him quiet. Her fingers stilled but remained twined in his hair, holding him against her. Now it was she who needed. Needed the closeness, the warmth. Not just any closeness, any warmth, but his. The warmth and closeness this one man could give her.

Even as she took what she needed, the questions, the doubts, the confusion began to crowd in. How could she need him? Was she so fickle, so inconstant, so shameless? Although she felt the loss like a physical ache, she began to edge away from him.

Theo drifted awake with the fragrance of verbena in his nostrils. Julie. Unaware that he had spoken her name aloud, he smiled and burrowed his face deeper into the inviting warmth of the mattress. Julie. He remembered falling asleep the night before, thinking that he could smell her scent as if he were lying next to her. This morning every breath brought him the fragrance even more intensely than last night, until his head spun with it.

Julie heard him murmur her name. Was he dreaming again? She halted her careful retreat almost before it had begun and cradled him against her again. But it was not like before, when she had held him as she might have held a child.

Now his breath was hot on her skin as if even the thin barrier of her cambric nightgown did not exist. The heat slipped over her skin, then under it and into her blood. Then it was traveling through her with a speed that stunned her, leaving her too shaken, too weak to move. By the time it had lodged in her belly, it had become a ball of fire that threatened to consume her.

She was still struggling to deal with the sensation when he nuzzled into her and whispered her name a second time. It seemed impossible, but the fire flared higher. It was so new that she could barely understand it or define it, but for a moment she wondered what it would be like to give in to this flame that beckoned with sweet, hot promises. She could almost taste that heady moment of surrender and her fingers tightened on the back of his head.

Then logic and her innate sense of order, of what was good and right, took over. Deliberately she let him go, although it took the last bit of strength she possessed, and began to shift away from him. When she felt the pull on the back of her head again, she realized that Theo's hand was still curled around her braid.

For the second time that morning she laughed softly, this time at herself. For the second time that morning she settled down to wait.

Chapter Eleven

The warmth and the scent of verbena faded a little and, wanting to recapture it, Theo flexed his hands. His fingers absorbed the sensation of silk. The memory of touching Julie's hair before he had fallen asleep floated through his sleep-drugged brain. Had he held on to it through the night?

The soft, husky sound of her laughter had him opening his eyes.

She was looking at him. There was a smile in her eyes that glowed golden even in the dim morning light. Desire slammed into him so quickly that it jolted the last traces of sleep from him. If he closed his eyes, he thought, perhaps it would go away. But the image of the golden eyes that held the promise of secret, fabulous pleasures stayed with him.

"Good morning."

There was a lilt of laughter in her voice. Without opening his eyes, he grumbled a response.

Theo's voice, still rough with sleep, seemed to scrape over her skin, sending yet more sparks toward the fire in her belly. Julie pressed her thighs together against it, but that only intensified the burning ache.

"I think it would be a good idea if you let go of my hair, Theo, so that I can get up."

There was still a hint of amusement in her voice that provoked his annoyance. It was fine for her to be amused when her scent, the thought of her soft body close enough to touch and the silk of her hair against his skin were driving him to the edge of control.

He opened his eyes, with a testy remark on his tongue, but when he met her gaze, he saw that if there had been amusement in her eyes, as well, it had fled. They had darkened and widened like the eyes of some small, fragile creature who has been backed into a corner by a predator.

His gaze lowered to where his fingers still curled around the dark plait, but only for a moment.

"What are we going to do, Julie?"

"What do you mean?"

"This is not the last time that we share a bed. Will we wonder every day what it's like to kiss when the softness of the night is still with us and the light is dim?"

Julie thought of the heat that still curled within her, teasing, tormenting. His voice alone had it soaring. The images that his words brought had it soaring further. She was innocent, but she knew instinctively that if he put his mouth on hers, the heat would become a roaring blaze that would consume all thought, all doubts, all scruples.

"Perhaps it is better to wonder than to know."

"Are you sure?" he pressed, not completely understanding why he felt compelled to do so. He had always preferred the straightforward in his personal relationships, but from the very beginning there had been nothing straightforward between them. Instead it had been as hazy, as unreal as a tapestry of dreams.

He was still touching her hair, his thumb rubbing up and down the braid, but she could feel his fingers as if his hands were on her skin instead. A new wave of heat arrowed down into her belly and lower.

It would be so easy. Just one word. Just one gesture of invitation. And they would both have what they wanted so badly. She could feel herself shifting toward him when some still-rational part of her brain, some pang of conscience broke through the sensual haze, replacing it with panic.

"What good is it going to do you to kiss me?" she demanded desperately. "What good is it going to do either one of us?" She dragged in a breath. "You will pretend I am someone else. As will I."

Blinding herself to the pain that shot into his eyes as she blinded herself to the fact that the words she had spoken were, for her at least, a lie, she grabbed her braid and pulled it out of his suddenly unresisting fingers. Her breath heaving, she lay on her back.

The guilt surged into him. It did not submerge the desire, but the pleasure went out of it, leaving only the edginess and the naked need.

"I don't know what kind of blackguard that makes me, but if I kissed you now, Julie, it would be you." He willed her to turn her head to look at him, but she did not. "God help me, it would be only you."

She said nothing, but as she stared up at the blue canopy of the bed, she knew that if Theo kissed her now, she would be kissing him and no one else, either.

Julie sat in front of the mirror with its ornate gold frame as the pert little maid dressed her hair. Avoiding her reflection, she kept her gaze instead on the ribbon she was methodically destroying with her nervous fingers. She'd looked into the mirror and seen her eyes, wide and glittering, echoing the sensations that were still jangling through her body. She had no wish to see them again.

She tossed the shreds of the ribbon onto the dresser. She would keep her distance from Theo, she swore to herself.

From now on she would be strictly business. After all, that was what she had offered him—a business proposition. No more and no less.

Oh, she remembered his warning. Too well. But she would not allow this to happen again. She could not. From now on she would make certain that she was asleep by the time he came to bed and up before he awoke. They would speak when it was necessary, touch when it could not be avoided, and they would be fine. Just fine.

Theo paced the lobby trying to come to terms with what had happened and what had almost happened that morning. No, he corrected himself, not what had happened. What he had done. What he had almost done, he added. What he had wanted to do. In passing he aimed a crack with his cane at a brass pot that held a small palm tree. The dull ringing sound earned him a nasty look from the doorman, who was wearing more gold braid than an admiral.

Even as some base part of him tried to shift at least part of the blame to Julie, he knew too well that if there was blame to be assigned, it should lie at his door. Yes, he had warned her, but it was he who was responsible for this whole charade. It was he who had all but begged for her kiss.

He remembered her last words. Did he have so little pride? he asked himself. So little pride that he wanted her, even though he knew that he would never be more in her eyes than a poor substitute for Max? He did not answer his own question, but he knew that what he had felt this morning had had nothing to do with pride.

But she had wanted him, some stubborn part of his brain argued. Him, not Max. He had seen her eyes darken with arousal. If he had pushed just a little— He gave a small grim laugh. Desire had little to do with love, he reminded himself. Was he not the very best example for that? Did he not want Julie while his heart belonged to Maryka?

Because something within him tripped over the last thought, he dug into his memory for Maryka's image and felt that familiar jolt of panic as he came up empty. He'd known her as no one else had known her. He'd touched her, loved her. He knew the texture of her hair and the scent of her skin. But he could not call to mind her face. He could not do it, he realized with a flash of resentment, because every cell of his mind was filled with Julie's image.

Then he felt the pain and grief surge through him, pushing the resentment aside, and he wanted to lower his face into his hands and mourn. For Maryka. For himself. For what they had had together. For what they would never have again. No matter if he found her. No matter if he exacted his revenge from General Boris Muromsky. Motionless, he stood in the middle of the lobby with its overabundance of marble and red velvet and stared at the far wall.

Trailing her hand along the wide marble banister, Julie walked slowly down the curved staircase. She was procrastinating and she hated herself for it. She rarely delayed diving into whatever had to be done, but how many times had she avoided Theo because of words they had had? It seemed to have become a habit.

It would be all right, she assured herself. It would be just as she had thought it through. She would be cool and distant and, because he was proud and stubborn, so would he.

Then she saw him standing in the middle of the lobby. A stranger would have seen merely a man absorbed in thought. She saw the desolation that seemed to radiate out from him like a gray veil. The strategy that she had so carefully mapped out flew out of her head as if it had never been and she ran down the remaining stairs.

Her heels clicked lightly on the marble floor, but he did not hear her approach. Although she knew that odds were high that he would turn on her with angry, cynical words, she did not brace herself against them. Instead she laid her hand on his arm and opened her heart.

"Theo? What is it?"

He started and turned slowly to face her. He saw the concern in her eyes.

"What is it?" she repeated.

What could he tell her? he asked himself. That her image, her scent so pervaded him that there was room for nothing, for no one else? After what had happened this morning, she would think it a clumsy attempt to flatter, to seduce.

So he only shook his head and offered her his arm.

With a small sigh, Julie threaded her arm through his and they stepped out onto the sun-washed quay.

Signora Laura Versini, her dress of violet taffeta rustling discreetly, escorted the young couple to the door of her small, exclusive dressmaker's shop. They called themselves Monsieur and Madame van Dam, but if she were wont to gamble, she would have wagered her last florin that they had never stood together in front of a priest.

She allowed a little of the disdain she felt to creep into her eyes, although she dipped into a curtsy that was a little lower than it might have been had times been better. But because of the cursed Austrians swarming all over her beloved city, half of her customers had fled to their country villas and the rest were using their money for things other than buying clothes in the latest fashion for their women. And the Venetian women who allowed themselves to be kept by Austrian officers were not breaking her door down, either. But the gold coins the tall blond man had tossed so negligently on the counter were good, and they, as well as those that remained to be paid, would more than recompense her for the fact that she and all her girls would have to work night and day to get the gowns finished.

The door closed with a light tinkle of its bell and she turned to shoo the whispering girls toward the cramped little workroom in the back.

They had barely taken a step when Julie heard the *signora* hiss at her shop girls much as she would have at a flock of pigeons on Saint Mark's Square. She had seen the shop girls exchanging glances and whispering behind her back and she had seen the carefully rationed contempt in the *signora*'s eyes. This was something she had not expected when she had set out on this adventure, she thought. But then, there was more she had not foreseen. Much more. A self-deprecating laugh rose to her lips.

Because her soft laugh reminded him of this morning, Theo stiffened. "Is there something in particular you find amusing?"

Julie looked up at Theo and saw that his eyes matched the cool formality of his voice. He was doing much better than she was, she thought. She had gone back on everything she had promised herself, but she was finding it difficult to be aloof when Theo had gone about the business of replacing all the clothing she had had to leave behind by dressing her from the skin on out with a matter-of-factness that had first amused, then embarrassed her. And now she found herself chafing under the knowing looks of those who had waited on them.

"Am I not allowed to chuckle when the shopkeepers cannot quite decide whether I am your sister or your mistress?" She watched as his eyes took on still another layer of ice.

"What are you talking about?"

"If it came down to a vote, I rather think they would vote for mistress." She did not understand why that thought hurt quite so acutely, and it was that more than the pain itself that made her tone sharper than it would otherwise have been. "No man plunks down a handful of gold coins for a sister without at least a small wince."

His eyes narrowed. "Would you care to explain why they would not believe you my wife?"

"Let's walk a little." Julie tipped her head toward the glass front of the dressmaker's shop. "I have had enough of audiences today."

Theo maneuvered her down the narrow street, trying to ignore the dull throb that had taken over his body. As soon as they had turned the next corner, he stopped her, his hand heavy on her arm.

"You planned everything down to the last detail, Theo, except one thing. No wedding ring. That is what the shop-keepers looked for the moment I took off my gloves."

"Why didn't you say something?" he demanded.

She bit her lower lip to prevent a smile. "I just did. Be-sides—" she paused "—I'm not sure a ring would change a great deal. I suspect that we don't look very married."

Theo gave her a long look. She was strung as tightly as he was, but because of her intrinsic softness, the edginess did not show quite as clearly. "No, I don't imagine we do," he finally said. "But we can remedy the matter of the rings at least."

He took her arm and steered her down the street. How could he have overlooked something that basic? he asked himself. If he had overlooked that, how many other things had he overlooked?

Since in Venice the next jeweler is never very far away, within minutes they were sitting in an elegant shop being served *biscotti* and sweet wine in goblets made of blue Venetian glass. When the jeweler invited them to move to a table covered with black velvet where he had prepared a display of rings, Julie shook her head.

"Go ahead, Theo. You choose."

She was tired, she thought as her finger was measured. Tired of the stiff formality they had maintained so carefully all day. Even as she reminded herself that it was what she had wanted, that it was the wisest course to take, she knew that it simply was not in her to keep up a facade that had nothing to do with what was happening underneath.

Subterfuge. It all came down to her ineptness at subterfuge, she mused as her gaze brushed over Theo. He was holding some kind of medallion on a chain and she stiffened. The clothes she could accept. That had been agreed upon. But now he was buying her jewelry. That hurt more than all the whispers, all the knowing looks. Now she felt good and well like a mistress.

It was simple to pick up two plain gold bands. Almost as an afterthought Theo quickly chose a few pieces of jewelry to complete the wardrobe he had bought her—a cameo carved of pale pink coral on a black velvet ribbon, a necklace and earrings of milky pearls, an amethyst pendant on a golden chain. He was already reaching for his money when his gaze happened to settle on a display case behind the counter.

The necklace and its matching earbobs, with stones that were shaped like oval discs, was simple and certainly less flashy and less valuable than most of the jewelry in the shop. But they were made of rich gold amber and had the exact shade of Julie's eyes.

The jeweler had seen the direction of his gaze and was already opening the case and placing the pieces on a velvet-lined tray.

"Those, as well." Theo gestured impatiently. He had bought the other jewelry for Madame van Dam. The amber was only for Julie. And he did not care to examine his motivation more closely. "I will take those and the rings with me. Have the rest in my hotel tomorrow morning."

The day still had a few hours of sun in it as they returned to the hotel, but the light was beginning to soften. By unspoken mutual consent they cut diagonally across Saint Mark's Square, avoiding the Café Florian, where a small orchestra played Viennese waltzes for an audience of Austrian officers and their ladies, whose favors had been paid for in coin. Lost in their thoughts, neither one of them paid attention to the Byzantine glory of the cathedral nor to the Gothic beauty of the Doge's Palace.

As soon as the door to their suite closed behind them, they moved into opposite corners of the sitting room, much as they had done the day before.

"Do you want to rest now?" Theo asked.

"No, but you should." Julie took off her bonnet and held it by the strings. "You've been having pain since lunch."

His head whipped toward her. "How do you know?"

"Because of the way you walk. The way you stand up or sit down. The way you breathe." She shrugged but did not look at him. "Take your pick." *Because of the way my nerve endings tighten when you have pain,* she thought, but did not say it.

She looked at him then and saw that the lines around his mouth had deepened. Everything that had passed between them today forgotten, she pitched her bonnet aside without looking where it landed and went toward him. Wordlessly she slid off his coat and unbuttoned and took off his waistcoat. Steadying him with a hand at his hip, she worked her other hand up and down his spine.

When she felt the pain begin to flow out of him, she stepped back. "You should stay off your feet tomorrow. The jolting of the journey and all that walking today were too much for you." She picked her bonnet up off the floor. "You're not healed yet."

He moved toward her, carefully at first, then finding the pain truly almost gone, more quickly. He caught her hands in his just as she was starting to turn away.

"Don't." She pulled away, but his hands tightened.

"Forgive me, Julie."

Her eyes flew up to his. "What for?"

"Have I done anything I should not beg your forgiveness for?" A corner of his mouth tipped up in a crooked smile. "From the very beginning?"

His lopsided smile made him look very young and it moved her so strongly that she had the sensation that he had reached out and brushed his fingers over her heartstrings as though they were the strings of a harp. Because the emotion vibrated through her so intensely, it made her feel that she was being petty. She shook her head. "Let us just leave it."

"It is not a matter of a few shopkeepers giving you knowing looks, is it?" he persisted, not understanding why he did so. All his life he had been content to enjoy women, content to simply give and receive pleasure with no demands, no questions. Why did he feel so pressed to understand this one woman when she puzzled him as no other had ever done? Why did he feel that it was so important to understand her, when he understood all too well that although she was not indifferent to him, it was his brother whom she loved?

"It's not even about what happened this morning."

She lowered her gaze again, but not before Theo had seen the hurt in her eyes. Suddenly, within the space of a breath, everything fell into place.

Chapter Twelve

"Of course. How could I not have seen it?" He shook his head at his own stupidity. "It was the jewelry, wasn't it? At first you took it all in stride, but—" He paused. "But when you saw me buying the jewelry, you saw yourself in a classic situation. A woman being bought with trinkets."

When she did not raise her gaze, he cupped her chin in his hand and tilted her face up to his. The stunned look in her eyes told him that he had been exactly on the mark. With a twinge of regret he thought of the amber he had wanted to give her as a kind of peace offering. That would have to wait.

"Will you believe me if I tell you that that was the furthest thing from my mind?" He could not resist running his thumb along her jawline, where the skin was so impossibly soft.

"Of course." With a twist of her head she broke the contact and began to move away.

"That does not sound very convincing. Or convinced."

Her only answer was a shrug.

He felt a jolt of surprise that a small thing like that could hurt so deeply.

"Julie." Theo forced himself to stay where he was, even though his hands itched to spin her around to face him. "If you don't believe I'm being honest with you, if you don't think you can trust me, tell me so. But look me in the eyes when you do it."

She rubbed the heel of her hand against her forehead. How could she explain to him that it was she herself she could not trust? How could she explain that feeling like his mistress was so hurtful because it was so nearly the truth? Suddenly everything she had felt that day from the moment she had awakened surged through her like a boiling spring shooting up from the red-hot core of the earth and she whirled around to face him.

"I trusted you at a time when you did not trust yourself, Theo, or don't you remember telling me that I should be afraid of you?"

"There is nothing about you, Julie, that I have forgotten. Nothing."

"All right. Since we're being honest with each other, then let's sweep the whole truth out into the open." She pulled in a deep, shuddering breath. "This morning I came within an inch of making it true, of making myself your mistress. I don't believe you were so blind or so naive not to see it."

Her words slammed into him, bringing the sharp taste of desire, and he had to fight to keep it out of his voice. "All I asked you for was a kiss."

The mellow sound of his voice had everything she had felt that morning pouring into her until she felt like a crucible full of molten metal.

"Yes, a kiss." The heat was rising, its power frightening her. "Do you really think it not would have become more?" Finding her hands fisted, she forced herself to loosen them.

"Perhaps you were right. Perhaps I really should be afraid of you," Julie continued. Fed by the heat and the fear, her words came quickly, leaving no time for thought. "After all, we will be in the same bed again tonight and you will forgive me for thinking you might have wanted to help things along."

Her hands flew up to her mouth as she gasped at her own words and shook her head wildly. "Oh God, I'm sorry." Even as she spoke the words of apology, a heaviness settled within her. She could not take them back. The words were said and they would forever hang between them. "That was an unfair thing to say."

She saw his eyes darken to a steely blue gray and she stood still, waiting for his anger. Wanting it. Needing it even. But no anger came. Instead he stood motionless, his eyes a bleak wasteland.

Her words hit him like a fist to his middle, robbing him of breath, robbing him of the ability to think. There was a moment of merciful numbness and then another before the pain broke through.

Julie felt the pain even before it reached his eyes and was already moving toward him. Reaching up, she laid her fingers against his face, needing to ease, to comfort. But he stiffened and she lowered her hands to lace them tightly at her waist.

"There is no excuse for what I said to you. There is never an excuse for causing pain." Although she wanted to look away, she met his eyes and held them. "But I will try to give you an explanation, if you want one."

He drew a long, careful breath. "Go ahead."

She wanted to touch him, she thought as she searched for words. But he was holding himself so straight and stiff that she did not.

"I lashed out at you because—" she swallowed and opened her hands in a gesture of helplessness "—because I am afraid of what I am feeling." She felt a sense of letdown at the lameness of her words. They did not begin to describe the tempest that was raging within her.

"And what are you feeling, Julie?"

"More than I bargained for."

She was hedging, Theo realized, and he felt something that teetered between amusement and relief. And underlying it was the hope he did not recognize. "And just what is that?"

"You are going to make me spell it out, aren't you?"

He met her eyes squarely. "Yes."

She sighed. "I needed to get away from Turin. No, I was desperate," she corrected herself. If the moment of truth had come, then it would be the complete, unmasked truth. "But that you already know."

He nodded, setting his jaw against the unreasoning surge of jealousy.

"I thought it would be easy. I suppose I knew even then that I was lying to myself."

"You said you wanted to go with me. That you needed to."

Surprise that he remembered her words so precisely was reflected in both their eyes.

"Yes, but I couldn't have explained why. I still cannot." The need for honesty pushed her to correct herself again. "At least not completely."

The barely perceptible lifting of his eyebrows, the faint amusement that came and went in his eyes both annoyed and eased her. This was the Theo she knew, the Theo she had become accustomed to, the Theo she had— Her thoughts bumped to a halt as if she had run into a brick wall. Her heart skittered, then soared, although she did not understand why.

"This morning I wanted you. I wanted you to—" She broke off. "It made me feel wanton and cheap. And today—" she threw up her hands in an impatient gesture "—today just confirmed it."

He had pushed her—farther than he had a right to push. Now, awed by her honesty, her courage, he was silent. What could he say to her? What could he offer her? Whatever it was, it was too little for a woman like her. But knowing it did not stop the wanting, the hunger he could feel down to his empty soul.

"Aren't you going to say something?" she demanded. "You've made me say things—" she gulped a breath "—admit things—" She felt the color flow in and out of her face.

"Julie." Theo took a step toward her. When she did not retreat, he closed the distance between them and took her hands in his. "Julie, there is nothing cheap or tawdry about the way you feel."

"But how can I—" She stopped.

"How can you want me to make love to you when you love Max?" he finished for her. Jealousy rose again, like a dull knife turning in his flesh.

Something was not right about the words, she thought, but she did not know what it was and nodded her agreement.

"How can I want to make love to you when I love Maryka?" Something was not right about the words, he thought, but he did not know what it was and he did not deny them.

An emotion flashed hot and hard through Julie. Not recognizing it as jealousy, she called it anger and tried to twist her hands out of his grasp. But his grip only tightened.

"I ask you again, Julie." He felt the quick, sharp jolt of panic and had to dig inside himself for the strength to push it away. "Do you want to go back?"

"No!" The denial rose to her lips without a thought. "No," she repeated. "But I will not be your mistress."

"No, you will not be my mistress," Theo agreed softly. Keeping his eyes on hers, he raised her hands to his mouth. Turning them, he pressed a kiss first to one palm then the other. "My lover perhaps, but never my mistress."

She was not sure what stirred her more—the way his lips moved over her palm or the way he kept his eyes steady on hers as he touched his mouth to her skin. Suddenly the heat was back, skimming over her skin, teasing, dipping inside her.

"You would seduce me?"

"Seduce? No." He smiled slowly, first with his mouth, then with his eyes, as well. "Mistresses are seduced. Lovers come of their own free will."

"Are you saying that you would not make love to me unless I asked you to?"

"I suppose that's one way of putting it." He traced light circles on her palms with his thumbs. "Weren't you the one who assured me that I would never take what you did not choose to give me?"

The thought was wicked, but the words were tumbling out before she could hold them back. "Then I could ask you for a kiss and it would not—" her breath caught "—not be more?"

Theo found himself wanting to give her anything, everything she asked for. He hoped he could. "Yes. Are you asking me for a kiss, Julie?"

"If I were a coquette, I could say I am only giving you the kiss you asked for this morning."

There was a trace of a smile in her voice, but her eyes were huge and serious.

"You could. But you are not, are you?"

"No," she whispered. "Kiss me, Theo. Kiss me now before the sun goes down."

He was still holding her hands in his. Lifting them again, he brushed his lips over her fingertips, once, twice. Then he laid her hands flat against his chest.

Cupping her face as gently as if she were made of glass, he tilted it up to his.

Julie forgot to breathe as she waited for the touch of his mouth on hers, but instead, his lips began a leisurely journey over her face. She sighed as he traced the curve of her cheek. Her sigh became a moan as he dipped to taste the skin warmed by the pulse that beat beneath her ear.

When his mouth found its way to hers she was already melting. He brushed his lips over hers, teasing, provoking them both. Even when her lips parted in invitation, he continued to tease.

Julie dug her fingers into his waistcoat, sure that if she did not find purchase, she would collapse at his feet. Sure that if he did not kiss her, truly kiss her, she would go mad. But he only skimmed his mouth over hers, watching her, always watching her.

Impatience became longing. Longing became need. Need became hunger. Desperate, she whispered his name.

Something eased within him as he realized that this was what he had been waiting for—this knowledge that it was his kiss she wanted. His kiss and no other. Then he deepened the kiss.

She thought she had remembered Theo's kiss—the taste, the texture, the sensations that it sent spinning through her. But as he took her mouth fully, she realized that her memories had been to reality as a single candle is to a blazing fire. As their tongues tangled, the heat arrowed through her. Here again was the power that she had felt earlier, but this time it did not frighten her. Perhaps because she knew it was too late for fear.

Theo could feel Julie's pulse race beneath his fingers. Even her skin seemed to quiver with the rush of her blood. He felt his own body stir. It was tempting, so very tempting. Another kiss, a touch, a caress and she would be his. His body hardened at the thought. But, he reminded himself, he had promised that he would not seduce her.

Slowly he ended the kiss. But, unable to sever the link completely, he allowed his mouth to linger on hers.

Julie felt the rush of her blood subside. The whirlwind within her waned degree by slow degree, but still it remained a small, spinning ball in her belly, sending out heat. It was no longer the frantic, violent heat that consumed everything in its path, but a solid, banked heat that would last through the night.

Her eyes were still locked on his and she saw the same feelings there that were pouring through her. Was she seeing merely a reflection of her feelings, she wondered, as she was seeing a reflection of her face there, or could he possibly be feeling the same thing?

"Theo?"

"Yes, *chérie?*" His hands were still cupping her face and he could not resist letting his fingers drift over her skin one more time.

"Thank you." She saw his questioning look. "If you had taken more, I would have given it. And given freely."

Her words sent a fresh rush of arousal racing through him, but it was tempered by a surge of tenderness so great, so sweet that it held him spellbound for a moment before he could speak.

"You have it the wrong way around, *ma petite.*" He brushed his thumb over her mouth. "You have to give first for it to count as not taking."

She thought about his words for a moment and gave a little shrug. "There are ways of giving that have nothing to do with words."

Her simple candor stunned him. "Do you have no guile, little one?"

"I don't know. I hope not." She smiled, and as her fingers loosened their hold on his waistcoat, she smoothed the brocaded silk.

Theo looked into her eyes, so open, so artless. No, he thought, she had no guile. What would she say, then, when she learned how false he had been with her? What would she say when she learned that she was additional bait in a trap for a man who was her blood relative?

Julie saw the shadow move through his eyes. In a gesture that was as natural to her as taking the next breath, she slid her arms around him and laid her cheek against his chest. She felt the leap of his heart beneath her ear, then the quickened, unsteady beat. The pleasure spread through her like a cup of warm, spiced wine on a cold evening.

Her movement had shifted his hands to the back of her head and he slid them down to the net-covered chignon the maid had fashioned that morning. His hands lingered for a moment as he indulged once more in the fantasy of removing the pins and letting her hair spill over his hands.

Then he felt her nestle her cheek still closer against his chest. Again the tenderness moved through him and his arms went around her to press her close.

The arousal was rippling through him still, no longer sharp and demanding, but constant and steady, like endless circles formed by a single pebble. Yet, at the same time, he felt a measure of comfort he had never before felt with a woman. But then comfort had never been something he had looked for. He had a sudden, distinct image of growing old beside her, but he pushed it away with almost panicked haste.

Julie loved Max, he reminded himself ruthlessly. And even if she were to stay with him, he would never be more than second best. And every time he took her into his arms, he would wonder if she was thinking of his brother. If she was imagining that she lay in his brother's arms. And he— he had obligations to another woman. It did not occur to him that he no longer thought of emotions when he thought of Maryka. All the soft feelings were gone. All he thought of were obligations—and guilt.

They began to pull back from each other simultaneously and Theo slid his hands along Julie's arms until he again held only her hands.

The last bit of cloudiness cleared away from her eyes, and when she smiled, the smile was rueful.

"I think it would perhaps be wiser not to repeat this experiment very often."

"Julie, I—"

She shook her head and with a light tug removed her hands from his before she turned and walked to the window. Now that it was all over her nerves began to jangle. Taking a deep breath, she concentrated on the tranquil water of the lagoon, which was beginning to darken, the tips of the ripples still gilded by the setting sun.

She had behaved shamelessly, she thought, and yet she could not bring herself to honestly regret what had just happened. It had been too—for a moment she searched for the precise word—too real, she decided.

How odd it was, she mused. Just this morning she had felt like a wanton when Theo had done nothing but touch her hair. She had been driven to hurt him with a lie to prevent him from kissing her. And now, just hours later, she had begged for his kiss, she had been so close to him that she had felt the stirring of his body and it had felt right. Yes, she thought, that was the precise word. It had felt right.

What did that make her? What kind of a woman was she to love one man and feel right in the arms of another? What had changed in just one day that she was willing to accept what had appalled her but hours before? There was no logic, no reason to it. Nothing she could hold on to.

Her life had always been so simple, she thought. Even when she had fallen in love with a man she could never have, it had remained simple because that love was so pure, so far removed from everyday reality. It did not occur to her how close her thoughts were to what he had said to her. Nor did she notice that what she felt when she thought of him was no longer painful but sweetly nostalgic.

Then Theo had entered her life and everything had become complicated, off balance. She, who had always known where she was going, found herself feeling that she had been put out into a dark forest without a light, without a map, to blindly pick her way. She, who had always known exactly who she was, found herself a stranger.

Theo felt a chill seep into him as he watched Julie look out the window. The moment was slipping away from him. He was afraid that she was slipping away from him, as well, and he had not the vaguest idea how to hold her.

As unsure of himself as he had ever been in his life, he closed the distance between them. His hand lifted to her shoulder, but he lowered it again without touching her.

Julie felt the warmth of Theo's body behind her before she focused her gaze on their combined reflection in the glass. He was the only familiar entity in a strange universe, she thought. More familiar than she herself.

It would be easy to lean back into him and let herself go. Too easy. And there were too many questions to be answered before she did.

"I think I'll turn in now."

"It's early yet. Don't you want supper?"

She shook her head and felt rather than saw Theo step back to give her room. As she turned around, she looked up at him.

"I'll need a little time." She tipped her head toward the bedroom.

"Take as much as you need."

For a long moment they stared at each other, realizing the double meaning of their words. Both wanted to give the other a gentle, reassuring touch. Neither one dared to.

"Good night."

"Good night, Julie."

It was a long time before Theo lay down on the far side of the large bed. It was longer still before he slept.

Chapter Thirteen

Hours had passed, or at least it seemed like it. Julie had turned this way and that, lifted her arms and been poked with enough pins to fill a pincushion.

When the shop door closed behind her with its little tinkle, she took a long, deep breath and wrinkled her nose at the damp, moldy smell that rose from the nearby canal. Then a gust of wind ruffled her pelisse and the next breath she took was scented with the salty smell of the sea. She smiled, satisfied that such a small thing could give her such pleasure, and began to walk.

She walked slowly, allowing herself time to browse through the shop windows, but her mind was back in the hotel room she had crept out of so quietly this morning. Theo had been asleep when she had woken and, although she would have wanted to indulge herself and watch him for a few minutes, she was mindful of what had happened the day before. Dragging her clothes into the other room, she had struggled into petticoats and gown, grateful that her slim figure could do without being laced into a corset.

Now she wondered how he had spent the morning and hoped that he had rested, as she had asked him to do in the note she had left propped up on the table. Smiling to herself as she walked up the shallow steps of the bridge, she barely noticed the two men in the green and red Austrian uniform who stepped away from the stone balustrade.

"The *bella signorina* looks like she wants some company."

Her gaze brushed over them and, although she did not know it, it held a good, solid dose of contempt. Flicking her skirts aside, she swept past them. Turning onto the sidewalk that bordered the canal, she had almost forgotten them, when she felt a tingle between her shoulder blades. For a moment she was tempted to look back to see if they were following her but she did not. Then she heard the click of boots on stone coming closer. She felt no fear, but the sound had her automatically quickening her steps.

The sidewalk was so narrow that, even though for practicality's sake she wore fewer petticoats than were fashionable, her gown scraped along the houses on one side and the metal guardrail on the other. Suddenly she found herself slammed up against the wall so violently that her breath whooshed out of her body.

"I think the *signorina* needs to be taught some manners."

A hand covered her mouth before she got even a small portion of her breath back and she found the world dimming in front of her eyes. She remained perfectly still as she desperately fought to pull in enough air through her nose, telling herself that her first priority was to make certain she did not faint. As long as she was conscious, nothing could happen to her. After all, this was the middle of the day on a public street in a civilized city. She felt a flash of panic and pushed it away, refusing to give in to it.

The grip on her shoulders eased a little. When, out of the corner of her eye, she saw two figures crossing the bridge that arched over the canal, she began to struggle.

"Let me go!" She pushed the hand covering her mouth away. "*Aiutatemi!* Help me!"

But the two figures only speeded their steps and continued until they were out of sight. Julie began to struggle even more frantically, managing to land a few kicks before she found herself pinned against the wall by a hand that pressed brutally against her windpipe.

"She doesn't seem to like us, Toni." The smaller of the two men smiled as he spoke, but his pale eyes remained ice-cold. "We'll have to use a little more persuasion."

The words were barely out of his mouth when he was knocked backward. His mouth opened in an inaudible cry as he lurched back against the metal railing, balanced for a moment and then tumbled back into the canal, his arms flailing.

Coughing and fighting for breath, Julie stared as Theo bore down on the second man like an avenging angel. The moment he had shoved the man away from her, he gripped the silver knob of his cane and whipped a thin, efficient-looking rapier out of the ebony casing.

The man moved backward, apparently giving no thought to defending himself as his gaze skittered to his friend, who was still sputtering in the water. When he reached the railing, his hand clutched the metal convulsively as he steadied himself. But Theo was already upon him, pressing the tip of the rapier against his chest.

"One false move and you're a dead man." His voice was soft and that made the menace that iced it even more distinct.

He needed all his control not to give in to the red haze in front of his eyes and thrust the rapier into the man's chest. He knew just what it would feel like—that one moment of resistance as it pierced the thick fabric of the uniform and then the soft give of flesh, as if one were slicing into butter.

"Are you all right, Julie?" When she did not answer right away, he almost spun away from his prey to look at her. "Julie?"

Rubbing her aching throat with one hand, Julie pushed herself away from the rough wall with the other.

"Yes." Her voice was hoarse and she coughed again. Needing suddenly to touch him, she stumbled forward. "Yes, I'm fine, Theo." Her fingers curled into his coat until she was sure she could stand on her own and, giving in to a moment of weakness, she laid her forehead against his back.

Theo felt her lean into him and fought off another wave of rage. His eyes flicked to the man who was struggling up over the slippery side of the canal, then returned to the other man, who was still gripping the metal railing so tightly that the skin stretched white over his knuckles.

"Help your friend," he snapped as he withdrew the rapier by enough inches to make it possible for the man to move without impaling himself. "But don't try anything."

The man did not move but instead stood staring at him.

"Well?" he barked. "Don't you understand French?"

Slowly the officer shifted to the side, but his eyes remained on Theo's face. Even when he bent to give a hand to his friend, his gaze did not stray for more than a moment. Nor did he pay any attention to the man as he stood cursing and dripping beside him. He stared at Theo as if he had seen a ghost.

Julie forgot that her heart was beating against her hand as if it were a hammer. She forgot that her breath was still labored and that her throat felt bruised. All she saw was the officer's pale blue eyes as he stared at Theo. She saw the curiosity there and the dawning recognition. And she saw that Theo was aware of none of it.

Her fingers curled into his arm and she leaned her face against his back, all the while watching the man over Theo's shoulder.

"Be careful, Theo." Her whisper was urgent. "That man recognizes you."

When he did not react, she dug her fingers deeper and repeated her words.

It took a moment for Theo to focus, really focus, on the man's face. When he had come around the corner and seen Julie being molested by the two men, he had felt such a frenzy of rage that he could have killed them both with his bare hands. He had the rage under control now—very thin control.

He was still rooting in his memory for a name to the man's face when the officer began to laugh.

"Well, well, Max von Berg's little brother. Word was that you had gone to your last reward in prison." He laughed again. "I'm certain that the military tribunal will be thrilled to learn otherwise."

Anton von Willner. The high-pitched voice summoned up the name and a new wave of rage. When he had set out on this journey, Theo had told himself that the chances of running into someone who would recognize him would be slim to none. Now he was facing Anton von Willner, who had fought with them in the revolution—until he had decided that his chances of survival were better on the other side.

"I don't know what you're talking about. What I do know is that the military tribunal will be less than thrilled when I deliver you to them." He was pleased to find his voice mild and even, although he could feel his heart hammering against his ribs. "I imagine that it will go against their grain to find out that Austrian officers go about trying to rape citizens of Belgium."

"Belgium? What are you talking about?" His voice rose. "I heard her call you Theo. You are Theo von Berg."

Theo saw Willner's hand jerk toward the hilt of his sword. He shifted quickly so that the tip of his rapier pressed against the man's tunic again and his hand fell back against his side.

"Thébault van Dam of Brussels at your service."

"I don't believe you." Willner swiped a hand at the sweat that had begun to bead his upper lip.

"That is not my problem." He curved his mouth in an icy smile. "But your superiors will believe me." And he had no choice but to believe his own words. With that realization a composure spread through him—that strange composure that comes when all preparations are made and you are riding into battle, the enemy already in sight. He knew from experience that doubt was fatal at a moment like this.

"You wouldn't dare." Willner gulped in air. "Prison wouldn't be enough this time. This time you would see the end of a rope."

"I don't know what you're talking about." Theo shook his head.

There was a clatter of boots from beyond the bridge.

"A military patrol. Excellent." Theo pulled in a long, deep breath. "And very timely."

Julie felt her blood freeze in her veins, as much from the sound of boot heels on stone as from Theo's words. Even as her fingers dug into his arm in alarm, she realized that brazening it out was the only way. Her fingers relaxed and she gave his arm a reassuring squeeze.

Theo felt the play of Julie's fingers on his arm. Confident now, he tucked his weapon back into the ebony casing and raised his arm to hail the officer who led the patrol.

"No! Don't do it." Willner was breathing hard. "If you don't say anything, I will not reveal who you are. I promise."

Theo sent him a withering look and called out.

A good hour later they were ensconced in a shabbily luxurious room in the *palazzo* that had been commandeered by the Austrians as their military headquarters.

They had told their story. Everything had been duly noted by a studious-looking young soldier whose handwriting looked like the fine engraving one finds on invitations.

When an officer who identified himself as Colonel von Hofmann entered the room and requested that they repeat what had happened for him, Theo decided that it was time to put on a small show.

He stood, cracking his cane down on the mosaic floor, which centuries of rising and ebbing seawater had made uneven.

"We have made our statement and it was noted by your scribe. I did not realize that it is customary in your country to treat victims as criminals." He threw back his shoulders and looked the officer straight in the eye. "Or do you seek to discount our statement to exonerate a fellow officer?"

Hofmann steepled his hands and tapped the fingertips against one another as he watched Theo for a long minute and then another. Then he gave a small nod as if Theo had passed a test.

"Captain von Willner insists that you are a certain Count Theodore Berg, who was thought to have died in prison in Hungary after the '48-'49 rebellion." His tone left no doubt as to his contempt.

"Yes, I heard him say that, but I am not responsible for his mistaken impression. You have my word and my papers." Theo's voice was steady and so were his eyes. "My wife has been through enough today. If there is nothing else, I would like to go now."

"I'm afraid that is not possible just yet." The officer gave a shrug and a smile so affable that it seemed ridiculously out of place.

Theo stiffened at his typically Austrian cordiality—so easy, so false. "May I ask why?"

Hofmann spread his hands in an apologetic gesture. "Captain von Willner has denied that he molested your wife." He gave a small bow in Julie's direction. "He says you recognized him and attacked him to keep him from giving you away."

Theo felt an icy shiver crawl down his spine. It was his word against Willner's. And it was up to Hofmann whose word he chose to believe.

"That's ridiculous." He struck his cane against the floor again. "Ridiculous! I demand that you allow us to go."

Julie stood and put her hand on Theo's arm. But instead of looking at him, she looked straight at Hofmann and gave him a demure smile. "You must excuse my husband. He is very protective of my well-being." Then she moved toward the officer.

She raised her head so that he could see her neck where the bruises were already beginning to form. "If you are in doubt, since it seems to be our word against his, perhaps you will believe this." She heard Theo make a sound and move toward her, but she continued.

"He pressed his hand against my throat to keep me from crying for help. I thought he was going to strangle me." She saw something flicker in the colonel's eyes and added, "Or do you believe that my husband inflicted these on me to make—" she paused slightly "—our lies more believable perhaps." She felt Theo's arm go around her shoulders and allowed herself to lean into him for a moment before she straightened again.

"My most sincere apologies, *madame*." Hofmann bowed deeply. "Of course, you and your husband are free to go. Rest assured that I will see to it that both men are dealt with appropriately."

"See that you do." Theo's voice was harsh. "Although I seriously doubt that your view of what is appropriate is the same as mine."

Hofmann smoothly ignored Theo's words and merely asked, "May I give you an escort to your hotel?"

"No, thank you," Theo snapped. "You will understand that my confidence in the honor of an Austrian uniform is not overly great at the moment."

Hofmann bowed with a discreet click of his heels. "As you wish, Monsieur van Dam."

When the door had closed behind them, he gestured to his aide.

"I have no doubt that Willner attacked the woman," he said, his eyes still on the door. "I never did. After all, he has a reputation for attacking women. But it would not hurt to examine the identity of this Monsieur van Dam more closely."

"Do you want Willner questioned again?" the aide inquired.

"By all means. With some insistence," Hofmann added. "And contact our embassy in Brussels."

"But they have booked passage from Venice to Greece in a few days. And their papers looked very genuine."

Hofmann sent the young aide a pitying look. "There is little you cannot buy if you are willing to bleed a little for it," he said with a shrug. "We cannot prevent him from leaving without evidence, but make certain that someone in Saloniki is warned to watch them."

Moving toward the window, he looked down into the narrow street where the young couple stood. The revolution and the ensuing civil war was five years past, but it would be a feather in his cap if he turned up an escaped revolutionary, he mused. And a man who had not made it past the rank of colonel by the age of fifty could well use such a feather.

Silently, not quite believing that they had done it and were free to go, they walked toward the massive door of the *palazzo*, flanked on either side by a guard in the scarlet tunic and plumed hat. They had barely stepped out into the narrow street when Theo stopped and turned toward Julie. Still silent, he tipped her chin up.

As he looked at the bruises on her delicate, pale skin, he felt the same red haze of fury he had felt when he had rounded the corner and seen her pushed up against the wall. Lightly he touched the backs of his fingers to the discolored skin.

"If I had seen this before, I would have killed him."

His voice was mild and that made the murderous look in the eyes he raised to meet hers all the more frightening.

Julie curled her fingers around his, understanding that he spoke no less than the truth. "Then I am glad you did not see it. I would not have wanted you to have blood on your hands because of me."

He turned his hand so that he held her fingers in his. As he lifted them to his mouth, he tried to forget that before this was all over he would have blood on his hands. And he tried to forget that she would hate him because of it.

Chapter Fourteen

Only a small, motley group of passengers came on board in Venice. In the midst of Levantine merchants, a few bespectacled, stoop-shouldered men, drunk on Homer and wanting desperately to sample the wonders of ancient Greece, and a few Turks trailed by their veiled women, Theo and Julie moved toward the gangplank. They saw that the passengers who had come on board in Trieste, the home port of the Austrian fleet, had lined up at the railing to gawk at the newcomers.

Theo felt Julie's fingers on his arm tighten and he tucked his cane under his arm for a moment and covered her hand with his.

"It will be all right," he murmured. "The odds of meeting up with someone else who will recognize me are not very high." His smile was ironic. "That has already been taken care of."

"I hope you're right." Wanting to believe him, Julie forced her fingers to relax under his hand.

Her gaze wandered down the row of people alongside the railing. Most were chatting with their neighbors, giving an occasional glance at the people straggling up the gangplank. Only one man, his back straight as a ramrod, spoke with no one. And he was staring straight at them without so much as a glance to spare for any of the other passengers.

"Theo?" Her hand tightened again.

"I know. I see him, too." He shrugged. "It would seem that Colonel von Hofmann is not as easily convinced as I had hoped."

"What are we going to do about him?"

Theo felt simultaneous jolts of pleasure and guilt. She had bound herself up in his life so thoroughly, he thought. And nothing expressed it more strongly than the simple, matter-of-fact use of that one small word *we*.

"*We* are going to do nothing," he murmured. "He's probably nothing but a flunky sent to watch me. I was expecting that."

"You were?"

"He had no choice but to let us go, especially after he had seen what Willner had done to you." A muscle jumped in Theo's cheek as he remembered the marks on Julie's skin. "But I knew he would try and pin my identity down."

"When Max and our father engineered my escape from prison, it was made to look as if I had died. Now that Willner has identified me, they want to trap me." He took a deep breath. "If they trap me on Austrian territory, they might try to lure Max from safety. He's the real prize.

"Don't worry," he said, seeing her eyes widen. "It's not going to happen. Besides, it's a long way to where we're going and once we're in Greece, we will disappear so quickly that he won't know what happened."

Before Julie could answer, there was a commotion further up the gangplank. A jowly man with oily, slicked-back hair began to shout in a jumble of mangled Italian, Greek and Turkish. Then there was the sharp sound of a hand meeting skin and bone and a small, thin figure stumbled down the gangplank. For a moment bony fingers grasped the rope that served as a makeshift railing, but the momentum was too great and the figure staggered further, finally careening into Theo and pushing him against the rope.

Catching his balance, Theo reached out to steady the boy. As his hand closed on a painfully thin shoulder, the boy looked up at him. His face was covered with a blotchy film of grime, and his eyes of a stunning aquamarine color and the dully reddish mark on his cheek were the only specks of color on his pale skin.

"Perdonatemi, signore." The boy's high voice trembled on the first word, steadying on the second.

Theo felt him shrink away from his grip as if expecting another slap, and automatically his hand gentled. "Are you all right?"

The boy nodded, his eyes darting to his right, where the man was bearing down on him, still shouting and gesticulating.

"Damn you, you clumsy little beggar." He lunged toward the boy and grabbed a handful of tangled black hair, which had been crudely chopped off just below his ears. "You made me drop my hat in the water. I should throw you in after it, you good-for-nothing little bastard!"

Theo recoiled before the reek of onions and sweat that the man exuded, but did not let go of the boy. Instead he rapped the silver head of his cane sharply against the man's knuckles. With a yelp he released the boy's hair.

"What do you think you're doing?" the man demanded. "It's none of your business." He curved his fleshy hand around the boy's other shoulder. "The brat belongs to me."

"Belongs?" Theo's eyes narrowed. "Is the boy your son?"

"Son?" the man squealed. "Never. He is the spawn of the very devil!" He passed his tongue over his red, shiny lips. "But he belongs to me nonetheless."

"*Signore.*"

Theo felt the urgent touch of thin fingers on his arm and looked down. There was a silent plea in the boy's startling eyes that he had no trouble recognizing.

"The gentleman is my employer." The boy paused to swallow. "And my benefactor."

Theo frowned.

"*È vero.* It's true."

Reluctantly he released the boy. Reaching into his pocket, he drew out a gold coin and held it out to the man. "Buy yourself a new hat and leave the boy in peace."

The man sent him a look of pure hatred before he lowered his heavy-lidded black eyes to the coin Theo held between thumb and forefinger. Greed was stronger than either pride or hatred and he pocketed the coin quickly before he turned away, pulling the boy after him.

Halfway up the gangplank he cuffed the boy on the back of his head to hurry him on and sent Theo a sly look of triumph over his shoulder.

Two of the ship's officers in their forest green tunics stood at the top of the gangplank to oversee the boarding and greet those passengers they deemed worthy. When he and Julie had reached the deck, Theo nodded to them.

"I suggest you keep your eyes on that man over there. He raises his hand a little too easily against the boy."

"These Levantines are all the same, *monsieur.*" The officer gave his cuffs of black velvet with their two gold stripes a discomfited tug. "But don't worry about the boy. These Venetian street urchins are used to worse." He raised a hand to his two-cornered hat with its black cockade in a casual salute. "A pleasant journey, *monsieur, 'dame.*"

Theo cursed under his breath as they moved away, aware of his own helplessness.

There was music—something as sweet as a Viennese pastry—playing in the salon, and the passengers who had been milling around on deck began to drift toward it. By unspoken mutual agreement Theo and Julie lingered on the deck, despite the strong smell of the coal smoke that the smokestacks of the ship were belching out.

The trembling of the deck intensified as the engines were turned up. Metal clanged against wood as the gangplank was pulled free. With a jolt and then another the ship moved away from the pier.

As Julie watched the strip of greenish water between ship and land widen, the finality of what she had done struck her with an intensity that had tears clogging her throat. Her thoughts flew to her parents, and even as she silently begged their forgiveness, she realized that part of what she felt could only be described as relief. Until that moment when the ropes had been loosened and the ship had pulled away from the wooden pilings of the dock, she had half expected her father to storm up on one of those half-wild horses he occasionally rode and snatch her away.

She felt Theo's hand curve around her shoulder. "They'll be all right. And you'll be back."

Something softened, then melted within her at the gentle, matter-of-fact way he comforted her, although she only half believed his words. Yes, she thought, her parents would be all right because they had each other. As for the other, yes, perhaps she would be back, but it would not be the same Julie Muromsky who had left Turin barely a fortnight ago. Already she had changed. She saw the change in her own eyes each time she looked into a mirror. She felt the change every time her pulse began to flutter when Theo was near.

She lifted her hand to his, contenting herself with a fleeting touch although she would have wanted to lace her fingers with his and hold on tightly. "And you?" she asked without looking at him. "Will you be back?"

Taken aback by her question, he did not answer immediately. When he did, his voice was hesitant. "I don't know."

"How like a man." She laughed softly, sadly. "To make plans for revenge half a world away without giving a thought to what comes after."

His tawny brows drew together. He had planned, no, he had lived, breathed his revenge for four long years. At times his revenge had been the only thing that kept him alive. The only thing that kept him from going mad from pain and grief. He had, in truth, given little thought to what would come after. All he had seen was Boris Muromsky's blood seeping into the ground. All he had seen was finding Maryka and freeing her from her imprisonment.

And afterward? Now, for the first time, he tried to move past his revenge and form an image of what his life would be like after everything was over. But no matter how he tried to focus his mind, he seemed surrounded by a thick fog that allowed him to see nothing. Slowly, step by careful step, he pushed himself through the haze, feeling like a dull-witted child trying desperately to understand something simple and basic.

Then the fog began to thin until it was no more than a whirl of misty scarves floating around him. But still no image rose. Suddenly he saw her. Far away yet, Maryka was only a slender figure surrounded by the wisps of fog. Then she began to run toward him and, berating himself for not feeling the joy that should have been making his heart fly, he opened his arms to her. She came closer quickly, as if her feet had wings. Then he saw her face. Saw that it was not Maryka but Julie who was running into his arms. The joy that had hidden itself a moment ago broke free as she flung herself against him.

Julie felt Theo's hand on her shoulder tighten and she tilted her head to look at him. He was staring beyond the railing, his eyes fixed on an image only he could see.

"Theo?" Shifting slightly, she put her palm against his chest. "What is it?"

She felt his body jolt as if something had slammed into it. Even as her concern rose, she watched his gaze clear, focus. Then he turned his head so that their eyes met.

As he looked at Julie, the tangle of emotion within him was so strong that he found himself short of breath. There was the need to pull her close—so strong that he had to strain against it. There was the way his heart pulsed with feelings he did not dare to look at more closely. There was the guilt that rose as bitter as bile to poison the moment.

Julie's breath caught in her throat as their eyes met. For the space of a heartbeat she saw everything mirrored in their blue gray depths—every need, every emotion. Then, so suddenly that she recoiled, they went cool and distant. She saw the coolness, the withdrawal, but not the guilt that had prompted them, and the hurt was as acute as if he had slapped her.

She stepped away with a jerky movement so that his hand fell from her shoulder.

"Julie, I—" Theo began, but fell silent even before she lifted a hand to stop his words. What could he say? How could he explain to her what he could not explain to himself?

The two-edged guilt was still gnawing at him as he stiffly offered her his arm to escort her to their cabin.

* * *

Julie looked around the tastefully appointed cabin where Theo had left her alone. She supposed that it was large enough as cabins went, but when she considered that she would be in these close quarters with Theo for almost three weeks, she wondered how she would stand it.

Ignoring the luggage, which sat in a large pile in the middle of the thin Bosnian carpet with its colorful geometric design, she went to the porthole and looked outside. The water had the color and glitter of fine aquamarines in the morning sunlight and she allowed the beauty to soothe her.

After all these months she should have been used to his sudden withdrawals, his moods. Why then, she wondered, did he have such a capacity to hurt her? Why did she have such a capacity to be hurt by him, now somehow much more than before? She answered her own question. Before, there had been the hospital, his pain, his impatience as reasons. Now there was only she herself.

She leaned her forehead against the cool glass. How much easier this would have been if it had remained the business arrangement it had been in the beginning. But, a small voice reminded her, it had never been a business arrangement. Then, because she was used to doing what had to be done, she turned to begin unpacking.

By the time Theo returned, she had unpacked what she could of her things, leaving the rest in the trunks she had pushed under one of the beds.

"I have left you half the room in the armoire, the chest of drawers and the cushioned chest over there." All business, her voice was as cool as her eyes, which met his briefly before she turned away to look out the porthole.

Theo deposited hat, gloves and cane on a tiny table near the door and walked to where she stood. He had spent the past hour trying to untangle the jumble of emotions and thoughts that wound through him. He had believed he had succeeded until he had seen her standing there, so lovely, so valiant.

He reached out to touch her, but lowered his hands when he saw her stiffen.

"Will you look at me?"

Slowly she turned around, her eyes wary.

"Julie, I don't want to hurt you." He saw the flicker in her eyes and, his voice rueful, added, "Any more than I already have." Even as he said the words, he knew he would hurt her again and he cursed himself for it.

"You were right when you said I had not thought about what will come after it is all over. I tried to do that out there on deck, before. I tried to imagine what it would be like to see Maryka again, to be with her, and—" he covered his eyes for a moment "—and all I could see was your face."

He saw the softness, the compassion flash into her eyes and spun away as the blackest of guilt punched into him again. "If I find Maryka—when I find her, my life has to be with her. I owe her that."

"Theo—"

He whirled back to face her and gripped her arms. "I have nothing for you, Julie. Do you understand me?"

His eyes had gone the color of ashes with only the barest touch of blue, and a muscle was jumping wildly in his cheek. She wanted to put her arms around him and just hold on, but instead she pulled her pride around her like a cloak and straightened.

"Have I asked you for anything you cannot give, Theo? Have I asked you for anything at all?" she asked softly. "Have you asked me if I would want whatever it is that you *do* have to give me?"

Her soft words struck him as cruelly as a whip biting into flesh. He stared at her for a long moment before he released her and took a step back. He deserved no less for his arrogance, he told himself. What arrogance it was to think that just because these last weeks had changed things for him that they had changed them for her, as well. What arrogance to think that just because she had kissed him with an eager innocence, just because her young body wanted him, that she was as lost in him as he was in her.

"I'm sorry. That was presumptuous of me." Asking himself why his heart should hurt so badly when it was only his pride, his male vanity that had been damaged a little, he took another step back. "I will stay out of your way as much as possible, Julie, for the remainder of our journey. I can give you that at least." With a curt bow, he left her alone.

Julie stared at the cabin door for a long time after it had closed behind him, not feeling the tears that filled her eyes and overflowed in thick trickles. When she felt the moisture on her face, she turned back to the porthole and the sea for comfort.

Theo remained true to his word. He did not return to the cabin until late at night and left early. They saw each other only in public—at meals, a walk on deck, an excursion on land when the ship docked at Ancona and then Ragusa before taking course for Corfu. They spoke with each other stiffly, impersonally, or not at all.

Although she promised herself every night that she would be asleep before he returned and would not waken until he was long gone in the morning, Julie was never able to find sleep unless she could hear Theo's breathing in the bed that was separated from hers only by a narrow nightstand.

Why were they doing this to each other? she asked herself as she lay awake. Why had they thrown away what had grown so stubbornly, so unerringly for months? She sat up and tossed back the covers. Refusing to give herself time to think, to reflect on the consequences, the implications, she slipped into her shoes and a white eyelet-trimmed robe and went looking for him.

The lamps had been extinguished at eleven as usual and the deck was deserted. The passengers were asleep and the officers and the men at their watch or asleep in their berths or hammocks. Theo lit a cigar, more from habit and to pass the time than because he wanted the taste of tobacco.

Julie, too, would be asleep now, he thought, but he still did not want to return to the cabin, which would be fragrant with the scent of verbena and woman. How many nights had he lain awake, much too aware of the woman who slept an arm's reach away? It was not just his senses that were filled with her, he realized. He was filled with her—with her nature, which was both gentle and tart, her mind, her courage and the power that always seemed to drift around her like a subtle perfume.

What would it have been like, he suddenly wondered, if they had met without all the burdens, the memories that weighed upon them now? Would their lives have meshed easily, without all the guilt, without all the stumbling blocks that were strewn around them now like rubble from buildings torn apart by some cataclysm? Would their lives have twined then like two vines growing together in the sunlight? What would it have been like to give? For her to be able to take what he offered?

He'd told her that he had nothing to give her and it was true, he mused. What irony that was. What irony when he had never wanted so badly to give. He had coasted through his life, accustomed to the easy affection of his family and the women who had succumbed to his facile charm and smooth tongue and who had seemed to want no more from him than the rich gifts and the pleasure he could give them.

If he were honest with himself, Maryka had been no different. It was only the end that had made it so. Now, alone, with the southern night dark and warm around him, with the stars and the sliver of a moon winking, he could admit it.

Julie found Theo quickly enough. He was leaning against the railing of the main deck, his tan suit and the red tip of his cigar a beacon in the darkness. Her feet slowed, but she forced herself to continue forward.

Lost in his thoughts, he did not notice her until she braced her hands against the railing barely a handbreadth from his side.

"Julie! Is something wrong?" His cigar tumbled overboard in a thin arc of light as he reached for her.

All of the sensible, logical things that she had been going to say flew out of her head as his arms went around her. "No," she whispered. "Nothing's wrong." Not anymore, she thought as she pressed her cheek against his chest. Not anymore.

"What are you doing out here, then?" He knew that he should let her go, but he stroked his hand down the slim line of her back instead, all too aware that she wore only the thin robe over her nightgown.

"Looking for you." She tilted her head back so that she could see his face.

He said nothing, but his eyebrows curved upward in question.

"It's late and I couldn't sleep. I can never sleep until you come in."

He felt rather than saw her shoulders twitch in a slight shrug. "Is that right?" he asked, finding himself caught between annoyance and amusement. "Then why have I been creeping into the cabin like a thief for the past week?"

"You don't really need an answer to that question, do you?" Her mouth was serious, but there was just a hint of a smile in her eyes.

"No. No, I don't." Slowly, he let her go, his hands trailing down the length of her arms.

They separated and stood facing each other for a moment, as if reluctant to look away, before they both leaned against the railing.

Julie lifted her face into the warm breeze, which smelled both of the sea and of the land ahead. In the distance she could see a few scattered lights, which told her that they would be docked in Corfu by morning.

"I'm not asking you for anything, Theo. We made a bargain and we both got what we wanted. You took me away from Turin and got the counterfeit wife you needed in return. But in the process we became friends and—" Because she needed to counteract the odd feeling that she was side-stepping the truth, she turned her head to meet Theo's eyes. "And I've missed you."

"Julie—"

Before he could continue, a door that led from one of the corridors burst open with a crash. A small, thin figure, clad in breeches and a billowing shirt, stumbled out and, with a cry, tripped over one of the slatted deck chairs. As one, both Theo and Julie started toward the boy they recognized from the day they had boarded the ship.

They had barely taken a step when the heavy man they remembered as well lumbered through the door, his shirt open to reveal a paunch, one hand holding up his half-fastened trousers. With a sound resembling the roar of a raging bull, he picked up the boy as easily as if he were a kitten and flung him against the railing.

"Damn you, you good-for-nothing creature," he bellowed, gripping the boy's shirt and smashing him into the railing again. "I bought myself a boy and you're nothing but a damned wench." He grabbed the child's shirt again.

Pushing Julie behind him with a sweep of his arm, Theo dived forward, propelled by fury, one hand closing on a bunch of oily hair, the other on a meaty shoulder. Ignoring the pain that shot through his back, he pulled the man away.

The man released the child's shirt and spun around with surprising agility. He launched himself at Theo, his eyes huge and wild. Unprepared for the quickness, the nimbleness of the man's attack, Theo found himself thrust backward before he managed to gain purchase and drive his fist into the man's gut once and then again. The flash of primitive satisfaction at the man's grunt of pain was so strong that it had him forgetting about his own pain, which was tearing through him like a hot knife.

Desperately Julie's eyes darted around the deck looking for a weapon. A forgotten ladies' parasol lay on one of the chairs. Wielding it as if it were a lance, she lunged forward, aiming it at the man's throat.

Theo caught her movement out of the corner of his eye. "No!" he shouted. "Get back!"

That split second of distraction cost him as a fist reached past his defense and clipped him on the chin, sending him sprawling. He slid along the slick wood of the deck, coming to a stop only when his head slammed into a metal strut with rope coiled around its base.

Dazed, he struggled up, the fear burning in his throat. When the man merely plucked the parasol out of Julie's hands, broke it over his knee as if it were a matchstick and turned away from her, pure relief had his stomach turning upside down.

As Theo staggered forward, his head spinning, he saw the man weave toward the child, who stood motionless, still pressed against the railing, arms thrown outward. Although he tried to move quickly, his feet seemed to be sinking into quicksand.

The man gripped the child by the shirt again and shook him, lifting him off the ground until the thin, frightened face was level with his own.

"You'll pay for this," he snarled. "And fully." Then he released the child with a push and turned away, swiping the back of his meaty hand over his split lip.

The child slid on top of the railing, tottered for a moment and then, with a thin cry, toppled backward and down into the water.

Not even bothering to turn around fully, the man made an obscene gesture and muttered, "Good riddance."

The words were barely out of his mouth when Theo's fist smashed into his face. The sound of fracturing bones was followed by an animallike howl as the blood gushed from his crushed nose like a fountain.

His fingers curling around the railing, Theo looked down and saw the telltale spot of white bobbing in the dark water.

"Go get help, Julie." His voice was oddly even, almost conversational. "I'm going over."

"No!" she screamed, and dug her fingers into his arm. "You can't do that. You'll hurt yourself."

His hand struck out, hitting her shoulder, sending her reeling. "Get out of my way."

Horrified, Julie watched him strip off his coat and turn toward the railing again.

Oh God, she thought, he would never make it. He would not swim two strokes in the cold seawater before his barely mended body, which he had already pushed much too far, gave out on him. She could not allow him to do this, she thought desperately. She could not lose him now. She could not lose him now when— The rest of the thought was lost as she searched, her eyes wild, for some way to stop him.

Suddenly her gaze fell on the deck chairs, the neat row now in disarray. Before she fully realized what she was doing, she hefted a chair and cracked it against the side of Theo's head.

Throwing off her robe and shoes, she climbed over the railing. As she dived down into the black water, she heard Theo cry her name.

Chapter Fifteen

Theo felt the panic leap straight up through him to lodge in his throat. His head was throbbing, but he did not notice it. Nor did he notice the trickle of blood that ran down his face from the cut on his temple as he scrambled up from the deck and ran to the railing. A second spot of white had joined the first, he saw. Even as gratitude that the sea was serene tonight streaked through him, he saw both heads go under.

The fear choked him as his body braced to go over the railing and dive after them, but common sense dragged him back. They would not be served by a half cripple going after them, he thought bitterly, swallowing his pride. Relief swept through him when he saw both heads bob up. Saw Julie hook an arm around the child and turn onto her back so that they both floated their heads well above water.

Shouting for help, he ran for the bridge.

Although it felt like hours, Theo knew that only minutes had passed when he ran back to the deck, two sailors right behind him. A glance over the side told him that Julie seemed to be holding her own, but the fear remained a huge, bitter lump in his throat. Helpless and furious at it, he watched the two men work together smoothly, speaking hardly a word. Quickly they uncoiled the rope from the metal support on deck, attaching what looked like a mass of leather straps and metal buckles to it.

Not more than a few minutes later, the leather straps had become a kind of seat and one of the men, a thick coil of rope looped crosswise over his chest, was being lowered over the side.

The deck slowly filled with people—officers and crew, passengers woken by the noise. Torches were brought, their flickering light spilling over the deck. Oblivious to all of it, Theo stood at the railing, his knuckles white, staring down at the water and the two spots of white. They had fallen behind, he saw, and his blood ran cold. They had been around the middle of the ship when they had gone over. Now they were somewhere in the last third, which meant they had lost a good fifty feet.

An officer shouted for the engines to be cut and a boat to be lowered, but Theo did not hear him. The panic that was blocking his throat was echoed in the panic churning in his belly. And yet emotion broke through it, as the sun breaks through black thunderclouds.

"Hold on, Julie. Just hold on. You're going to be all right." He sent the words down to her, unaware that he spoke them aloud. "I love you."

With a jolt he recognized the emotion. With recognition came immediate acceptance, allowing the emotion to pour through him as the sea pours over sand, erasing all the markings that had gone before. How could he not have seen it? he thought. For months he had wanted her, needed her. How could he not have seen the love that had been there all along?

As if she were responding to the feelings that were spinning inside him, he saw Julie shift, her free arm cutting cleanly through the dark water so that she was a few feet closer to the sailor swinging alongside the ship in his rig. She rested for a moment and then pushed forward again with a few strong strokes.

He saw her head turn as the sailor called out to her and tossed the rope so that the looped end landed an arm's length in front of her.

She was tiring. Because she had only one arm free, Julie had to make every stroke count double and that sapped her strength more quickly. So for every few strokes she made, she had to turn onto her back and float for a few moments to rest.

Although she had not felt the cold after the first shock when she had dived into the water, she knew that, even in the relatively warm water of the Mediterranean, her time was limited. At some point her muscles would become stiff and begin to cramp. She had a distinct childhood memory of swimming too far out and then going down like a stone because she had become overchilled, but, refusing to let it distract her now, she pushed the memory away.

Theo. The thought of him shot into her mind, warming her like a glass of brandy, bringing strength back to her tiring muscles. She couldn't die now, she thought. She had to get back to Theo. She had to see him again. There were things she had to say to him, although at the moment she could not remember what they were.

She was surrounded by sounds. The rush of the water. The rasp of her own labored breathing. The slap of her hand against the surface of the water. The rumble of the ship's engines. But Julie heard the splash of the rope in the water ahead of her as clearly as if it were a shot.

Her eyes full of seawater, she reached out for it blindly. As her fingers closed over the hemp, she felt herself go weak with relief. The rope felt so solid in her hand, so wonderfully reliable. Forgetting to tread water, she simply held on, letting the rope take her full weight, not even considering the possibility that the man holding the other end had not yet taken up the slack.

Face first, she went under. Stunned, she could do nothing to prevent her fingers from opening, allowing the rope to slip through them, as she could do nothing to prevent the gasp that had her sucking in treacherous seawater. The arm holding the child went limp, as well, if only for a split second. But it was enough so that the child began to slip out of her grasp. Panic streaked through her and she brought both arms tightly around the thin body. Gagging on the water she had sucked in, she held on, but the uncoordinated movement and the breathing which had grown even more ragged, had both of them going under again.

She came back up, salt water burning in her throat and lungs. With her last bit of strength she turned onto her back again. Still coughing, she focused her mind on breathing carefully until the urge to gag had become a controllable struggle for air.

They had lost most of the distance she had gained, and fear rose, making her head light. She knew she had to start swimming again, but she knew, too, that just keeping their heads above water took almost more strength than she had left.

When she heard the rope hit the water behind her again, she bit down fiercely on her lip to control the overpowering urge to flip around and, forgetting everything else but survival, grab at it with both hands. Instead she held on to the child with both arms and kept floating.

Again she heard the slap of the rope on the surface of the water. And again. Once she thought she felt the rope graze the top of her head.

Theo. She closed her eyes tightly. He was there calling to her. She had hurt him, she thought. She had hurt him physically and she had hurt his pride. But she would rather

have him hurt than dead. She felt her muscles weakening
and it occurred to her that she could die in his stead. But
there was still hope. She held on to that.

On that thought the loop of the rope settled around her.
Because that overpowering urge to grip it with both hands
was there again, she tightened her arms around the child.

Then the loop tightened and she felt herself being pulled
through the water.

The moment the sailor rolled onto the deck with his burden, Theo was crouching next to Julie, gathering her up in
his arms. He saw her eyelids quiver and touched his hand to
her face.

"Julie, *chérie*, can you hear me?"

She wanted so badly to open her eyes and look at Theo,
but she needed all her strength to fight the shivering. She
had barely been aware of the cold before, but now with the
contrast of Theo's warm body against hers, his hand on her
cheek, the cold that had chilled even her blood was taking
over her body. But then the last of the strength flowed out
of her and she gave in.

The shivering began so suddenly, so violently that Theo
felt the bitter taste of panic in his mouth.

"It's a good sign, if she's shivering. That means she's
fighting back against the cold."

Theo jerked up his head and saw a white-haired man with
a kind, wrinkled face bending down over them. "What?"
he managed to ask, thinking that the man's words sounded
absurd.

The old man put a hand on his shoulder. "She'll be all
right. I'm a doctor." He smiled. "I know what I'm talking
about." He put his fingers on Julie's wrist and then nodded. "Now take her to your cabin, wrap her up warmly and
give her some brandy." He gave Theo's shoulder a quick

squeeze. "And thank the good Lord that he has gifted you with such a wife."

Struggling against the shivering, against the weakness that was threatening to overwhelm her, Julie opened her eyes, which were blurred and burning from water and salt.

"I-is th-th-the child a-all right?" It occurred to her that her teeth were chattering so loudly that they sounded like castanets. If she had had the strength, she would have laughed.

The doctor looked over to where two sailors were bent over the child, pumping the water out of her thin body with hard, quick thrusts to her back. She was coughing up water now, but her lips were no longer bluish.

He took Julie's hand and smiled directly into her eyes. "She'll be all right. I will personally take care of her." The doctor gave her icy hand a squeeze. "I promise."

Julie tipped her head to the side, saw the child's coughing spasms, and everything in her yearned to help. But knowing that she was in no condition to do it, she did not protest when Theo picked her up and, wrapping her up in a blanket someone handed him, carried her away.

In front of their cabin, Theo almost fell over Fritz because his attention had been focused solely on Julie.

"I brought hot water." Fritz gestured at the two large buckets at his feet. "You got to wash the salt off her."

"How did you manage to bring it here so fast?" Theo asked as he shouldered the door open.

"Went off while she was still down there." Fritz said laconically as he set the buckets down at the foot of one of the beds. "Knew she was going to make it." At the door he turned back and fisted his rough hands to hide the fact that they were not quite steady. "She is going to make it, ain't she?"

"Yes." Theo heard the door close behind Fritz. "Yes, she's going to make it."

He laid her down on his bed, feeling helpless for the second time that night. He knew that he had to get her out of the dripping nightgown she still wore and do it quickly, but his hands hesitated. How many women had he undressed easily, casually, with no other thought but an hour of pleasure? Why did he feel this uneasiness, this timidity even, when it was a matter of life and death? Life and death of the woman he loved.

"Julie?" He cupped her face, feeling an absurd need to apologize. "I need to take your nightgown off. Do you understand me?"

She opened her eyes, and if she gave him a nod of agreement, it was lost in the shivering that continued as violently as if she had some kind of palsy. With fingers that were suddenly clumsy, he began to unbutton the thin cambric. But when the cold, dripping fabric was gone, her trembling did not abate.

Tamping down on the desperate feeling of inadequacy that rose, Theo swabbed her with warm water to wash off the worst of the salt. Then, wrapping her up in a clean, dry sheet, he tucked her into the bed and piled every quilt and feather tick he could find on top of her. But the shivering went on as before.

Even when he crooked an arm around her head and held a glass of brandy to her lips, managing to get at least part of the liquid down her throat, nothing changed. Beginning to sweat with exertion and fear, Theo threw off his coat. God, he thought, cursing silently as he paced, his own body was like a furnace and Julie was still shivering so badly that if the bed hadn't been nailed down, it would have been shaking.

Suddenly he stopped in his tracks, remembering his father's reluctantly told tale of the battle of Austerlitz—how the wounded had crept together on the icy December ground to share body warmth and perhaps survive. An idea dawning in his mind, he knelt next to the bed and touched the backs of his fingers to Julie's face.

Julie could feel the weight of the quilts on her body, knew they should be warming her, but no matter how she concentrated, she could feel no warmth. The cold seemed to pour out of her body in an endless supply to ice over her skin and negate any warmth that came from the outside.

She was tired, so tired, and she wanted to rest so badly. Just lie still and forget the nightmare of the last hour. Yet the shaking of her body continued as if she were a windup doll, depleting any energy she might have had left. Then she felt Theo's fingers on her face, the warmth from just that one small touch seeping into her body, giving more heat than all the blankets piled on top of her.

"Julie, love, can you hear me?"

When she opened her eyes, Theo almost groaned at the exhaustion, the misery that were mirrored there. He took a deep breath and spoke quickly before he lost his courage.

"The blankets aren't doing you any good. The only way I can think of to help you is with the warmth of my body." He turned his hand over so that it cupped her cheek. "Will you trust me enough to let me do it?"

A surge of warmth washed through her blood just at the mere thought. Or had she imagined it?

"Y-yes," she managed to reply. "T-trust you."

Brushing his fingers over her face one more time, he stood and, turning away from her, began to take off his clothes.

Julie remarked his movement and her mouth twitched in a shadow of a smile. Had he forgotten, she wondered, that there was not an inch of his body that she did not know from the months she had cared for him? Now he would care for her. And he would know her body. She let her eyes fall closed again.

Theo threw back the blankets and slipped into the bed beside her.

He hesitated, but only for the space of a breath, before he put his arms around her and drew her closer. As he pulled her against him, as flesh met flesh, he felt the power pour into him. And the pleasure. For the first time in years—ever since he had received the wound that had crippled him for so long—he was giving something to another human being. And for the first time in years he felt like a man.

Twining his body with hers, his hands stroking up and down her back to give warmth and comfort, he tried to focus totally on the task of easing her. But he found it difficult not to remember that he was holding the woman he loved.

Loved. Closing his eyes, he remembered that moment on deck when love had filled his heart. No, he corrected himself. It had not filled it. It had been there all along, but he just had not seen it. Had perhaps refused to see it. When had he begun to love her? he asked himself, thinking back all the months. It had been the first time he had seen her, he decided. When he had opened his eyes and thought he was dead and looking at an angel.

Time passed, but it could have been minutes or hours. Slowly, bit by bit, Julie's shaking began to subside. Theo felt her skin warm. He even imagined that he felt her blood pulsing faster, more strongly. When she finally lay still, he shifted away and prepared to rise.

She would sleep now, he thought. And it was better that she sleep alone. Now that the throb of fear in the pit of his stomach had faded, it was too easy to remember that they were lying there skin to skin. And it would be too easy for the hint of desire that was already whispering through his blood to burst into full arousal. He had asked her to trust him. Suddenly there were too many reasons for her not to.

Even as he drew away, she shifted closer with a soft, unintelligible murmur. The arm she had pressed to her chest in the effort to conserve warmth stretched now and slid over his rib cage. Her breath feathered over his skin like a caress.

Even as he cursed himself for a beast, Theo bit back a moan of pleasure as his body responded. Once again he pulled away, intending fully to leave the bed, but Julie's soft whimper of protest stopped him more effectively than anything else could have.

How much had she given to him and how little had she asked in return? he thought. She was asking now and what kind of a man would he be if he denied her? Turning onto his back, he pulled her snugly against his side.

It was a long time before he slept.

The absence of movement woke Theo long before dawn. He and Julie were twined as intimately as if they had fallen asleep, their bodies still joined, after making love. Even as he extricated himself from her, he could feel his blood heat. Leaving his arm tucked under her head, he rolled over onto his back and waited for the fierce taste of desire to recede.

But, as if loath to give up his nearness, Julie followed him. She spread her hand on his chest, and as she settled against him, her hand drifted downward. He pulled in a quick, sharp breath as her hand lingered low on his belly. Perilously low.

Julie came awake slowly, her system still sluggish with exhaustion. Jumbled memories of the night before flooded in, too quickly for her to unravel them, and she tensed, unsure of what had really happened.

Had it been a dream, a nightmare? she asked herself. But the memory of the water closing over her head was too vivid and her hand flexed in instinctive defense. When she found her wrist caught in a tight grip, she came fully awake, the first spurt of unease giving way as her eyes flew open making her realize that it was Theo who held her.

"For a moment I thought I might have dreamed it." Her throat was parched and scratchy from the salt water she had swallowed. "But some things were too clear to have been a dream."

"How do you feel?"

She stretched a little, testing her muscles, finding them uncomfortable, but not painfully so. "A little the worse for wear, but I'll live." A shadow came into her eyes. "And the child?"

"The doctor said last night she would be all right. We will go look for her in a little while." He felt her skin slide against his as she stretched again. The pleasure, the arousal that skittered through him had him edging away carefully.

His movement brought home to her that they lay as close, as naked as if they were lovers. She should be feeling embarrassment, she thought, or shame. But instead she felt gratitude because she remembered how he had taken her into his arms to warm her. And she remembered that he had asked her to trust him.

"Theo, thank—"

He silenced her with a touch of his finger to her lips. "Don't. It was little enough after what you've done for me."

She gave a little nod, accepting his words and the sentiment behind them, and let her eyes drift closed again.

He thought she had fallen asleep when she spoke again.

"I was so tired down there. So tired that it would have been much easier to let go than keep fighting." She opened her eyes then and looked into his. "Then I thought of you and knew that I couldn't die. I had to see you again. There was something I needed to tell you." She frowned. "But I can't remember what it was."

Her words moved him incredibly. Moved him and made him want to tell her things of his own. The words were on the tip of his tongue, so close to being said that he could almost taste them.

No, he thought. He could not do it. He could not burden her with his feelings when she did not love him. Oh, he did not doubt that she felt something for him, but the memory of how she had looked at Max, her eyes lambent with so much love, so much anguish, was still much too clear in his mind.

So he contented himself with brushing his fingers over her cheek before he cloaked his feelings and smiled into her eyes.

Julie looked into Theo's eyes. They were dark, so dark that there was the merest trace of blue within the gray. She had seen them cold and angry, but she had never seen them glowing with enough warmth to feed a dozen fires.

She could see her own reflection in the luminous depths that seemed to beckon to her, and she felt herself move to the edge. She knew that now she should take a step back. If she did not, it would be too late. Her eyes on his, she took a step forward and fell off the edge into love.

Chapter Sixteen

They found the child in the cabin of the kindly doctor of the night before, being cared for by the doctor's plump wife. The girl looked frail in the white bed, her aquamarine eyes dull, her cheeks hollowed, one cheekbone marked with a purple bruise. Even her straight, unevenly chopped-off hair did nothing to detract from her budding feminine beauty and Julie wondered how she had ever believed her a boy.

"This is the lady who saved your life, *piccolina*. You must thank her." The doctor's wife clapped her hands lightly as the words spilled out of her mouth at a breathless speed. "Go ahead, thank her."

Gesturing to the woman to keep silent, Julie went forward and bent down toward the girl. "May I?" she asked, pointing at the edge of the bed.

The girl shrugged and, her mouth sullen, stared down at her hands.

"Are you all right? Did he hurt you?" When the girl did not answer, she covered the thin, rough hands with her own.

Suddenly the girl jerked her head up, her eyes furious. "If you mean did he rape me, no, he didn't. You heard him. The filthy swine only likes boys." She dragged in a breath. "Why did you do it?" she demanded. "Why did you pull me out?"

Her voice broke on a half-suppressed sob. "It would have been all over then. Now he'll make my life hell and some night, when he needs an amusement, he'll slit my throat!" Defiantly she lowered her eyelids over eyes that were suddenly brimming with tears.

Julie looked at the doctor's wife, who was staring, eyes and mouth round with shock, at the child. "Would you please leave us alone, *signora?*" she asked with an apologetic smile. "For a little while?"

The woman nodded, finally managing to close her mouth, and scurried out of the cabin.

Julie waited for a few moments, but the girl kept her eyes stubbornly lowered. Finally she sighed softly and spoke.

"Will you tell me your name?"

"Lucia." The girl did not raise her eyes. "Lucia Damiani."

"You don't have to go back to him, Lucia."

"I don't?" The girl's eyes flew upward, hope streaking briefly through them before it died. "'Course I do. He bought me from Lesto. I saw the coins." She leaned back against the pillows and stared upward at the ceiling.

"I thought it'd be all right. They believed I was a boy and I figured I'd be safe." She lifted a thin shoulder. "I thought maybe I wouldn't have to steal anymore. I thought I'd have a pallet of my own to sleep on instead of the hole where Lesto kept us penned in like animals." Her voice sank to a whisper. "Sometimes there were so many of us in there that we didn't even have room to lie down at night."

Julie bit her lip to hold back tears at the bleak hopelessness in the girl's voice. "Who is this Lesto?"

"They called him that 'cause he had the fastest fingers in the district of San Marco. 'Twas a privilege to work for him." She looked at Julie with a spark of pride in her eyes. "It meant you were good."

"Whether or not the Levantine paid for you, you don't have to go back to him," Julie said briskly. "After what we saw him do to you, he can thank God if he isn't handed over to the next magistrate."

"Will I have to go back to Lesto then?" Lucia whispered, her eyes huge. "He said he couldn't use me anymore. That I was getting too big." She swallowed audibly. "He'll whip the skin off my back. Or sell me to one of the pimps. Or both."

"How old are you?" Theo spoke for the first time.

"Fifteen. More or less." She shrugged again, but her eyes skittered uneasily up to Theo. "Don't really know."

"Where are your parents, Lucia?"

"My mother died three Easters ago."

The wave of compassion that went through Julie almost robbed her of her voice. "And you've been fending for yourself ever since? What about your father?"

"Never knew him. Don't think my mother ever really knew him, either." She stared defiantly at Julie, her eyes daring her to make a disparaging remark.

Although she would have wanted to take the girl in her arms, Julie understood that such compassion would not be welcome. So she met the girl's gaze squarely and kept her voice brisk. "As I said, you don't have to go back."

"And where would I go?" Her voice rose. "Are *you* willing to take me with you, knowing that I'm a street child whose only skill is picking pockets?" Despite her callous words and insolent tone, her eyes lit up with hope.

"No, Lucia," Julie said softly. "We cannot take you where we are going, but the doctor and his wife have said you could go with them."

The light in Lucia's eyes died. "Where are they going?"

"To Athens. Their daughter lives there. They said she has several children and can use an additional pair of hands."

Julie squelched a feeling of unease that the doctor's wife had agreed with such alacrity only because she saw the girl as naught but cheap labor.

When Lucia let her head fall back and closed her eyes, Julie sent Theo a distressed look.

"You should have let me drown."

"Don't say that." Julie covered the girl's hand with hers. "Life is a gift."

"Even if you're a slave?" Lucia lifted her eyelids and met Julie's eyes. "I was Lesto's slave. Then I was the Levantine's slave." Her eyes filled. "And soon I will be someone else's slave."

Julie wanted to contradict her, but the words stuck in her throat.

"You can't deny it, can you?" The anger had gone out of her voice, leaving it dull. "You can't tell me that I won't be a slave."

Before Julie could answer, Lucia sat forward and gripped Julie's hands. "You wouldn't make me a slave." Her hands tightened. "Would you?"

"Oh, child." Julie's heart broke a little. "Where we're going is no place for you."

"Please. I'll go anywhere with you." Her thin shoulders began to shake with her sobs.

Julie took the girl in her arms and looked at Theo. "Can we?" she mouthed.

Theo saw the sadness, the pain in Julie's eyes. He heard Lucia's heartbreaking sobs and he nodded.

"All right, Lucia. You can come with us."

"*È vero?* Is it true?" Lucia looked at Julie, her eyes mirroring hope and a flash of joy. Then her gaze darted over to Theo and registered fear. "Does *he* like girls?" She tipped her head at Theo.

"*He* is my husband and you may apologize for that remark, Lucia," Julie said softly. Although she understood the girl's reasons, she understood, too, that discipline would be necessary.

"*Scusate,*" the girl mumbled.

"We will see about accommodations for you, then."

As Julie began to rise, Lucia grabbed her sleeve. "I don't want charity."

"We are not offering any. You will learn to be a girl again and you will learn to be my maid."

Julie saw a rebellious flicker in the girl's eyes.

"There is no shame in being a servant. It is an honorable way to make a living."

"You would pay me?" Lucia's eyes widened.

"Yes." Julie stood. "But I expect you to work diligently and keep your fingers out of my purse and my jewelry box. And other people's purses, as well." She turned away and reached for Theo's arm.

She had not gone two steps before the girl called out, "*Signora?*"

"What is your name, *signora?*" she asked when Julie turned.

"Giulia." She gave her name in its Italian form. "My name is Giulia."

"I'll try hard, Signora Giulia." She made a quick sign of the cross over her heart with her thumb. "I swear I will."

Touched by the childish gesture and the flash of desperate hope in the girl's fabulous eyes, Julie returned to the bed. Unable to resist a small touch, she cupped her hand to the girl's face. Lucia could not quite control a flinch before she went very still. Her heart breaking, Julie swore to herself that she would make certain that this child never had to flinch again.

* * *

When they had left the cabin that morning, they had had the sense of purpose of finding the child to cover the sudden awkwardness that had sprung up between them as they had risen. Now, having accomplished their mission, they walked along the deck and found the awkwardness returning and the silence between them growing long. And longer yet.

They stopped, not far from the spot where they had stood the night before. Leaning against the railing, they kept their attention on the bustle down on the dock. The awareness between them was almost palpable and yet they both kept their eyes straight ahead, both afraid that their newfound emotions would be too easily legible there.

Did love always have to hurt? Julie asked herself. Already the ache was drifting through her. Would she always love men who did not love her? Men whose hearts belonged to another woman? What a tangled web, she mused. First one brother then the other. No, she corrected herself, only Theo. Max had been right. She had never loved him. Or if she had, it had truly been no more than a girl's hero worship.

She remembered how they had lain together this morning, skin against skin, as if they were already lovers, and the ache tugged at her again, stronger this time. What sweetness had been there. Sweetness underlaid by the sharp pull of desire. Oh yes, she knew that he wanted her. She knew that a word from her and he would make love to her. The corners of her mouth tipped almost imperceptibly upward in a sad little smile. He would feel guilt, but he would make love to her because he wanted her too much not to. She wondered if she could take that and make it be enough.

Theo felt his heart overflow with his newfound feelings, and for the first time in his adult life, he cursed his brother.

Why did he, who had so much, have to have Julie's love, as well? he demanded, even as he chided himself for his own childishness.

She wanted him, he reminded himself with a sulky kind of pride. She might love Max, but it was him she wanted. He pressed thumb and forefinger to the bridge of his nose where a headache was beginning to form. It was him she wanted, he repeated with a kind of desperation. He wondered if he could take that and make it be enough.

Because she needed to make some kind of contact, be it ever so casual, Julie spoke.

"It was kind of you to let me take the girl with us."

Because he needed to touch her, be it ever so lightly, Theo traced his fingers across her knuckles. "Kind? No, Julie, I'm not particularly kind." He lifted his eyes to hers. "But I find it difficult to deny you anything. Especially something you want so badly." He ran his fingers over her hand again. "I just hope that you're not priming yourself for a disappointment or worse."

He shrugged. "But then women apparently have rather good instincts on these matters."

Julie raised her eyebrows in question.

"Years ago my mother adopted a child in Vienna who was being abused by her stepfather. My father warned her that if he found the family silver missing, it would be on her head."

"What happened?"

He grinned. "Poldi diapered every single one of us and considers it her prerogative to hand out unsolicited advice at the least provocation."

The smile on Julie's face died as she noticed the man watching them. Had he been close enough to overhear them, as well? she wondered. Turning her hand over quickly, she squeezed Theo's fingers in warning.

Theo turned and sent a brief, dismissive nod in the man's direction.

Choosing to take the nod as an invitation, the man moved closer. "Fellner's my name. Good day." He snapped his heels together in a military bow that belied his civilian clothes. "You and your wife have caused quite a stir on board ship."

"We just happened to be in the right place at the right time," Theo answered him in the slow, accented German that he affected as part of his persona of Thébault van Dam.

"Admirable," he said. "Most admirable. Not many would have done the same."

"I find I am rather tired, *mon cher.*" Julie looked up at Theo. "You will excuse us." She sent a vague nod toward the man.

As they moved away, Julie could feel the man's sharp, calculating gaze on their backs.

Their journey continued—Crete, Cyprus, Rhodes, Piraeus. The tension between them grew, and although they both used the excuse that their final destination was drawing nearer, this had little to do with it. And they both knew it.

The nights grew warmer as the ship wound its way between the islands scattered through the sea that separated Greece and Turkey, as if some mythological giant had sown a handful of pebbles. Sometimes they sailed close enough to an island that they could see the whitewashed houses rising up steeply from the pale sand or a herd of sheep grazing in a rocky meadow.

Julie slipped out of her gown and her petticoats and unfastened the coil of hair at her nape. As she began taking out the pins, the star-spangled night sky called to her again and she moved toward the porthole.

The light from a lighthouse winked at the passing ship. Suddenly she was seized with the wish to stop the ship and flee onto the island with Theo. Surely it would be possible to live in one of those sparkling white houses, with nothing but the deep blue sea and the azure sky around them, and forget that the rest of the world existed. Surely she could make him happy then. Surely— She froze at the soft sound of the cabin door opening.

Oh God, she thought. She had always been in the narrow bed when he returned, the covers pulled securely up to her neck, pretending to be asleep. Julie looked over her shoulder and met Theo's eyes as he stepped into the cabin.

She stood very still, her unbound hair spilling over her naked shoulders like a dark cloak. Theo knew that he should turn around and go. Instead he took a step forward and closed the door behind him.

Even in the dim light of the cabin he could see her eyes— golden like the eyes of a cat. But there was no coolness there, no distance. There was only warmth. Warmth only she could give. And in her eyes shone the answer to the question he had not yet voiced.

"Julie, if you want me to go, tell me so now."

He wanted her. She recognized the desire in his eyes. Would that be enough? she thought. Would it be enough to be desired for one night? To be given the gift of his body? To give him the gift of hers? Even as she asked herself these questions, the answer blossomed within her and she knew that she wanted to give as much as she needed to take.

Theo's gaze traveled down, over her skin. He knew that her skin was as soft as the inner petals of a rose. Just by looking at her, the sensation of how she would feel tingled in his fingertips.

He was only looking at her. Why then could she feel his hands on her skin? Her muscles seemed to loosen as if she had had too much wine.

Julie turned to face him. Neither one of them heard the soft clack as the hairpins she held scattered over the floor. She lifted her hands and held them out to him.

It took only a few steps to cross the cabin to where she stood, but to Theo it felt like an eternity. When he stood in front of her, he took the hands she held out to him. He had dreamed of this moment. Long before he had admitted to himself that he loved her, he had dreamed of her like this.

Keeping his eyes on hers, he lifted her hands to his lips and pressed a kiss first to one palm and then the other. Then he watched her golden eyes widen, darken as he let his mouth drift down to taste the tender skin of her wrist.

He felt her pulse flutter against his mouth. As he touched the tip of his tongue to her wrist, he felt it begin to race.

A jolt of pain, hot and sharp, shot through him as he watched her eyes begin to cloud. She was slipping away from him, he thought. Even as her pulse was pounding from the touch of his mouth, she was slipping away from him. She would give herself to him, but he would possess no more than her body. When he took her, her mind, her heart would be elsewhere.

As Theo's mouth caressed her wrist, Julie felt the pleasure pour through her like warm honey. When he began to trace his tongue over her skin, her blood began to swim. Even so, the doubts, the painful knowledge that she would only be a substitute for the woman who lived in his heart were subdued for the moment but not silenced.

"Julie, look at me."

"I am," she whispered, feeling his fingers tighten on her wrist.

"Tell me what you want," he demanded.

There was a strange light in his eyes, an urgency in his voice. One more time the doubts came flooding toward her, but Julie swept them aside and her heart filled with love. Filled and overflowed.

She shifted, closing the space between them.

Theo swallowed a groan as her soft body pressed against his. "I need you."

"I know." Julie felt the ache twist her heart. Felt it and accepted it.

"And you?" With his thumbs he traced circles over the pulse that throbbed at her wrists. "Do you need me?"

"Yes." She stretched upward until they were almost mouth to mouth. "And more."

Already seeing the question come into his eyes, afraid that she had said too much, she pressed her lips against his.

What had she meant? But even as the question flared up, her mouth was on his, her taste already seeping into him. Beckoning to him. Tempting him. Unable to resist, he took her mouth fully.

The heat blazed up between them like a solid wall of flame, threatening to enclose them, consume them. Because no more than a breath separated reason and madness, Theo forced himself to end the kiss. He released her hands, but they remained caught between them.

A protest already forming on her lips, Julie looked up at him. "Why did you stop?"

Theo traced the line of her neck and shoulders with his fingers. Because that made him want more, he took his hands away.

"I have not made love to a woman in a very long time. I don't know if I can be gentle enough with you." Because he could not stay away, he lifted his fingers to touch her cheek. "You deserve someone who will be gentle with you the first time."

Julie looked at him. She saw the edgy passion that made his eyes gleam and his nostrils quiver. He did not love her, she thought, but he wanted her. And tonight he needed her. He needed her so badly that she felt the need as if it were a wave of heat emanating from him.

Surely, she thought, surely it would be enough if one of them loved.

She reached for his hands and curled her fingers around them. Keeping her eyes on his, she lifted his hands and pressed his fingertips against her mouth.

The way his breath caught made her bold. The glitter in his eyes aroused her. No, she thought again. He did not love her, but he wanted her. If that was all he had to give her, she would take it. Perhaps it would not be enough, but it would still be more than she would otherwise have.

Slowly, her eyes still on his, she drew his hands down. She hesitated for a moment as the heels of his hands brushed the tops of her breasts. If she continued, she knew that there would be no turning back. She slid his hands down and curved the long, slender fingers over her breasts.

Chapter Seventeen

Theo's breath tripped as Julie lifted his hands and pressed his fingertips to her mouth. It was such a simple touch and yet, with her eyes on his, so erotic that he felt his blood begin to heat.

Then she began to draw his hands downward. When the heels of his hands grazed the soft skin above her corset, the uneven thud of her heart had his own heartbeat pounding. When her hands trembled in hesitation, he found that his own hands were unsteady. But then she was guiding his hands further.

When the ruffle at the top of her bodice scraped over his palm, he shuddered. When she curved his fingers over her breasts, his breath came out in a moan.

The soft give of her flesh beneath the stiff fabric had the desire clawing at him. Her hands fell away from his. He used the freedom to mold his fingers to her breasts even more closely. Just the thought of what it would be like to touch her skin had his arousal spiraling upward.

One more step, one more touch and there would be no going back for him. Because he knew just how close he was to losing control, because he knew just how much he loved her, the doubts, the guilt surfaced. He loved her, but he had nothing to give her in the long run, he thought. Suddenly he knew that no matter how badly he needed her, he needed to give her one more chance to back away.

"Julie—" he began, falling silent when he saw that although her eyes were still on his, her gaze was unfocused. Did she see him at all? he wondered. Or was she seeing Max's face? Was she imagining that it was Max's hands that were touching her? He had no reason to reproach himself, he thought bitterly. They were even. She had nothing to give him in the long run, either.

But the love that he carried secreted in his heart surged up like a spring of clear, pure water to wash away the bitterness. The hurt remained, but with the bitterness gone, the words came easily.

"Julie, are you very sure?"

His voice was very soft, but it cut through the haze of desire that surrounded her as cleanly as if he had shouted the words at her. For the first time since he had entered the cabin, she felt exposed. Hurt flashed through her. And anger.

"How can you stand here like this, with your hands on me, and ask me that?"

Theo saw her eyes clear. Saw the anger but not the hurt. Perversely pleased, because now, at least, he was sure that she was looking at *him*, he removed his hands from the temptation of her breasts. When he had slid them up to her shoulders, he realized that this was not an improvement. Here, without the barrier of the fabric, the skin was naked and as soft and cool as rose petals at dawn, making him want to taste it.

She stared at him. He was looking at her as if she were a sinfully rich dessert and yet he had had the cool presence of mind to ask her if she was sure, as if it were a matter of choosing between pearls and diamonds. She had offered herself to him. She had put his hands on her body. And he asked her if she was sure. Even as she had the wild urge to flee, pride kept her where she was. Pride and love.

"Perhaps I should have asked *you* if you were sure."

"No. No, I'm not sure." The words burst out of him before he could hold them back, and he felt her begin to move away from under his hands. The quick jolt of panic that went through him had his fingers tightening. "I have no right."

Julie went still. His eyes were dark—like a summer sky before a storm. There was something there. Something she could not quite read. But whatever it was, it gave her the courage to take the next step.

"I'm not talking about rights, Theo. Not rights, not promises." She swallowed and opened herself up to whatever he would deal her. "It's a question of whether you want me enough. No more and no less."

The love surged through him, love threaded with a hope he would have denied. He ran his hands over her shoulders and up her neck to cup her face. "Yes, I want you." His thumbs feathered over her mouth. "And more," he added, not realizing that he was echoing her words of a few moments ago. "Will you let me show you?"

He replaced his thumbs with his mouth. "Will you?"

Julie felt his words, his breath flow through her parted lips. Felt the heat arrow through her as if he had touched her most secret place.

"Yes," she whispered into his mouth. "Show me."

He began to touch her, tracing tantalizing circles over her bare shoulders, sliding his fingers beneath her bodice to skim over her breasts, while his mouth made love to hers. When his hands wandered down the graceful line of her back, he urged her closer and closer still, until not a breath could have passed between them.

His body was already painfully aroused, but as he pressed against her, he found that there was more. And still more.

Already spinning helplessly in the vortex of desire, Julie found herself incapable of coordinated movement as he maneuvered her toward his bed. Her blood swimming, she could only hold on as he bent to lay her down.

Theo knelt next to the bed and, giving in to temptation, tasted the soft skin at the curve of her shoulder. The taste, the scent made him greedy and his mouth trailed down. Unsure of his control, he had sworn to himself to wait until the last possible moment to unveil her, but now he broke the vow and undid the top fastenings of her bodice. With a sound that proclaimed both longing and satisfaction, he buried his mouth between her breasts.

Her hands were weak and heavy with the desire that seemed to have melted her bones, but Julie lifted them, as much to weave them through his tawny hair as to keep his mouth where it was doing indescribable things to the hollow between her breasts. Needing to touch, she slid her fingers down to his neck and found herself frustrated by shirt collar and cravat.

"I want to touch you." Her hands trailed back up and fisted in his hair. "I want to touch your skin."

Her words sent a new surge of desire to swell his body. He rose and began to shed his clothes. Tonight he did not turn away. Instead he kept his eyes on hers, as if that contact could ensure that she remembered exactly who was making love to her.

When his clothes were gone, he lay down beside Julie, but he made no move to undress her further. Instead he nestled her against his side and let his fingers roam over her, seemingly without purpose.

He measured her still-covered breast with his hand, then allowed a single finger to slip under the fabric to circle the crest. He ran his hand down her flank, then trailed his fingers up the inside of her thigh. When she moaned with pleasure, he took the sound into his mouth and filled her with his tongue. And all the while his fingers idled at the apex of her thighs, barely skimming over her.

Surely she would go mad, she thought as his fingers teased her, feathering over the fabric of her drawers. Her thighs parted in unconscious invitation, but still his touch did not change. She was burning, and as she arched against the heat, his fingers slipped between her thighs.

They both stilled. She in wonder at the almost unbearable pleasure that flashed through her. He impossibly aroused by the heat and dampness that filtered through the fabric.

His mouth on hers, he began to slide his fingers back and forth over the thin cotton.

Stunned by that first onslaught of pleasure, Julie found that she could only lie there, trembling lightly in anticipation of the next touch. Then his touch changed, his fingers pressing, provoking. The pleasure grew sharper, more acute, sparking the need to move with it. Shifting toward him, she began to slide her hands over his smooth skin.

The sight of her pleasure drove his arousal higher, but Theo mercilessly held it in check. But when she began to touch him, his control began to fray.

"You're playing with fire, touching me like that."

"There's no part of your body that I haven't touched before." She lifted her heavy eyes to his. "But it never felt like this." Looking down, she watched her hand travel down his side, over his lean hip. Her fingers trembled to a stop when her gaze reached his sex.

She knew the human body better than most women, and the trip of anticipation in her belly carried only the slightest trace of fear. Suddenly the air was thick, her breath clogging her throat.

Theo heard the change in her breathing. "Don't be afraid, love."

When she did not answer, he tipped her face up to his. "Do you want me to stop?"

She shook her head before she found her voice to whisper, "No."

To prove her words, she took his hand and drew it down to her half-open bodice. "I want to feel your skin against mine."

"Julie, wait—" The words dried up in his mouth as she, still holding his hand in hers, unfastened the next hook. And then another. The bodice fell open, revealing the curve of her breast.

His control snapping like a bowstring pulled too tightly, he pushed the fabric aside and lowered his mouth to her breast. The taste of her skin went straight to his head. His blood swimming, he slid his hand down again toward the heat. But this time a teasing touch was not enough and he covered her with his palm.

Instinctively, she mimicked his motion. She felt the throb of his flesh. Felt rather than heard his moan against her breast. Fear that she had hurt him faded as he lifted his head and she saw the desire smoldering in his eyes.

The sensation of her hand on his flesh had touched off a desperation in him. The desperation of a man dying of thirst just inches away from a pool of sweet water. Kneeling beside her, he began to peel away her underclothes.

He wanted badly to touch, to taste the skin he unveiled, but he knew that that pleasure would have to wait for another time. Hooks, buttons, tapes, laces melted away before his quick, clever fingers until Julie lay naked before him.

His flesh quivered with the need to bury himself within her. As he fought for control, he closed his eyes against the beauty of her gentle curves, her skin as pale as milk, her hair spread across the pillow like a dark curtain.

Julie felt the cool air on her skin as he undressed her with a skill, a swiftness that she found both exciting and terrifying. His features were taut, his eyes, which he kept trained on his task, were brilliant with desire.

She reminded herself that she had wanted this. She reminded herself that she had known he did not love her. But her young heart, which was so full of love, still hungered for a tender kiss, a gentle word. As he drew away the last bit of clothing from her, she watched his gaze travel upward. Quickly, before his eyes reached her face, she lowered her eyelids, not wanting him to see the unfulfilled wishes in her eyes. Wanting to be able to pretend that there would be love for her in his.

But then he was touching her again. His hands, his mouth seemed to be everywhere, seducing, tempting, promising, until she was so drugged with aching pleasure that she moaned with it.

She felt him lift her and settle her between his thighs. She felt him nestle his sex there, where the heat, the ache, the pleasure were greatest. Although some still-lucid part of her mind told her she would feel pain now, her body was floating free, languid and lax with all the new, wonderful sensations, and she did not tense against the first gentle probing.

His control straining, he probed her hot, slick flesh with his. Where he had expected tension and resistance was only welcome, as if she were opening for him, inviting him in. As he fought back the urge to plunge into her, the panic flashed through him.

"Julie." He framed her face with his hands. "Look at me." Suddenly he had a deep need for her to look at him. Him. He would not let her take him inside her and pretend that he was someone else.

Julie opened her eyes and looked into his. The desire was still there, but now it was edged with desperation and something else that called to her. He'd said her name, she thought. He'd said her name. As her heart gave a little skip of joy, her mouth curved in a smile. Perhaps he was making love to *her* after all.

"Now, Theo." Her hand, which lay on his hip, tightened. "Come inside me now."

Her smile, her words, which were for him alone, were a precious gift. Slowly, his eyes on hers, he completed their joining.

Julie felt him slide into her, fraction of an inch by fraction of an inch. The pain was no more than a twinge before even that was blanketed with pleasure. Suddenly she felt Theo tense, saw his eyes widen. Then he shuddered and moaned her name.

Theo felt the sorry remainder of his control unravel as he slipped into her. When he filled her, when he was fully surrounded by her tight, slick heat, he was lost. He could only hold on and moan her name as he poured himself into her.

The aftershocks of the cataclysm were still vibrating through him when he began to move again. Gently he rocked against her, wary of causing her pain, wary of his own arousal, whose razor-sharp edge had barely been dulled by his climax.

When he slipped his hand between them, she bucked against him and tensed for the first time. Even as his hand stilled, she moaned.

"What are you doing?" She pulled in a ragged breath in anticipation of the next wave of pleasure, but his fingers lay motionless against her flesh. "Don't stop." Her hand fluttered down to his. "Please, don't stop."

Even as he began to touch her again, her hand stayed where it was. The juncture of their bodies joined as one fascinated her and drew her touch again and again.

The pleasure, the hot, sweet pressure were coming in waves, ever stronger until she could do no more than let herself be tossed upward. Higher and higher still.

He watched her, holding himself back. Even when he felt her begin to pulsate around him, he held himself back, needing as much to feel her climax as he needed to feel his own. She arched against him and called his name as she climbed that final peak. Only when the throbbing of her body began to fade, only when he felt her body begin to slacken, did he let himself go to join her in fulfillment.

Although drowsiness was pulling at her, Julie kept her eyes open, afraid that if she closed them, the past hour would dissipate and become a dream.

Her body was heavy with the aftermath of extravagant pleasure, which was only intensified by an occasional twinge, reminding her where the pleasure had come from. She felt a stab of well-mannered guilt as she wondered how soon she would feel it again.

The physical pleasure twined around the love she carried in her heart as wild roses twine around a trellis, and both were so real that she almost felt she could reach out and touch them. She wanted so badly to tell him what was in her heart. Would it be so terrible, she thought, if she spoke the words? She wasn't asking for promises. She simply wanted to share, to give.

"Theo, I—"

Had he ever felt quite so alive? Even as he asked himself the question, he knew that he had not. He had felt a certain affection, a tenderness for every woman he had made love to, but he understood that he had never truly made love until tonight. Tonight had taught him what a union of the body and the heart was like.

A measure of unease crept in as he watched Julie. The dazed contentment cleared slowly from her eyes and was replaced by a pensiveness he could not quite read. Was she feeling that vague sadness one felt after a coupling that existed only on the physical plane? Was it shame that was dulling her eyes? Was she regretting giving him what she would be able to give no other man?

The love welled up inside him so suddenly that the words began to spill out onto his tongue before he realized it.

"Julie, I—"

They began to speak simultaneously and it was that that had them both falling silent, the rush of words stemmed as abruptly as it had begun. Grateful that they had not said the words that would have burdened the other, they both tucked them away in their hearts.

"Are you all right?" Theo cupped his hand to her cheek.

"Shouldn't I be?" Julie covered his hand with hers.

"Well—" his brows drew together "—I didn't have much finesse."

"You mean there's more?"

"Yes. Oh God, yes." Curling his fingers around her hand, he brought it to his lips. "I didn't show much self-restraint, either." Their bodies were still joined, and as if to confirm his words, Theo felt his sex flex within her.

Her body pulsed in answer and Julie's breath caught in her throat.

Theo heard her breath trip and cursed himself for being a barbarian. "I'm sorry. Are you sore?"

She began to deny it, but she saw the knowledge in his eyes. "A little," she admitted. As he began to withdraw from her body, she stayed his movement. "But not only that." She felt the color flood her face at her own boldness.

Even in the dim light, Theo saw the flush stain her cheeks. "And what else are you feeling?" Relief had his mouth curving into a smile.

For a moment she hesitated, her teeth worrying her lower lip. Then she felt his hand run down her hip in invitation and she smiled. She couldn't give him the words that were inside her, she thought, but she could give him this. "Excitement, desire, need." Shifting, she pressed her mouth against his. "Take your pick."

"Julie—" He groaned as she moved against him. "If I made love to you now, I would be a savage."

She laughed, suddenly feeling very strong, very much a woman. "You're not making love to me." She nipped at his lips. "I'm making love to you."

Tightening his arms around her, he rolled onto his back, taking her with him.

"What are you doing?"

"I'm not doing anything. You are." He gave her a devilish grin. "At least you said you were."

She struggled up, propping herself on his chest. "But—"

He caught her behind the knees, bringing her forward so that she straddled him. The slow trailing of his hands up over her derriere and her back cut off her protest even before he closed his mouth over hers.

"This way you choose. How fast, how slow. How much, how little."

The husky invitation in his voice had her shifting over him in an experimental little move. Their breath mingled as they both gave a soft moan.

"Does that mean I'm doing it right?"

"What do you think?"

He slipped his hand between them and rubbed a finger over her slick flesh. She moved against it, pleasing them both.

Slowly she began to move, feeling wanton and voluptuous and wonderful. Glorying in the pleasure that rippled through her belly, glorying in the pleasure she saw in Theo's face, she took them to the edge. For a long, excruciating moment they hovered there before they plunged down together.

Chapter Eighteen

A few stars still winked, but the moon had already gone
down, leaving the night the pitch-black of that dark hour
before dawn. The silence was broken only by the slap of oars
on the water and an occasional creak of the mast.

In the narrow bow of the fishing boat Theo and Julie
stood close but without touching. Although they could not
yet see it, they both knew that the Russian coast was drawing nearer. And they both watched for it.

It had been laughably simple to find someone in Saloniki
who would take them to the Crimean coast. The city, after
all, lived from smuggling, especially now with English and
French troops just to the east in Turkey and to the north up
and down the coast from Varna. Here it was just as easy as
in Paris or London to purchase the best French brandy or
an excellent after-dinner port—only much cheaper. And the
smuggler they had hired cared little if the cargo he carried
was human.

And it had been just as simple to evade their Austrian
watchdog, leaving him watching a couple of empty hotel
rooms.

The last leg of their journey had been uncomfortable, but
mercifully quick. Sailcloth smelling vaguely of fish had
protected them against the watchful eyes of British and

Turkish sentries as they had passed the Dardanelles and the Bosporus. Now, as the boat cut boldly across the Black Sea, they knew that they would go on land before the sun came up.

His eyes stared ahead at the invisible line where the inky sky merged with the inky water, but Theo saw only Julie's face. She'd become important to him, he thought. So important that he found himself regretting that he had ever begun this quest. So important that he found himself speculating on what it would be like to tell the helmsman to turn around. He cursed silently, knowing that he could not do it. Knowing that, even if he did, he would never be able to live with himself.

Theo fisted his hands in the pockets of his coat to stop himself from taking Julie into his arms. How could he pretend that they were still the heedless lovers of a few nights ago when he knew that once they had reached their destination everything would change? How did he know if those last two nights on board ship had not been moments out of time that could never be repeated, never be duplicated? How did he know if Julie wanted his hands on her at all?

They were standing close enough that he felt her shiver. "Cold?" He glanced at her, but looked away almost immediately because it made him want too badly to touch her.

"No, not really." The night was mild, but there was a chill inside her. A chill that had begun to grow and spread when they had left the ship. A chill only Theo could warm.

But he was already there at their destination, she thought, where her part in his life would no longer be more than merely incidental. Tucking her arms close to her body, she cupped her elbows. "I was just thinking how full of strange coincidences life is. My parents left Russia from Gurzuf. And now I'm coming back to almost the same place."

Because she'd heard the story so many times, she could see her parents in the boat, watching the coastline recede in the distance, as clearly as if she had been there herself. Because she had grown up with the pain of exiles far away from their beloved country, she felt some of their joy in coming home.

"I still have relatives in Russia," she continued in a soft, dreamy voice.

Theo stiffened.

"*Maman* has cousins and *papa* had a brother."

"Had?" His heart began to hammer. Before he could stop himself, he had whipped his head toward her, wondering if she somehow knew more than he did. "Is he dead?"

"I don't think so." Feeling the sudden strange tension in Theo, she looked up at him. "But he's dead for my father."

"And why?" He looked back out into the distance and willed his pulse to quiet.

His eyes did not return to her, and after a moment she, too, looked back out to sea. "My mother forced him to help her get my father out of prison after the December rebellion, but he betrayed him as no brother should betray another."

Tell her, a voice inside him urged. *Tell her the truth now. It is late enough as it is.* But Theo let the moment pass and remained silent.

When the first bluish shadow of the coast appeared, Julie slid her arm around Theo's waist, unable to stand there alone as the end drew nearer. When he pulled her closer, her breath shivered out in a small sigh of relief.

"It will be all right," she whispered with all the generosity of her loving woman's heart. "We will find her and it will be all right." Turning her face into his chest, she closed her eyes against the tears.

* * *

"You sure this is where you want to go on land?" At Theo's terse yes, the swarthy-faced smuggler grunted an order to his men. The course of the boat shifted to the south, aiming for the flat, treeless plain between the Kacha and the Alma rivers. "Further north you could get a guide who would take you through the mountains," he muttered. "Here you won't have a chance to take two steps before you're picked up by a patrol."

"That is my business." Theo did not add that that was exactly what he was counting on.

"Isn't that a bit unorthodox?" Julie gave a shrug and a lopsided grin at Theo's look of surprise that she had understood his exchange with the Greek boatsman. "The advantages of a classical education." She paused. "I mean, why *are* you counting on us being arrested by a patrol?"

"You've never asked before what happens once we are on land," Theo hedged. "Why now?"

"Perhaps it never seemed real until now. Perhaps I didn't ask because I knew it would become real if I did." She saw Theo's eyes shift away from hers and knew suddenly that he was deliberately hiding something from her. "Are there questions I should have asked before this?"

"What do you mean?" The bitter taste of guilt on his tongue made him bristle.

"I offered to make the journey as your wife." She put her hand on his arm. "I did not volunteer for a suicide mission."

"No!" He swiveled toward her and gripped her arms. "Do you think I would knowingly put you in danger?" The guilt surged up again, reminding him that he had put her in danger from the moment they had left Turin.

She lifted her chin. "Nor will I watch you go on a suicide mission."

"Why?" he demanded as a spark of hope flamed.

"I've put too much effort into you," she snapped, fighting to keep her emotions out of her voice, out of her eyes. "Damn you, I'm going to see to it that you're around to bounce your grandchildren on your knee." Realization of how badly she wanted his grandchildren to be hers, as well, had the pain slamming into her with such force that it took her breath away.

Theo felt his heart leap, but her eyes had a dazed, empty look and did not offer what he wanted so badly. Fighting disappointment he had no business feeling, he let her go and stuffed his hands into the pockets of his coat.

"There is no orthodox way for us to get where we're going. How orthodox do you suppose it is to arrive on a beach with a pile of luggage? How orthodox is it to travel to a godforsaken peninsula that is surrounded by three armies just waiting to start shooting?" he demanded. If the confines of the boat would have allowed it, he would have paced.

"You're not telling me anything I don't know, Theo." She met his eyes. "I want you to answer my question."

"It's really quite simple." He returned her gaze—not because it was easy to do so, but because she deserved it.

"This is the best way to get us where we need to go. My identity precluded traveling by land through Austrian territory. If we had sailed through the Russian fleet into the harbor of Sevastopol, we could have been fired on before anyone thought to ask questions. This way, we can be certain that we will be taken directly to the authorities and we won't have to worry about how to get there."

"And the man you're looking for is among these ... authorities?"

"Yes."

"Why should he—or anyone—believe that a Belgian arms merchant comes here, in this manner, instead of going through official channels in St. Petersburg?"

He almost smiled at her relentless logic and her ability to boil the matter down to the basics. "He doesn't have to believe it. He'll be intrigued and greedy. I'm counting on learning from him what I need to learn. And I'm counting on killing him before he kills me."

Theo stopped, sucking in his breath as if someone had sent a fist to his middle. Saying the words aloud brought home that he would be killing a man in cold blood. He told himself that he was entitled. "You see—" his voice rose "—I have a strong desire myself to bounce my grandchildren on my knee."

"Will you tell me who this man is?" She asked the question, although Theo's phrasing made her all but certain that the man he was looking for was whoever was in charge.

"No." Theo turned away. "No." Somehow, the irrational hope had not died that he would be able to keep her from finding out that he was going to kill her uncle.

The boat that had brought them was still within hailing distance when the patrol circled them.

The fear was an acrid, vile taste in Theo's mouth as the memories of the last time he had been surrounded by Russian uniforms swirled up within him. Memories so distinct that he could feel the heat of the August sun, smell the dust and his own blood. He battled the fear back, and as an officer rode toward them, he stepped in front of Julie.

Behind him, Julie moved closer to Lucia. With a reassuring murmur, she put an arm around the girl's shoulders.

"Lieutenant Yuri Naumov at your service." Seeing Theo's blank look, he repeated the greeting in French, his polite tone belied by the hand that lingered near the hilt of his sword.

"Thébault van Dam." Theo returned the bow. "My wife. Our servants."

"How do you come to be here? And why?"

"I represent a Belgian arms producer and I have come to do business."

"Business? Here?" The officer frowned, obviously familiar with the official channels. "With whom?"

"With your superiors, Lieutenant."

Naumov nodded, impressed despite himself by the unflinching steel blue gaze and the soft voice obviously accustomed to being obeyed. "I do not answer to the army commander, Prince Menshikov. I report to the commandant of Sevastopol."

The flash of fierce joy that went through Theo was so strong that he could almost taste his revenge. "*Tant mieux.* All the better. I am certain that he will be just as interested in what I have to offer."

Julie watched Theo mask whatever he was feeling under a casual shrug, but she had felt the ruthlessness of the emotion that had sliced through him as clearly as if it had been her own. Why was it, she thought, that she could feel this violence in him so vividly, and yet when she sought to distinguish his softer emotions, she found everything growing hazy? It was almost as if he were deliberately trying to conceal them. And perhaps he was, she mused. Perhaps he was merely trying not to hurt her by letting her see that his softer emotions belonged to someone else.

"I will escort you and *madame* to the commandant."

The sound of the officer's voice broke into her reverie. She watched him wheel his horse around and give orders to his men.

"What is he saying?" Theo demanded over his shoulder, keeping his eyes trained on the officer.

She stepped closer to him and translated the officer's words in a low voice. A curt nod was all the acknowledgment Theo gave her, never taking his eyes off the soldiers, never reacting to the hand she slid down his arm.

Swallowing the ache that twisted up through her to lodge in her throat, Julie reminded herself that this was why he had taken her with him. He had taken her with him because he had needed her and her knowledge and not because he had felt anything for her. The fact that they had become lovers was nothing but a random happenstance. Fate, her Russian soul whispered. Fate. She smiled a little at her own foolishness.

Still, she could not help remembering what she had seen in his eyes when he had looked at her across the dim cabin. What she had seen when he had framed her face, demanding that she look at him, in the moment before he made them one. What she had felt when her heart had sped toward him in that final surrender. She closed her eyes. She would always have that.

Within an hour the riders had returned from Kacha, the nearest village, where they had commandeered a *telega*, a flat wagon large enough for both luggage and passengers. Impatient to present his quarry to the commandant, Naumov set a quick pace. The ruts the wagon wheels had dug during the spring rains had dried hard and dusty and the unsprung wagon jolted them unmercifully against its low sides, which offered no support.

Even without looking at him, Julie knew how the abuse was affecting Theo's still-unhealed body. Silently she moved closer to him and slid her hand under his jacket to lie against his spine.

Theo felt the physical pain ease under Julie's magic touch even as the ache in his heart grew, as if his heart were being squeezed by a merciless hand. It was his last chance to tell her who the commandant of Sevastopol was. His last chance to admit that he had known it all along. His last chance to confess that he had considered using her for his revenge.

She would hate him, he thought. It would not matter that everything had changed. After all, he mused bitterly, he could not even tell her just how much it had changed. How much time did he have, he asked himself, until Julie began to hate him? An hour? Two? If he told her now, he would not even have that. Because there were no words he could say, he took her free hand in his and lifted it to his mouth. Because there was nothing else he could give her, he laced her fingers with his.

Julie willed him to say something, anything, but he said nothing. She willed him to look at her, but he did not. But his thumb brushed back and forth over her palm.

Their hands were still laced when the wagon clattered into the city.

The city rose from the wide harbor up toward the foothills of the mountains that towered behind it. Neither one of them had eyes for the trees and shrubs that flowered in a symphony of bright reds, corals and pinks, nor for its European elegance, which was in counterpoint to the bright-colored, highly decorated oriental-looking buildings that remained from the time when it had been little more than a Tartar village.

They pulled up in front of the governor's palace, the rough wooden wagon incongruous against the classic facade of white marble. The bright blue water of the bay was barely visible from the street, but the windows of the top story would command a full view of the harbor.

"Your servants can wait for you here until his excellency assigns you a place to stay."

Julie felt Lucia shift closer to her and she caught the young lieutenant's gaze and held it. "The girl comes with me." Her voice was firm.

"Of course, *madame*." He bowed. "As you wish."

They mounted a wide, elegantly curved staircase, not speaking as Naumov led them quickly through a series of dim, spartan anterooms. In the last room, where half a dozen people sat on the edge of their chairs waiting to be admitted, he spoke in low tones with an aide, who disappeared behind heavy, ornate doors guarded by fierce-looking cossacks, their red coats trimmed with Persian lamb.

The only sound in the room was the sound of breathing—their own and the others who waited. As the minutes stretched, Julie kept her arm hooked around Lucia's, but she watched Theo. Lost in his thoughts, he stood apart from them, frowning fiercely.

Theo focused his attention on the task before him. He would have to be careful, he reminded himself for the hundredth time, not so much for himself, but for Julie. He had to play his role with strict precision, allowing no emotion to slip through. This revenge would have to be taken cold.

When the aide returned and beckoned to them, Theo felt a quick prod of excitement and controlled it. As he offered Julie his arm, he felt her questioning gaze on him, but he ignored it. He could not afford opening himself now.

The guards threw open the high double doors, revealing a large, airy room, its baroque superfluity of furniture and knickknacks and the light streaming through the high windows all the more striking after the bare, shadowy rooms they had passed through.

At the other end of the room a lean, gray-haired figure in a forest green uniform tunic sat, very stiff and straight, behind a large, gleaming desk.

If her attention had not been so fully trained on Theo as they stepped over the threshold, Julie might not have noticed the slight, quickly controlled tensing of his arm beneath her hand or the way his breath stumbled. So, she thought, they had arrived where they were going.

Prepared to feel loathing, she looked across the room and consciously fixed her own gaze on the man's face. Her eyes widened with horror.

The face was a grotesque mask, the scarred skin stretched tightly over nose, cheekbones and forehead, which had obviously been crushed too badly to reknit properly. Even the mouth was misshapen, its contours blurred. The only undamaged feature in his face were the eyes.

The first quick surge of hatred that had billowed up within her faded into pity, heightened by a revulsion that was almost physical. Then her gaze was drawn again by his eyes—golden brown Tartar eyes. Understanding, recognition began to dawn within her, but she pushed them away.

No! The protest rose so loudly, so clearly within her that she was surprised not to hear her own voice crying out. It could not be, she screamed to herself. It could not. Theo was not capable of such lies, such betrayal.

She looked again at the man's eyes. And the terrible certainty snapped into place like a prison door falling into its lock.

Chapter Nineteen

"Monsieur and Madame van Dam. May I present the commandant of Sevastopol—"

Naumov's clear young voice rang melodiously through the room, but in Julie's ears it was like a drumroll announcing catastrophe.

"His Excellency General Prince Boris Muromsky." With a salute toward the desk and a bow for them, he left the room, closing the door soundlessly behind him.

Theo felt the jolt go through Julie a fraction of a second before Naumov finished his introduction and understood that somehow she had recognized this man even before she had heard his name. Had she recognized, too, that this was the man he was looking for? The knot in the pit of his stomach tightened and grew.

She did not look at him as they moved forward. He felt the hand that lay on his arm tremble lightly before she removed it to press it against her middle. She still walked beside him, but it was as if a solid wall had gone up between them. And then he knew that she had made the connection. She had understood that this was the man he had come to kill.

He almost welcomed the pain that whipped through him. Surely her withdrawal, her rejection would make it easier for him to do what he had come here for. He forced himself to concentrate on the man he had hated for almost five years, but his attention kept skittering to the woman who walked at his side, slipping further and further away from him with each step.

He wanted to stop, to shake her, to tell her that he had not meant to lie to her. But that in itself would be a lie. Desperate, he reached out and touched her elbow with his fingertips in a silent plea. Without looking at him, she shifted away.

Because it was all he had left, he struggled to grasp the hatred he had nurtured for so long. Like an old, faithful friend, it did not disappoint him, and by the time they had crossed the room and stood an arm's length away from the desk, he could all but feel his fingers closing around Muromsky's throat.

"Please sit down and tell me what brings you here." General Muromsky's deformed mouth curved in a hideous smile. "And in such an unusual manner."

Julie felt the color drain out of her face at the sound of the mellow voice that could have been her father's. Because she was not sure that her legs would hold her up much longer, she lowered herself awkwardly into a chair that was upholstered in ostentatious turquoise velvet.

"It was the most expedient manner," Theo said briskly. "I would have been hard put to find a boatsman willing to bring me directly to Sevastopol no matter how much I paid him."

"You could have traveled by land."

"I could have." He forced himself to lean back in the chair and lace his hands lightly because the desire to hurt, to kill was so strong that he could taste it. Then he met Muromsky's eyes straight on. The startling resemblance to Julie's eyes had his breath tripping and it took him a precious moment to recover his composure. "But I had business to dispatch in Italy and it would have been too troublesome to travel overland," he finished with perfect truth.

Muromsky gestured him on with elegant, perfectly manicured hands.

"I represent Viannet. The name is familiar to you?"

"Of course. Who does not know Belgium's premier arms producer?"

"As I told the lieutenant, I am here to do business." Theo heard his own voice, clear and self-confident, and the nerves began to drain away.

General Muromsky's eyes narrowed to slits. "If you do represent this company, then you must be aware that all decisions are made in St. Petersburg." He gave a short, mirthless laugh. "Even if they do not always make the right ones."

"Exactly." Pleased that he had been given the perfect opening, Theo smiled. This was a resentful and bitter man, he thought. Perhaps it was going to be easier than he had thought. "That is why I have come here."

"Explain yourself." He stood abruptly. "The decision will be made in Petersburg nonetheless."

"A recommendation from you could be quite beneficial, I imagine." Theo paused. "And rewarding for all concerned."

"Are you offering me a bribe, Monsieur van Dam?"

"No." Theo heard the chill indignation and kept his voice easy. "I imagine that it would be reward enough for you to know that your soldiers are armed with modern weapons and your city protected by effective artillery."

"You know what kind of weapons and artillery we have?"

Theo shrugged. "It's common knowledge."

"Not that common." Tapping the tips of his steepled fingers against one another, he watched Theo.

Then, slapping the palms of his hands on the desk, Muromsky leaned forward with all the suddenness of a snake striking. "You are a spy, *monsieur*. A spy!"

Theo just barely controlled a sound of surprise, but he felt a muscle jumping wildly in his cheek.

"If you think about that for a moment, General, you will see how illogical it is." For the first time since he had entered the room, he felt fear. "I would hardly travel with my wife if I intended to do any spying."

"On the contrary. What a perfect cover a wife is. Besides, what if she isn't your wife at all? What if she is also a spy? What responsible man would drag his wife along with him anyway?" Muromsky's voice rose. "There's a war on, for God's sake."

Theo raised one tawny eyebrow. "With all due respect, General, it doesn't seem like much of a war yet."

"It will be."

"Your word in God's ear, General. Viannet is depending on it."

"And where do your allegiances lie, Monsieur van Dam?"

"I am a businessman, General. I cannot afford to have allegiances."

Dazed, stunned, Julie sat perfectly still, her eyes going from one man to the other as she listened to the thrust and parry of their words, which were as skillful and dangerous as swordplay. She did not know what she had expected. But it certainly had not been this.

Within the space of minutes Theo had become a stranger. Something wild and primitive within her had understood the man with the blazing need for revenge. But this man with the cool eyes and the easily nimble words had nothing to do with the man she had fallen in love with. If she had felt anger or hatred or even violence smolder beneath the casual coolness, she might have been able to accept it. But this calculation, this portrayal of a greedy arms merchant, which seemed too perfect to be anything but real, were terrible for her to see.

He had lied to her, she thought. What else had he lied to her about? But then she remembered that he had made no promises.

She started when she felt the touch on her arm. Turning to the side she saw Lucia looking at her with understanding in her eyes, which had already seen too much. She covered the girl's hand with hers, taking comfort.

"Perhaps it would benefit you to reflect on your allegiances in a cell."

The underlying malice in the quietly spoken words had Julie's head snapping upward. The same malice was reflected in the golden brown eyes that were so like—and so unlike—her father's. Malice and more. She understood that this man would be cruel and enjoy it. And she understood in one blindingly clear instant that, no matter what Theo had done to her, there was nothing she would not do to protect him.

Perhaps Theo had betrayed her. Perhaps he had not told her any outright lies, but he had lied to her by omission. He had dealt her a terrible hurt, but the love in her heart was still a living, breathing entity. And she would protect him— even more fiercely, perhaps, because the man who threatened him was her own flesh and blood, making her feel absurdly responsible.

"But it would not benefit you to put my husband in one." Slowly he turned his head toward her and pinned her down with his gaze as if she were some kind of specimen under glass.

Fighting the urge to squirm, she tilted up her chin instead. The discomfited surprise in his eyes made it easy to stare back at him.

"And why would that be, *madame?*"

"Because he has something you want. Because a stay in a cell would not dispose him to procure it for you."

His mouth twisted into the hideous smile again. "You would be surprised, *madame,* what a man in a cell is prepared to do."

"I do not doubt it. But that would still not get you your weapons." Her voice was clear and steady. "We do not carry them in our baggage, after all."

Uncomfortable with the young woman's direct golden gaze, Muromsky turned around and strode to the row of windows behind his desk. He had never been comfortable with self-confident women, he mused bitterly. He had never been comfortable with women, period.

The memory of how Irina Golovin had browbeaten and blackmailed him into getting his brother out of prison returned to haunt him. Even after almost thirty years he could remember just how she had looked, her determination and her cunning at odds with her dreamy beauty. He passed his fingers over the scarred skin of his face, which stretched over the unevenly knit bones beneath it. He knew that he and his own powerless rage had done that to himself, but he had never stopped blaming her and his brother.

"You will remain here as my guests," he said, turning around to face them. "We will speak further and then I will take my decisions." Because there was something about the young woman that made his flesh creep, he sent her an exaggerated, ironic bow. "Will that be satisfactory, *madame?*"

"That will be most satisfactory, General. Thank you." She stood, and with an imperious nod she turned and, taking Lucia's hand, moved toward the door.

They had not yet reached the door when it was thrown open, the two cossacks stepping into the doorway to block their path.

"*Otoidit'e*. Step back." Muromsky's voice was like the crack of a whip. "Naumov."

The cossacks moved back to their post on either side of the door and the young officer took their place.

"Escort our guests to the blue apartment on the second floor and see that they have everything they need."

The young lieutenant saluted.

"And, Naumov—" the hideous smile appeared again "—make certain that our guests are well protected. I would not want an international incident because citizens of a neutral country came to harm."

Theo turned and gave Muromsky a cool nod. "Your sentiment is greatly appreciated."

Naumov gave another snappy salute and moved aside to let them pass through the doorway.

The apartment indeed did its name justice. Chairs and sofas were upholstered in velvet the color of an Indian summer sky and the color was repeated in the drapes that framed the windows. The Tabriz carpet had an intricate design the color of sea and sand and the ice blue Chinese silk that covered the walls was embroidered with songbirds in sapphire and gold thread.

"We need to talk, Julie."

"Do you really think so?" The first dazed hurt was gone now and she gasped at the full pain of a gaping wound. "Did we have too little opportunity to talk before this?" Her fury rose so suddenly that it made her head spin. She jerked open the ties of her bonnet and flung it on the sofa, sending her gloves after it.

"How long have you known that the man you are hunting is my uncle?"

"From the very beginning. Max told me." Theo watched her lace her hands and turn away as he spoke his brother's name. The jealousy sliced through him like the slash of a sword and he wondered how long it would take for him to begin hating his brother, whom he had loved all his life.

"I remember." And she did remember. She remembered very clearly, even though it felt very far away, her memory colored with that undertone of bittersweet melancholy that every woman reserves for her first, unrequited love. "He told me that you had questioned him. I thought it was only because I was Russian."

"No. Max neglected to give you that little tidbit of information."

"I see." She pressed her lips together. "So in his own way he manipulated me just like you did."

"I cannot be sorry that he did. If you had known the full truth, you would have not made the journey with me. And we would not have become lovers." He fisted his hands at his sides because he wanted to touch her so badly.

"And now we are lovers with lies between us." She shivered a little, thinking that some of the lies were her own.

"Julie—" He gave in, reaching out to touch her shoulder.

She heard the sadness in his voice. She felt the tenderness of his touch. Because she could already feel herself softening, she held on to her anger.

"Your acting abilities are truly excellent, Theo." She heard his quick intake of breath and forced herself not to turn around. "You should have no trouble making the general believe you."

"Julie, I wanted to tell you, but—"

"But what?" She whirled around to face him. "Did you think to use me because he is my uncle? Is that why you took me with you in the first place? Will you use me as a hostage? As leverage?"

She filled her lungs with air in the vain attempt to stop the tears that were already burning in her eyes.

"Julie, listen to me." Theo gripped her shoulders. "I knew you would hate me when you found out. At first I thought I could somehow prevent you from finding out. Then—"

"When I spoke of him on the boat, why didn't you tell me then?" The first tears began to course down her cheeks. "You heard what I said. He betrayed my father. Did you think I would condemn you for hating a man like that?"

She twisted out of Theo's grip. Because she wanted to pace and throw things, she stood very still.

"My mother forced him to help her get my father out of prison. In my father's cell they exchanged clothes and my uncle was to say he had been overpowered." Her mouth twisted into a bitter smile. "He put a little extra into the overpowered part."

Taking a deep breath, she continued. "In order to make my father into the lowest kind of criminal, he smashed his own face against the wall of the cell. He must have done it again and again until he lost consciousness. And all because he wanted my father to be hunted like a mad dog, not just for his part in the rebellion but for doing such a terrible thing to his own brother."

Theo stood silent. There was nothing he could say now, he thought. Nothing.

She stepped back from him and stiffened her spine. "You need not be afraid for your plans, Theo. I promised you my help and I keep my promises."

Her head high, she beckoned to Lucia and left the room.

* * *

Theo stared into the glass of Crimean wine, so dark that it was almost black. He was a coward, he told himself. If he was any kind of a man, he would go to Julie now and beg her forgiveness. And if she had no words of forgiveness for him? What would he do then? He set down the wine untasted. At least he would know.

The minute he stepped into the dim dressing room, where a lone lamp burned, Lucia sat bolt upright in her narrow cot.

"Leave her alone." She hissed at him like a half-grown kitten. "You made her cry, and if you go to her now, you'll only make her cry again."

Theo looked down at the girl, who was staring at him, her aquamarine eyes glittering with hostility.

"You're probably right. But, nevertheless, there are things I need to tell her."

"*Sì.* You'll tell her you love her. You'll beg her forgiveness," she spat, her lips curling with contempt. "And like all men you'll think you have done enough."

Theo's mouth twisted in a sad smile. "So young and already so wise."

"Don't laugh at me."

"I wasn't laughing. I meant it." He crouched down next to the cot so that his eyes were level with hers.

She checked a movement to shrink against the wall, but her fingers curled tightly into the blanket.

"Don't worry, *piccolina,* I'm not going to hurt you." He met the girl's eyes and waited for her to understand that he was telling the truth. "You love her very much, don't you?"

"*Sì, signore.* Very much. No one has ever been so good to me." Without being aware of it, she lifted her hand to the almost faded bruise on her cheekbone. "Not my mother, not anyone."

"Can you keep a secret?"

Lucia nodded.

"I love her very much, too. But I can never tell her that."

"Why not?" she demanded with all the frankness of a child of the streets. "You are her lover."

"What—how—"

"I saw it in her eyes." She did not add that she had seen the blood on the sheets, as well.

"There are reasons." Theo shook his head at the absurdity of explaining himself to this beggar child, but her eyes held all the knowledge of an ancient woman who has seen too much. "Besides, she loves another man."

"But—" She fell silent, unsure of why she did not continue and tell him that she was certain that Signora Giulia loved him, too.

"I will go to her now, *sì?*"

"*Sì.*"

Theo rose, wincing at the pain in his legs. He saw that the hostility in Lucia's eyes had faded to a wariness.

"Do you know any prayers, Lucia?"

"I know one."

"Then say it for me."

Chapter Twenty

The room was dark and at first he thought that Julie was already asleep. As his eyes adjusted to the darkness, he saw that she stood at the window. A little of the hope he had felt died when he saw that she did not move, but still stared through the glass.

So it had come to this, he thought. No one knew better than he how much softness, how much kindness lived within her, and yet now, when he needed something, anything from her, she had nothing for him. Not a glance. Not a word.

Silently he called to her. He asked for nothing. He knew only too well that he had no right. But his heart called to hers the way an animal in the wilds calls out to its mate.

Lost in the heartache, Julie stood at the window, staring out into the darkness. She had tried to shut off her mind, to submerge herself in some unconscious world where she would no longer think, no longer feel. But the thought that Theo had not trusted her enough to tell her the truth still spun round and round in her head like a sorcerer's curse.

Oh, she knew that he was not for her. She'd known it from the beginning. And she had accepted it. But was it too much to ask for honesty? The anger that she had felt earlier had long since fled, leaving behind a weariness that weighed down every single cell of her body.

She surfaced from the abyss of her thoughts so suddenly that she had to close her eyes against the dizziness. He was here, she realized as her heart began to race. She had not heard the door open or close. But she knew that he was here as surely as if he had touched her.

"Julie?"

"What is it?" Because she had to fight the urge to run to him, her voice was brusque.

His courage almost left him. "I've come to ask your forgiveness. I know you have every reason to refuse to give it to me, but I'm asking you anyway."

She felt the pain in his heart as clearly as she had ever felt the pain in his body. Because she had no defense against it and because the love in her heart was so great, she nodded. "You have it, Theo."

He stared at her as if she had struck him. "So simple?"

She almost smiled. "Would you rather I made it hard?" She turned toward him and regretted it, finding him much too close and much too pale in the milky light of the moon.

He shook his head. "I don't deserve it."

"We don't always get what we deserve." Her shoulders lifted in a shrug. "Sometimes we get more. Or less."

"Julie—" Needing to touch her, just once, he took a step toward her.

She felt a quick flash of panic and threw up a hand, palm outward, to stop him. "No. I gave you what you wanted, Theo. What you asked for. Go now, please." Because it was too hard to look at the naked longing on his face and keep her distance, she turned back toward the window.

"Don't turn away from me, Julie."

"What more do you want?" she demanded. "Didn't you just say that I'd already given you more than you deserve?" Because she felt the pull as if he were a magnet and she a pin, she curled her fingers around the windowsill and leaned her forehead against the cool glass.

"Go away, Theo." Using every bit of her self-control, she held back the tears. "I don't want you here."

It was her right to send him away, Theo thought as he looked at her. The thin nightgown did not hide the tension in the lines of her body nor the light trembling of muscles strung much too tightly. He'd done this to her. The guilt welled up—and the knowledge that if he pressed, if he reached out and took, she would give him everything.

"Julie—" He had not meant to speak, but her name slipped out, all his longing, all his love echoing in that one word. He wondered that she did not hear it.

She shook her head and lifted her hands to press them against her ears to escape the mellow seductiveness of his voice. There was tenderness there and it would be so easy to pretend that that tenderness was love. It would be so easy to allow herself to be pulled in again and she couldn't afford that, she reminded herself. She was in far too deep as it was.

It was as if she had struck him. He watched her block her ears and saw rejection where there was only desperation. His heart died a little as he turned away and moved toward the door.

They had so little time left. The thought streaked through her mind as she heard him move away. And she had so much love to give him. Should she punish herself by punishing him for a single lie? Later, when he had found Maryka and she was alone again, would she be any happier, would it hurt any less because she had denied this time to them both?

Again she felt his pain. The pain she had dealt him. And intertwined with it were her own emotions. Suddenly the love poured through her veins like a torrent of lava—warming her, soothing her, making her strong enough to take what she knew would not be hers to keep.

"Theo."

Her voice stopped him in his tracks, but he remained still, afraid to move, afraid he had imagined that she had called out to him.

Julie moved forward, her steps soundless on the soft carpet. When only an arm's length separated them, she paused. Would he think her coy? Would he think her a silly woman who did not know her own mind? No, she thought. She would make him understand. She would make him feel.

Closing the distance between them, she slid her arms around his waist.

Theo bit down on his lip to silence the moan that was both pleasure and relief as he felt Julie's arms go around him. As she laid her cheek against his back, her hands moved up his chest. He lifted his hands to curl them around hers.

"I was not being coy a moment ago, Theo, when I sent you away."

His fingers tightened on hers as he felt her warm breath seep through his clothing and spread over his skin.

"I wanted to punish you. But I realized that I would be punishing myself, as well. When I said that I didn't want you here, it was a lie."

"You have forgiven me, then? Or are you letting me stay because you feel sorry for me?" He was driven to ask the question, barely daring to breathe as he waited for the answer.

"I have felt many things for you, but pity was never one of them. Never."

She slipped her hands out of his and stepped back, the pressure of her fingers on his hips urging him to turn around.

"As for forgiveness, didn't I already give it to you?" she said when he faced her. "Or don't you think I meant it?"

He said nothing and she lifted one hand to touch his face. "You were right, you know. If I had known from the beginning I would not have gone with you. But I'm glad I did." She leaned forward so that her forehead rested against his chin. "Very glad."

"Why, Julie?" His hands curved over her shoulders. "Tell me why you stopped me from going just now?" The compulsion to question her burned within him. Somewhere in the back of his mind, the suspicion—and still more the fear—that she saw him as a stand-in for Max still lived. And anything would be preferable to that—even her pity.

Julie tensed. What could she tell him? She could not tell him she loved him. She could not burden him with the knowledge that for her everything had changed. He would feel obligated and guilty and she did not want that.

It had been her responsibility and hers alone. She thought back to the moment when she had knowingly, perhaps even willfully, taken that last step and fallen in love with him. The memory was sharp and clear, etched into her brain forever, and she smiled to herself, pleased with the thought that loving Theo had been her conscious decision as well as a necessity of the heart.

Theo felt Julie's shoulders tighten with tension. "I'm sorry," he whispered into her hair. "I'm making it difficult for you."

"Yes, you are." Julie tilted her head back to look into his eyes. They were turbulent with emotion, the color of the sea on the verge of a storm, and she could not read them. "Why is it that you want to know that so badly?"

"It may be a mean-spirited thing to say when I'm the one holding you in my arms—" he did not allow his gaze to steal away from her eyes "—but I need to know that you are here with me because of me and not because of Max."

He lifted a hand to trace the backs of his fingers down the side of her face. "I know that you love him, Julie. But I need to know that you are here with me—not only your body, but your mind, as well."

Now, finally, Julie understood. Understood why he had demanded that she look at him when he had made love to her the first time. Her mouth curved into a smile.

"I want you, Theo." She lifted her hands to frame his beloved face. "I want you to make love to me. You." Stretching up, she whispered the last word against his mouth.

He looked into her lambent golden eyes and felt the exquisite pain wind through him. Perhaps she did not love him, he thought. Perhaps she still loved Max. But her desire, her passion belonged to him.

His arms went around her fully and he lowered his mouth toward hers.

Julie's hands tightened on his face. She hadn't been going to ask him, but suddenly the question was burning on her tongue. "And you, Theo? Are you here with me completely?"

"Oh God, yes." His hands slid upward and fisted in the hair she had left unbraided. "Can you doubt it?"

He looked down at her. Her eyes were already darkening with passion, her lips parted in anticipation of his kiss. "Julie, I—" The words in his heart almost slipped out. "I need you."

Passion was blazing in his eyes—a streak of lightning in a stormy sky—and she felt a flash of triumph. This was hers at least. Hers and no one else's.

"Show me," she demanded. "Show me how much you need me."

There was invitation in her eyes and the promise of all earthly delights. In that moment she was the quintessential seductress—Lilith and Eve and Circe.

His hands slid down her back to press her more closely against him.

A sound—somewhere between a gasp and moan—escaped her when she felt his aroused body against her belly. Then he was gathering her even more closely, lifting her so that his body was pressed intimately against hers.

Theo felt something dark and primitive swirl up in him as he held Julie. This was passion—pure and unadulterated and utterly basic. This was desire, so hot and urgent that he wanted to tear open his clothes and take her where they stood. This was madness, this was greed that made his hands rough and his mouth frantic as he tasted the impossibly soft skin at the base of her throat.

Her taste, her fragrance rose to his head like sweet, heavy wine. He opened his eyes and looked at her. She lay in his arms, her head thrown back in surrender, her body open to him. Arousal was already a hot, heavy knot in his belly and the picture of female submission she presented triggered every base, primal instinct within him, urging him to take and plunder.

He was already reaching for her, when his hand slowed, his touch gentled. Shaking his head as if to clear the haze of lust from his eyes, he saw just how vulnerable Julie was to him at this moment. Horror at what he had almost done filled him, and within the space of a heartbeat the male ready to take became the man in love wanting only to give pleasure. Cradling her against him, he moved toward the bed.

Had she had the strength, she would have cried out when she felt Theo press her intimately against him. But she was floating, floating in a wild, untamed world that promised boundless, glorious pleasure. Just for the moment it took to draw a breath she felt a flash of regret for the tenderness she knew him capable of. But the passion was coming from him in hot, pulsing waves, allowing no respite, giving no quarter, and she was swept up again in the anticipation of the wildfire.

Letting her head fall back, she waited for him to take her. She would give him what she could, she thought, and take what he had to give her.

When she felt the give of the soft mattress beneath her, her eyes flew open in surprise.

"Can you forgive me? Again?" Picking up her hand, he brushed his mouth over the back.

Her eyes clouded in confusion and she shook her head.

"I almost took you where we stood. All of a sudden I felt like a savage slavering before a virgin sacrifice." Still holding her hand in his, he let his other hand drift down her throat.

"You would have let me take you like that." His words were not a question. "Why?" he demanded. "Why didn't you stop me?"

"It was exciting to be wanted like that." She shrugged and lowered her eyelids.

"I could have hurt you."

"No." Her eyes returned to his. "Not the way you mean."

He opened his mouth to question her further, but she shook her head and reached up to him.

"No more talk, Theo." Lacing her fingers behind his neck, she pulled him down toward her. "Kiss me."

Her fragrance had his head reeling again. But now he knew how close to the edge of control he was. Determined to give her pleasure before he took his own, he allowed himself no more than a brief sip of her lips before he took his mouth down her neck.

The pulse that fluttered in the hollow of her neck heated the skin, giving it the dark flavor of secrets to be shared in the night. Unable to resist, he nipped at it. Her moan had his head flying up, afraid that he had hurt her.

"Don't stop." Through the aching pleasure that was already curling through her, she remembered what he had said, remembered what he needed. Fighting past the weakness that had turned her into a puddle of need, she opened her eyes to assure and reassure him.

"Theo." She found the strength to lift her hand and ran it down the front of his waistcoat. "I think you have too many clothes on." Hooking her fingers under the placket, she managed to open two of the embossed silver buttons before he caught her hand.

"No. This time is just for you."

"I don't understand."

"You will."

Keeping his eyes on hers, he lifted her hand to his mouth and scraped his teeth lightly over her knuckles. He turned her hand over and pressed his mouth to the palm. Still watching her, he traced a circle with his tongue and was pleased to see her eyes widen as he sketched a damp line down one of her fingers and then drew the tip into his mouth.

He felt her shift and he looked down to see that she had pressed her thighs together.

"When you put your tongue to my skin, I felt it all the way down—" Her teeth worried her lower lip.

"And it felt good?"

Julie nodded, although she wasn't at all sure that good was the right word to describe the voluptuous ache that had taken root within her. She watched him run her fingers back and forth over his open mouth. That simple gesture combined with his passion-dark eyes on hers and his warm breath on her skin had her shifting against the ache again.

He gritted his teeth at the telltale movement of the nightgown as she pressed her thighs together again. A few more touches, he knew, and she would be ready for him. Even as his aroused body protested at the constraint of clothing, he reminded himself of what he had promised her.

Loosening the satin ribbon that gathered up the neckline of her nightgown, he slipped the tips of his fingers beneath the fabric. Slowly he swept his hand from shoulder to shoulder so that his fingers brushed the top curve of her breasts. Then he traced his way back, allowing his fingers to dip in far enough this time to graze the crests.

He could feel her skin begin to vibrate. Or was it the pulsing of his blood beneath his own skin? He could hear her heartbeat begin to drum. Or was it his own that was pounding?

"Will you let me look at you now, Julie?"

"Yes."

The single word floated out on a sigh, more seductive than any siren's song. Lifting her a little, he slid the nightgown down to her waist.

Julie felt the cool air brush over her skin, but only for a moment. Then his hands and mouth were covering her, warming her. The ache within her grew until her body seemed to be a mass of flame.

But then her nightgown was gone and Theo's hand was sliding down her belly, down, toward the ache that had become the center of her existence.

He had never seen anything quite as beautiful, anything that had given him quite as much pleasure as the sight of Julie stretched out beneath his hands and mouth. Her skin shimmered in the milky moonlight like the finest alabaster.

Her hair was spread out on the white sheet like a length of dark silk.

But it was not her translucent loveliness that touched him most strongly. It was watching her shift beneath his caresses. It was seeing her skin throb with pulses he had sent racing. It was hearing her sighs and murmurs from pleasure he was giving her. The power—and the love—poured through him until he was drunk with it.

Slowly he trailed his hand down her belly. When she raised a hand as if to stop him, he slowed still further. But her hand fell back bonelessly to the sheet, and as his fingers slid into the curls at the apex of her thighs, she opened for him, her hips arching upward.

Twin gasps of pleasure echoed through the stillness as his fingers slid over her slick flesh.

He began to touch her carefully, slowly. He might have touched a fragile, precious musical instrument with the same skill to coax a melody from it.

At first she lay quiet, unable to move, so steeped was she in the incredible pleasure that he was creating. Then, suddenly, everything changed as she slipped into a vortex of sensation that was all dazzle and movement.

Her breath jolted as the sensations spiraled upward and upward still and she began to move with them. Every time she thought that surely now there could be no greater pleasure, he was driving her on until the pleasure was so acute that it was almost pain.

She was soaring. In some still-lucid portion of her mind she wondered if it was possible to die from too much pleasure. As if in answer to her question, the quicksilver pleasure scaled yet another peak. For a moment it trembled on the summit. Then, as it arrowed out from her core to every single point of her body, she began to shudder.

"Theo."

Awed and humbled, he heard her moan his name as her body stretched like a tightly strung bow, quivering with pleasure for long moments before the final release had her crumpling down.

Stunned, as weak as if her muscles had turned to liquid, Julie lay still. It was her mind that cleared first, bringing both the awareness of the incredible contentment of her body and the awareness that the pleasure had been hers only. And it was the thought that Theo had not shared those earthshaking moments with her that brought tears to her eyes.

"Julie?" Theo's breath stumbled as he saw the telltale glitter of her eyes.

She reached for him, the urgent movement pushing her onto her side so that she trapped his hand between her thighs.

"It was beautiful, Theo." She rubbed her hand over his still-clothed leg. "But I was by myself."

"You were supposed to be." His hand was caught in her moist heat and he shifted in a vain attempt to ease his body.

"This time it will be for you."

"No. In a little while it'll be for us both."

Sure that she was too weak, too depleted to feel anything even remotely like what she had felt, Julie said nothing. Gathering what strength she had left, she shifted onto her knees and began to unknot Theo's cravat.

Theo remained motionless as she worked slowly, methodically, to divest him of his clothes. Motionless, because he reveled in having her small, soft hands on him. Motionless, too, because he was afraid that his aroused body would explode at the least movement.

When her hands were at the waistband of his trousers, he gripped her wrists.

"I am at the end of my tether, Julie." He dragged in a ragged breath. "If you keep touching me it will be over before it's begun." He lifted her hands to his mouth. "Do you understand me?"

"Yes."

Again, that one breathy word was almost his ruin. While he still could, he stood to shed the rest of his clothes.

Kneeling on the bed, she watched him. Although her body was still heavy and languid, she felt a flicker of excitement. Wanting, needing to give him in return the pleasure he had given her, she held out her hand.

He knelt in front of her and skimmed his hands down her shoulders toward her breasts.

"Theo, no," she protested, retreating a little.

"Is it unpleasant when I touch you?" He cupped her breasts and feathered his thumbs over the crests. "Does it hurt?"

Her quick intake of breath and the tiny twist of her hips told him everything he needed to know.

He was making her drunk with pleasure again, she thought as his hands glided over her skin, mapping every curve, every angle. Surely it was impossible for her to want his touch again so soon. But she felt the ache spring to life and shimmer through her and she swayed toward him.

They both stilled as the tip of his sex touched her belly.

Theo shifted back, pressing his hands, which were suddenly damp and unsteady, against his thighs.

"Will you lie down for me, Julie?"

The soft question sent another quiver of anticipation through her. Keeping her eyes on his, she slid back over the smooth linen and lay down.

The angles of his face were stark with passion just barely controlled. If she had not loved him so much, she might have been afraid. Expecting him to seek his own fulfillment, she shifted her thighs apart.

Theo bit the inside of his cheek, drawing blood, so great was the need to plunge his body into hers. Instead he reached for one of the pillows and slid it under her hips.

Words of protest at her shameless posture rose to Julie's lips. But as she watched Theo run his hands along the inside of her thighs, as she watched him spread them apart for his entry, the heat that rose within her burned the protest away before it reached her tongue to be spoken.

He touched her once and then again. Her head fell back as she waited for him to fill her.

Theo looked down at her, his heart overflowing with love. He was beyond arousal, beyond desire. Lowering his head, he filled her with his tongue.

"Theo!" Julie reared up, her hands lifting to push him away. But instead they caught in his hair to hold him fast.

When he felt her slick flesh begin to tremble with those first tiny pulsations, he rose and, lifting her hips, melded their bodies to one.

Needing to touch him, Julie reached toward Theo's hands, which bracketed her hips, and circled his wrists with her fingers.

He moved slowly, wanting, needing her to accompany him on this journey. But she was too tight, too wet, too hot, and the last shreds of control slipped from his grasp.

On a wave of pleasure Julie saw Theo stiffen and stop moving.

"Oh God, Julie. I can't wait." The words were punctuated by his raw, harsh breathing. "I can't—"

He surged into her one more time and she felt his seed pour into her like a hot caress, pushing her up and up and over the top.

Time stood still as the aftershocks of release rippled through them both. And then there was only a wondrous contentment that wound through them, wrapping around them like tendrils of a soft mist.

Theo levered himself down and they lay face-to-face, their bodies still joined. They did not speak, but they breathed as one.

She—her fragrance, her taste, her very essence—filled him completely, leaving no room for anything else. It was as if they were the only people in the world. No, they were the world.

"We go back," he whispered. "Tomorrow we go back."

Confused, her senses, her mind still clouded with passion, she looked at him.

"We will be together." He propped himself up on an elbow and ran his hand possessively down from shoulder to waist. Then swamped with the love that surged through him in wave upon wave, he buried his face in her throat. "I'm never going to let you go. Never."

She knew that it was only the aftermath of passion speaking, but for a moment she lay there, her fingers twined in his hair, and let herself believe his words.

They were still twined together when sleep took them.

Chapter Twenty-One

They had forgotten to close the drapes the night before and the bright, unforgiving southern light was pouring over the bed when they awoke. They lay close enough to share a single pillow, but they were not touching, as if their bodies had somehow sensed that daylight would bring a distance the night had not known.

"I meant what I said last night, Julie."

She knew exactly what he was talking about, but because the night during which they had spent more time making love than sleeping had made her sentimental and weepy and impatient with herself, she lifted her eyebrows in question. If she let herself, it would be, oh, so easy to want to hold him to the promise he had so rashly made. And because he was the man he was, he would feel bound to keep it.

Theo raised himself on one elbow, a frown already digging two vertical lines between his eyebrows.

"I said that we leave here today." He watched her roll onto her back, tipping her head away from him, and tamped down on the sharp desire to grab her and bring her back to face him. "I meant that—" he fought to keep his voice even "—and everything else I said."

Julie curled her fingers into the sheet to keep from reaching for him. Because she judged she owed him that, she shifted so that her eyes met his. "Yes, I know you did. It is a great gift, Theo, and I will treasure it always."

"And you're saying that you cannot accept it." He felt the pain in his belly as if she had taken a quick swipe at his vitals with a knife.

"You know I can't." She shifted away from him and sat up, lifting the sheet to cover her breasts. Somehow it no longer seemed fitting that she allow his anger-filled eyes to rest on her nakedness.

"Can't or won't?"

Julie dragged in a breath. "Can't."

He looked into her eyes. He saw the distress there and understood that whatever she had come to feel for him, it was not enough. Horrified, he felt the first flame of hatred for Max flicker to life within him.

Julie saw his eyes go dull with pain and a tiny, desperate hope wound through her that perhaps whatever little he felt for her could be enough. But then that last hope died as the pain faded and was replaced by the hard glitter of something much like hatred before he turned away from her.

"Listen to me, Theo." As she reached out to him, the sheet she had held to her breasts fell to her waist. "If I said yes now, if we left, how long would it take you to start hating me? Or hating yourself?" She gave him a small shake. "Or both?"

"That's not the point!" he shouted, throwing up his arm so that her hand was flung aside.

She heard something in his voice, something of the same desperation that lived within her. "And what is the point, Theo?" She found herself holding her breath.

"The point is that I—" Words of love on his tongue, he faced her again, met her eyes and held them. There was a light there that made them gleam like burnished gold and he wanted that light for himself so badly that the need was as tangible as a physical ache. But the memory of how her eyes had shone precisely that way when she had looked beyond the garden grate at Max was seared into his memory and he shook his head. "Never mind."

Withdrawing into himself, he let his gaze travel coolly down her body to where the sheet had pooled at her waist before he turned and pushed himself off the bed.

"Lieutenant Naumov tells me that although you have only been here three days, you are already getting impatient." Muromsky kept his eyes on the diagrams of Viannet-produced artillery that Theo had brought to him. The cool, straight lines of the weapons made him feel the same covetousness another man might have felt when looking at a beautiful woman. "I told him to make certain you had everything you wished." He looked up to meet Theo's eyes. "If he did not do so, tell me, and I will reprimand him."

"The lieutenant has done everything in his power for our comfort these past days." Theo emphasized the word *everything* because he had seen the malicious gleam in Muromsky's eyes at the prospect of administering a reprimand. "You will forgive me, General, but a prison remains a prison even when it is a luxurious one."

"Elegantly said, Monsieur van Dam. However, I fear I cannot accommodate you until I am quite certain you are who you say you are and your purpose here no other than to sell us this wonderful machinery." He brushed his hand over the diagrams on his desk in a gesture that was almost a caress.

"If the papers and letters I have already given you do not convince you, I regret I have no other proof, General."

"I have a suggestion." His ruined mouth twisted into a caricature of a smile. "It would, however, entail extending your stay here as my guest." He leaned back in his chair and scrutinized Theo's face. "Would that be a problem?"

Theo took a moment to make certain that the fierce satisfaction he felt was not audible in his voice. "No, General, it would not be a problem. Not unless hostilities begin. Needless to say, I would mislike it if my wife were placed in danger."

"Bon." Muromsky gave a curt nod. He took a sheet of paper out of a thin portfolio of red morocco leather and, his eyes on Theo, slowly pushed it across the desk with two fingers.

The gesture and the sly look in his eyes reminded Theo of a gambler who has a pair of aces up his sleeve.

"Take it, take it, *monsieur.*" He fanned his hand loosely at the wrist.

Picking up the paper, Theo saw that it was a bank draft. His eyebrows arched at the amount and at the fact that it was issued personally by the general.

Muromsky watched Theo over his steepled fingers. If he was lucky, he mused, he would get what he wanted and prove to those senile incompetents in St. Petersburg what he could do. If he was not—*eh bien,* it would be a simple task to rid himself of this man and his wife, whose alert cat's eyes made his flesh crawl.

"Since you are apparently well-informed, you know perhaps that percussion rifles were ordered three years ago, but—for whatever reasons—we have yet to see a single one here in the Crimea. And as far as the breech-loading field guns are concerned, our logistics people have seen fit to order none at all."

Theo nodded, but said nothing.

"If my mathematics are correct, this draft should cover five hundred rifles and one such field gun. If you can produce the sample merchandise within, say, four months, and make a promise of prompt delivery of more merchandise, I will demand that St. Petersburg place orders with Viannet immediately.'' He paused to let the information sink in.

''Then you will have your business and my soldiers will be armed with real weapons. You were quite right, you know. Our men might as well be armed with slingshots.''

Theo's mind raced as he tried to calculate the risks and possibilities. His chances of actually getting his hands on the arms were zero, but with a little help, he could simulate the procedure well enough to give him the time he needed to do what he had come here for.

''You will have your arms, General.'' He gave a curt nod. ''And I will have my business. However, I have some conditions of my own.''

Pleased, Muromsky gestured for him to continue. If the man had not had conditions, he would have had him shot for a spy within the hour.

''Freedom of movement for my wife and myself.''

''Within reason.'' He raised his hand to silence Theo's protest. ''Within reason,'' he repeated. It would be simple enough to monitor every movement they made.

''Should hostilities begin during this time, safe-conduct for my wife out of the country. Your word as a man of honor.''

''Done.'' Promises, after all, were made to be broken. He almost laughed aloud.

''Recompense for the months I will not be doing business elsewhere.'' It galled Theo to say this, but he knew that it would have been out of character not to do so. ''Unlike you, I am not a rich man.''

''What amount were you thinking of?''

''Ten percent of the bank draft.''

"Steep, but worth it, if you deliver." He stood. "Done, Monsieur van Dam." He held out his hand. "I hope I will not regret doing business with you."

"I hope so." Theo smiled coldly, pleased at the ambiguousness of his answer. Swallowing the revulsion, he gripped the general's hand.

Unable to sit still, Julie tossed aside the gown she and Lucia had been stitching and paced to the window. All she could see were rooftops and an occasional small patch of street. The mountains rose like a dark wall behind the last houses and the closed-in feeling the view gave her made her skin itch.

They had been confined to their apartment ever since their arrival three days ago. Every time they had looked at each other they had seen the memory of the words that had passed between them in each other's eyes. And neither one of them had had the strength to forgive.

She had hurt Theo, Julie mused, although she had only given him what he had needed. Now there was no more talk of leaving and that was as it should be. And he—instinctively she crossed her arms over her chest in a self-protective gesture. That last cold glance he had trailed over her body had hurt more than if he had struck her.

"It will be all right, Signora Giulia."

Julie felt Lucia's shy, fleeting touch. She dug inside herself for a smile and the corners of her mouth tilted upward.

Lucia hugged the smile to herself and wondered if she should tell the *signora* what she knew. But her life had taught her that keeping her tongue to herself was the best rule, and she remained silent.

Both the woman and the girl stiffened as the door opened. As one they turned toward it.

Julie squelched the need to go to him, waiting instead until he had almost crossed the room before she moved.

"You spoke to him?"

"Yes."

"And?" she prompted after a few moments when he had still not spoken.

"You seem to have more interest in my revenge than I do," he barked, regretting both his words and his tone the minute he had spoken.

"I have even more interest in getting out of this apartment," she snapped back. "I'm tired of being locked up."

"Then perhaps you can imagine what it was like to spend more than two years in a filthy prison."

"Just what is it that you are reproaching me for, Theo?" Her voice was even and just lightly tinged with irony. "For understanding your need for revenge or for the exact opposite?"

Theo laughed harshly at the contradiction of his own words. "Forgive me." He pinched the base of his nose with thumb and forefinger. "It would seem my mind is not working properly. I haven't been sleeping well."

"I know," she said softly. "Neither have I."

Lowering his hand, Theo turned to face her. As their eyes met and held and clearly read the other's suffering, they almost reached out to each other. But the moment passed and then it was too late.

Briefly, with no embellishments, no explanations, Theo recounted his conversation with Muromsky.

"What are you going to do?"

"I will say that I cannot contact Viannet directly and I will write to the man who procured me the information I needed for this journey. All I need is a little time." With his right fist he beat a tattoo on his left palm. "If his promise is to be trusted, we will be given freedom of movement." He laughed mirthlessly. "Within reason."

"Good. Then I can begin asking questions about Maryka." Julie felt the pain of loss curl through her and she knew that somewhere inside her was the terrible wish that Maryka would be forever lost.

He whirled toward her and gripped her shoulders. "But discreetly, Julie. Take no chances." His hands gentled. "Will you promise me that?"

For a moment she allowed herself to savor his touch before she took a step back so that his hands fell away from her. "Life consists of taking chances, Theo."

It occurred to her that she had taken a chance three days ago, and because they had both been hurt, she had retreated to someplace safe. She had taken no more chances—and she was no happier for it. Perhaps—she took a deep breath—perhaps the time had come to take another chance.

"What do you mean?"

"Just what I said. No more, no less." She closed the distance between them again and took his hands in hers. Because there were so many words inside her—words she could not say—she said nothing.

"Talk to me, Julie."

She shook her head. "We have already said so many words, Theo. And every time we succeed only in hurting each other. Perhaps talking is not such a good idea."

He sent her a rueful smile. "Any suggestions?"

"Will you hold me? Don't say anything and just hold me."

Theo lifted their joined hands to his mouth and brushed his lips over her knuckles before he lowered her hands, resting them palm downward on his chest. He wanted badly to kiss her, to taste the honeyed sweetness that would intoxicate him and blur his reason. But he understood that she needed tenderness now and not passion.

Julie saw the desire spark in his eyes. She felt his heart begin to pound beneath her hands. He wanted her, she thought, and told herself that that was enough. She tipped her head back to offer him her mouth.

He cupped her face and brushed his thumb over the mouth she was offering for his kiss. But he did not take it, and it cost him. Then his fingers slid into her hair and he pressed her head against his chest.

Her heart filled with love and overflowed. She had seen the desire in his eyes, and the knowledge that he had understood her need and checked his own was a precious gift. She closed her eyes and pretended.

"What is the meaning of this?" Theo's voice vibrated with anger. "Yesterday you promised us freedom of movement and today we are told, no, ordered, to prepare to journey to Gurzuf."

"My dear Monsieur van Dam." General Muromsky raised his hands as if to appease Theo. "I suddenly find myself desiring a change of scenery and I merely asked you for the pleasure of your company." He rubbed his hands together. In Gurzuf it would be easier to keep an eye on these two and their odd entourage, he thought. And far less for them to see if they were spies after all.

"And if we do not wish a change of scenery?" How would he ever find Maryka if Muromsky kept him on a leash? Theo suppressed the thought that his anger stemmed from a sense of relief that the possibility of looking for Maryka was being taken out of his hands.

Muromsky smiled his hideous smile. "I said 'within reason.' And I find it quite within reason to request your company on this little excursion. Or did you have other plans?"

Theo saw the flash of suspicion in Muromsky's eyes and subsided. "No, of course not."

"Then—" Muromsky spread his hands. "I request that you and *madame*—" he bowed in Julie's direction "—be ready in the morning."

Julie looked into her uncle's eyes, which were so like her father's, and waited, as she did each time, to feel a kinship, a trace of affection. And if not that, then at least a little compassion. But all she felt was a loathing that made her blood run cold. And yet—and yet she knew that she did not want his blood on Theo's hands.

"We will look forward to the trip, General." Julie managed a smile.

"*Madame.*" Muromsky masked a shiver beneath another bow. The woman's knowing cat's eyes made him want to squirm.

"Aren't you coming to bed, Julie?"

Julie's fingers tightened on the blue drapes. A feeling of dread lay within her like a lead weight. Was it the journey to Gurzuf tomorrow, she wondered, or was it something else?

"Julie?" Theo raised himself up on an elbow and turned up the wick of the petroleum lamp on his nightstand.

As her mind stumbled, Theo's voice faded as if it were coming from very far away. Gurzuf. Of course, she thought. It had been a fateful place for her parents and it would be a fateful place for her. Whether Maryka was dead or alive, Gurzuf would bring that knowledge to them.

She felt the strength drain out of her legs until she had to lean forward against the window seat for support.

Theo sat up and sent a worried glance to where Julie stood. Feeling her need for solace, for comfort, as if she had asked for it, he rose to go to her.

"What is it, love?"

Unable to speak, Julie shook her head.

He turned her within the circle of his arms. Because he knew that she would respond more to his need than her own, he whispered, "I need you tonight."

Julie felt the power pour back into her. No matter what tomorrow would bring, she would take what this night offered her and it would nourish her forever.

"Make love to me, Theo." Her hands strong and desperate, she pulled him down to the rug where they stood. "Make love to me here, now." She spoke the words against his mouth. "Make love to me so that there is room inside me only for you and the moment."

Her breath spilled over his mouth like a sultry breeze. The fragrance of verbena that always clung to her darkened to a dangerous perfume that made his head swim. Her hands were running over him—tantalizing, provoking, arousing. Theo heard a moan and realized that it was he himself who had made that sound. Another minute of her touch and he would explode.

Even through their nightshirts, she could feel the pulse of his blood. Needing suddenly to touch his skin, she began to work open the buttons. Quick and impatient, her fingers slipped into the opening. As they slid over his skin, she made a soft sound of pleasure.

"Julie, please. How much more do you think I can take before I—" He caught her hands at the wrists, but her agile body still moved against him.

"Before you what?"

There was no fear in her voice, nor in her eyes, which gleamed in the dim light like Florentine gold. "Before I take you with greed instead of tenderness." He closed his eyes as he fought for control.

She hurt with need. She burned with desire. And she knew that this was a night for passion, not for tenderness.

"Look at me, Theo." Twisting her hands free, she gathered the edges of his nightshirt in her hands and gave him a little shake. "Look at me." She echoed his words of their first night together, but neither one of them realized it.

He met her eyes. The desire there had his own desire spiraling upward. He was already reaching for her when she spoke.

"Now."

With one tug she ripped open his nightshirt.

For the space of a breath they both remained perfectly still. Then, as one, they plunged into the vortex.

Much later, when they lay side by side, Julie felt Theo nuzzle her shoulder as one hand made its lazy way down to her belly. Her limbs were heavy, but she managed to raise a hand to cover his.

As their fingers linked, the thought streaked through her without warning. The first moment of shock gave way to a joy so great she could have shouted with it. She pressed their joined hands a little more firmly against herself, knowing that they rested against the place where the child they had just made together would lie.

Chapter Twenty-Two

Julie leaned back, exhausted from the almost sleepless night and the long drive over the narrow mountain road with its breathtaking scenery, which seemed to explode in a constant succession of thick, primeval forest and bizarre rock formations. As they began their descent, glimpses of tiled roofs and bright walls hinted already at the town that sprawled down below at the base of the mountains.

Almost without warning the landscape changed from the wild rocks and forest to carefully cultivated vineyards and orchards. Just as suddenly, a feeling of *déjà vu* had Julie jolting forward.

How many times had she heard her parents' story of their flight from St. Petersburg, through the snowy Russian steppes to the Crimea? This last part of their journey had always fascinated her, perhaps because it had been so full of the colors and scents of flowers and blossoming trees. Now, as their carriage bumped and swayed through the same landscape, she felt as if she had traveled this road before.

When they alighted from the carriage in front of the large house, its walls of gray stone partially covered with wild roses and wisteria, she knew that she would have recognized it by the scent alone. Just that fact moved her beyond words.

Theo watched Julie as she looked at the villa. Her arm was hooked through his, but there was a remoteness about her that was like a knife in his gut. He tamped down on a desperate urge to shake her and make her look at him, really look at him, for the first time that day.

Something had happened last night. Between the first time and the last time they had made love, she had in some way stepped away from him. That was good, he told himself. Distance was something she would need. As would he. And yet he found that anger and resentment smoldered within him that for her it was apparently so easy, while he felt as if his heart had been hacked out of his chest.

He hadn't asked for this, he thought as the sudden, irrational anger flashed through him like a bolt of lightning. He hadn't asked to love her. He hadn't asked for this ache that was so bitter—and so sweet. The ache that accompanied his days and threaded through his sleep. The ache that made him grieve for what would soon be lost, even as he held her close. He paused. No, he hadn't asked for it, but without it he might as well be dead.

Julie looked at the house where her father had spent so many happy boyhood holidays. The vague feeling of dread she had had the night before had crystallized to the certainty that behind these walls Maryka waited for Theo. A few moments, she thought, a few more moments and Theo would be reunited with the woman he really loved and she would be alone. Then she touched her free hand to her middle. No, she thought, she would not be alone. She would have the child Theo had given her. She smiled, as much as a defense against the threatening tears as a response to the soft joy drifting through her.

Theo saw the smile without seeing the tears behind it and his heart broke.

* * *

Within moments, the doors of the villa opened and servants in Tartar dress poured out and arranged themselves in a fussy formation on either side of the staircase as precisely as if they were performing a well-choreographed dance. Both the men and the women were garbed in wide oriental trousers and bright-colored shirts or tunics. Only their headdress distinguished them—astrakhan hats for the men, while the women wore small gauzy veils from nose to chin, attached to small embroidered caps that perched on their dark, henna-tinted hair.

"Where are they?" General Muromsky's voice rang out like the crack of a whip. "Why aren't they here?"

He had barely spoken when a man and a woman appeared at the top of the stairs. They, too, wore the Tartar dress, but their light coloring and blond hair set them apart from the others.

Julie knew. Even without the tensed muscles in Theo's arm, even without the hiss of his breath, she knew that the blond woman who stood framed in the doorway was Maryka. Unable to stop herself from staring, she saw the woman's eyes widen and a gamut of emotions run through them—joy, chagrin and something she would have sworn was panic. Then Maryka bent to the waist in a bow and the eyes were hidden.

Her own emotions and Theo's and Maryka's seemed to make the air around them crackle, as strongly as it crackles before a summer storm. A wave of grief that was so hot, so bitter, rose to clog her throat. She felt rather than saw her uncle shift beside her. Despite the emotion swirling in and around her, she picked up on the vague suspicion that simmered within him. She had to divert him, she thought as a flutter of desperate fear for Theo's safety pushed her even closer to the edge.

She fought herself. She fought to concentrate, to focus as an explorer does when he fights through a thick, tangled jungle with brutal slashes of a machete. It seemed like hours, but it was only moments before she turned to Muromsky.

"How unusual." Her voice was light, steady. "Is there a special reason why they do that?"

"The very best reason in the world. I enjoy power. I enjoy having my orders obeyed." He smiled his hideous smile, the very hideousness of it hiding the madness that lurked behind it. "It is one of life's greatest pleasures." It is life's only pleasure, he told himself grimly. Life's only remaining pleasure.

Out of the corner of her eye Julie saw that Maryka and the man beside her had straightened again, and she felt the light quivering of Theo's muscles as he fought for control. Even as her fingers stroked the inside of his arm, wanting to soothe him, she tortured herself wondering what he would do now if no one was watching and he was free to do as he would. Would he run to Maryka? Kiss her? Swear that he would save her, that they would spend the rest of their lives together?

"And why are they dressed in the oriental manner?" Despite the thoughts tumbling through her brain, despite the pain shooting through her heart, she continued without losing a beat.

"I have always had a weakness for the Tartars and the Mongols. Perhaps because some of their blood flows in my veins, as well." He smiled again. "Perhaps because I have always appreciated their capacity for cruelty. For such wonderfully dispassionate cruelty." He chuckled. "And creative, too."

Anything she might have wanted to say died on her tongue as the thought struck her that she, too, might have this cruelty, no, this madness in her. For surely he was mad, she thought. He had to be.

Unable to move, Theo stared at Maryka. He recognized her, of course, but he recognized her with his mind only. The pretty, doll-like girl had become a pleasantly plump woman but that had nothing to do with it. When he looked at her, his heart saw a stranger and the thought terrified him. She had become a stranger because he had changed. Because Julie had changed him.

He had desired Maryka, and even if he had never loved her, he had had affection for her, he reminded himself. Now he desperately searched inside himself for whatever remained of it. Surely some trace was left—a flash of desire, a wisp of fondness. But all he found was the ashes of memories. Memories so far away that they felt as if they had never existed. Instead, all he felt as he stared at her was a terrible, consuming guilt. And the horror that his honor demanded that he spend the rest of his life with her and not with the woman he loved more than life itself. He felt his muscles begin to quiver as he silently raged against the thought.

At a gesture from Muromsky, as abrupt, as deprecatory as if he were ordering a pair of dogs to heel, the couple descended the stairs and bowed deeply again. As Muromsky moved closer, both stiffened, in expectation of the punishment they knew he could mete out so casually. When he cupped Maryka's chin, his fingers digging cruelly into her cheeks, burning hatred flickered into the eyes of the man who stood beside her, but everyone was looking at the woman and no one noticed.

"You know how I value discipline, my dear." His voice was mellow and friendly. "I have told you before that I want you out with the others when I arrive." He heard her soft whimper and, satisfied, eased the pressure of his fingers. "I shall have to take you with me when I return to Sevastopol. Perhaps I can think of a new exercise or two for you."

He slid a possessive hand down her neck before he let her go and turned back to his guests. "A nice collection, wouldn't you say?"

"Collection?" Julie almost choked on the word.

"Yes. I always made it a habit to bring back a souvenir from each campaign—Turkey, the Caucasus, Uzbekistan." He smiled. "And I especially prize these two." He gestured toward Maryka and the man at her side. "I took them in Hungary in '49."

At the thought that the same blood that ran in her veins also ran in the veins of this beast, Julie felt a wave of nausea, followed closely by a wave of the blackest rage. "Collection? Why don't you call it what it is?" She paused for breath. "Slavery."

Muromsky threw back his head and gave a bark of laughter. "Oh, you Europeans are so self-righteous. At least we Russians are honest. You have slaves just like we do. You just like to call them free."

Knowing that if she spoke now, she would not be able to control her tongue, Julie said nothing. But she had no control over the expression in her eyes.

Muromsky squelched the urge to squirm beneath the fire in the woman's strange golden eyes. When she looked at him, the feeling that she knew every vile thing he had ever done crawled over his back like a scorpion waiting to strike. With a small shiver, he looked aside at her husband.

"And you, Monsieur van Dam? Do you share your wife's moralistic opinion?" He watched Theo tear his gaze away from his little Hungarian trophy and smiled to himself. So he wasn't immune to feminine charms, despite the calf's eyes he made at his wife.

Theo started, realizing that he had no idea what Julie and Muromsky had been speaking of. "I agree with my wife in all matters, General."

Muromsky raised his eyebrows, stretching the already taut skin over the ruined cheekbones. "Ah, yes? What harmony." With a smile he gestured toward the stairs. "Let us go in now and refresh ourselves."

Maryka lay on her knees in front of General Muromsky and wept. "Please, *barin,* I beg you, do not make me do this."

He reached down and, winding her blond braid around his hand, jerked her head up to the level of his knees.

"You will do as I say. I saw the way he was looking at you." His hand on her braid tightened. "You will speak to him. You will make promises. If you are clever, I can barter you to him for more arms." He pulled her further up until they were almost face-to-face. "I wish you good fortune, *ma petite.* I would not wish to be in your shoes if you fail." Letting go of her hair, he pushed her away so that she fell back to the floor.

Cursing, he rose and paced away, his heart beating hard and fast with anticipation. There were so many things he had never had. Fury rose, blurring his senses, his mind as he remembered that it had been his brother who had had everything. It was Alexei who had had the success, the affection, the power that should have been his. And even in defeat, in the filthy cell where water ran down the walls and rats scurried, the aura of power had still surrounded him.

Then when he had thought himself finally, finally to be the winner, he still had lost. His face had healed to a ravaged ruin. He had lost the trust of his superiors. And his body had become incapable of making love to a woman. His face would always be the face of a monster. Nothing would ever change his impotence. But now, if his gamble paid off, he would be a hero. Yes, he thought as his pacing quickened. He would be a hero, respected, honored, greeted everywhere with adulation. His eyes began to shine with a mad gleam.

Maryka covered her face with her hands, pressing them against her mouth to muffle the sobs that were tearing out of her lungs. How could this be happening to her? Why had Theo happened to turn up now, now when she had real hope for the first time in more than four years? Two more days, two miserable days and she and Janos would have been on their way to freedom. A small keening sound escaped her and her body tensed automatically in expectation of a kick, but the boots kept clicking faster and faster on the marble tiles.

Her bunched muscles eased marginally. She would talk to Theo. She would tell him everything. She would explain that she loved Janos. Theo was good man, a gentle man. Surely he would not stand in her way just because some incredible coincidence had brought him here.

The thought soothed her and she lay quietly on the floor until she heard the door open and close. When the click of the general's boot heels faded away down the corridor, she sat up and began to plan.

"You're tense." As she had so often, Julie put one hand on Theo's hip and pressed the other to the small of his back. "But that's small wonder after the jolting we've been subjected to all day."

"Julie—" Theo started to turn toward her, but her hands tightened and kept him in place.

"Shh. Let's get rid of the kinks before your back seizes up." Julie squeezed her eyes shut. She could almost hear him saying something sweet and meaningless, meant to comfort her. No, she thought, she wouldn't be able to stand that.

She stood quietly, waiting for the emotions, the pain to flow away from her so that she would be empty and free for the power to move through her. But instead of draining away, the feelings filled her more and more densely until she seemed to be nothing but a compact mass of emotion.

When her palms began to tingle and she felt that first marginal easing of Theo's muscles, she understood that it was her own energy that was pouring out of her to help him. How simple, she thought as her mind began to cloud. How simple it would be just to let go and let her life force spill into him. Dispassionately, she stood apart from herself and watched herself empty.

Even as he felt himself relax under her touch, Theo knew that something was wrong. Her hands fell away from him as he turned sharply.

Panic shot through him as he saw her veiled, opaque eyes. Gripping her hands, he pressed them, palm downward, against his chest, willing her to take from him what she needed.

The energy skimmed back into her, as easily, as lightly as a sailboat skimming over the water, and with it came a boundless sadness.

Theo watched her eyes clear and focus. Suddenly he understood.

"You did it on purpose." Releasing her hands, he gripped her shoulders. "You knew exactly what you were doing this time."

The accusation, the fury in his voice hurt, but she would far rather have his anger than his pity.

"Why, Julie?" He shook her. "Why?"

Trying for a smile, she managed to tilt a corner of her mouth upward. "It seemed like the thing to do at the time."

"Don't you ever do that again!" The panic he had felt a moment ago was still pumping through his blood and his fingers dug into the soft flesh of her upper arms. "Do you hear me, damn it? Do you?"

No, she thought, as the realization of what she had almost done streaked through her. She had almost destroyed herself. She had almost destroyed her child. How could she have misused her gift so sinfully? It had been wrong to touch him now, when he was no longer hers. But then he had never been hers, she reminded herself.

No, she thought, she would never touch him, never give him comfort again. The pain moved through her that this, too, had been taken from her.

"You're hurting me, Theo."

He released her as suddenly as if her flesh had turned to fire and singed him. Horrified, he looked at his hands as if they were murder weapons. "I'm sorry." Self-disgust was bitter on his tongue. "Will you rest for a while?"

Julie nodded, knowing better than to try to fight the debilitating weakness she felt. Like a sleepwalker she moved to the wide divan that stood in a corner of the room and, unmindful of her travel-dusty clothes, lay down on the colorful Tartar rug that covered it.

For a moment the terrible wish that a miracle would make Theo hers and hers alone wound through Julie, but she pushed it back. She told herself that she wanted them to be happy together. And she did, for the simple reason that she loved Theo enough to put his happiness before her own.

Theo sat down on the edge of the daybed. She looked so small and fragile and exhausted, her eyes shaded with violet smudges that hadn't been there just minutes ago. The wave of tenderness that engulfed him was so huge that he could have drowned in it. She needed him, he thought with something very much like gratitude. If she did not love him, then at least she needed him, and he found that he, in turn, needed that small consolation very badly.

For a moment Theo wished for a miracle, but he knew that no matter what happened, there would be no miracle for him in the end. They had found Maryka and he would do what was honorable and make her the best husband he could. And yet what made it so hard was that he could not help believing that he could have made Julie at least content. And perhaps in time she would have loved him.

The love welled up in him. Once, he thought, just once he would say the words. No matter that he had no right to say them. No matter that she did not want to hear them. "Julie." He laced his hands with hers. "I want you to know that I—"

She shook her head. "No words, Theo. We've hurt each other with words so often. No more words." She lifted their joined hands to brush her cheek against their entwined fingers. "Please."

Something inside him twisted at the deep sadness in her voice. "I don't want to hurt you, Julie. I want to tell you that I—"

"No." Her fingers tightened on his, echoing the tightness that banded her chest. She could stand anything, she thought. She could stand anything but the gentle words of consolation she could almost hear him saying.

"All right," he acquiesced. "Will you let me lie down with you until you sleep?"

It was tempting. It was, oh, so tempting to feel his body against hers one more time. But she was afraid. Afraid that if she felt his embrace once more, she would not be able to let him go.

"No, Theo. We said goodbye last night. It's better that way." The first tears blurred her vision, and she did not see the pain that turned his eyes to the gray of ashes. She had nothing left but her pride, and that had her turning her face into the soft pillow that someone's hands had embroidered so lovingly with lush roses.

Her words, so lightly said, struck him like a knife in his vitals. And the way she turned away, as if she couldn't wait to be rid of his presence, was that knife tracing a slow, torturing curve. The urge to crawl away and howl like a wounded animal was so great that he fisted his hands against it.

He stood. Was it that easy for her? Of course it was, he answered his own question. She might be fond of him, but it wasn't him that she loved, he reminded himself.

When he looked down at her again, the temptation to touch her was so great that he knew that he could not stay here and not reach out for her.

The pain wound through him as he strode into the next room, where Lucia was unpacking their valises.

Chapter Twenty-Three

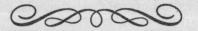

"I'm going outside for a while. Look after her when she awakes. She's exhausted."

Lucia looked at his haggard face and her heart gave a little twist. "You should rest, too."

Theo gave a snort of a laugh. "I'll have time to rest soon enough. Soon I'll have nothing but time."

The girl frowned, not quite understanding his words. But she understood well the pain she saw in his eyes. And she was so sure that if she told him that Signora Giulia loved him, the pain would go away.

"*Signore—*"

Theo turned in the doorway. "Yes? What is it?" He saw her aquamarine eyes light up for a moment before the spark flickered and died.

The courage left her and she shook her head. "Nothing, *signore.*"

The door closed behind him and she sighed as she tucked the undergarments she was holding into a drawer. If only she could be sure what was right. They were both so kind to her and asked for almost nothing in return. For the first time in her life, she had decent clothes and a full belly. For the first time in her life, the constant fear of being slapped or whipped or raped did not dig into the back of her neck like the talons of a rapacious bird of prey. And she wanted so very badly to pay them back for their kindness.

She would talk to Signora Giulia when she awoke, she decided. If she told her that the *signore* loved her, then surely everything would be all right.

Pleased with her decision, Lucia drifted over to the window. Pushing the heavy lace curtain aside, she looked down into the lush garden. The *signore*, his angular face grim, the thin cigar in his hand forgotten, stood staring at the jets and cascades of the fountain. She felt a small leap of joy and pressed her hands to her heart, which suddenly felt light, so light. Yes, she would tell Signora Giulia, and when he returned, the *signore* would smile again. They would both smile again.

Humming a tuneless little song, she started to turn away from the window, when a blur of color caught her eye. She stilled as the blond woman who had stood at the top of the stairs at their arrival, her bright, gauzy oriental clothes now fluttering in the breeze, glided up to the *signore* and touched his arm.

He turned toward the woman, they spoke. Because she needed to believe it, Lucia told herself that they were exchanging the meaningless words of two strangers. Still she watched them, as quiet, as alert as a small wild animal who senses something wrong.

When he lifted his hands to cup the woman's face, Lucia's world began to crumble and fingers closed on the curtain, crushing the lace. When he lowered his head to kiss her, Lucia turned away, the sharp sense of betrayal turning the joy in her heart to hate.

The jet of water shot up in a strong stream through the mouth of a plump fish to fan out and ripple down in a fine bell-shaped mist, which enveloped the cherubs prancing on the outer rim. Theo stared at the fountain but he saw neither the limpidness of the water nor the finely carved Carrara marble of the figures. He saw only Julie's face.

It was over. Irrevocably and finally over. Any hope that he might have nourished was gone now. But then he had had no right to hope, he reminded himself. His duty lay elsewhere and he had known that from the beginning. And even if he had forgotten his duty, he thought with a rueful half smile, Julie would have not allowed him to neglect it.

But what he hadn't known was that he would fall in love. He hadn't known that it was in him to love as completely, as absolutely as he loved Julie. And he hadn't known that he could hurt so badly at the realization that she could reject him with a few lightly spoken words.

The touch on his arm sent a reflexive flash of joy streaking through him. Then he turned his head and saw Maryka. His cigar fell unheeded to the white gravel of the path and he turned to face her fully.

He looked down into her face, which was so familiar and yet so alien, made more alien still by the half-transparent veil that fluttered gently from her breath. They had so many memories together, Theo thought. Tender memories, amusing memories, sensual ones. Why was it that he could remember nothing but the panicked horror on her face when one of Muromsky's soldiers had picked her up and flung her over the front of his saddle?

"Theo."

Gooseflesh rose at the sound of her slightly breathy little girl's voice. The memory of both her laughter and her easy chatter was gone. But the memory of how she had cried his name when she had run out of the cabin was present with a horrifying clarity. That and the memory of how her voice had risen in a single terrified scream. How a soldier had raised her skirt and stuffed it into her mouth to silence her.

A line of sweat ran the length of his spine as he fought his way past the nightmarish memories. "Maryka." His voice was rough. "Come away from here. If you are seen here with me..." Although he had not spoken Hungarian for years, the words came easily.

His gaze made a quick sweep of the garden and the windows. The garden seemed deserted and the windows only threw back the reflection of the late afternoon sun, but the prickling at the back of his neck was an unmistakable warning.

She shook her head. "I have to be seen here. I was told to come here and speak to you."

"What?"

"He saw you looking at me." Her teeth nipped at her lower lip as she tried to decide how much to tell him. But because she was a woman without guile, the words spilled out. "I am supposed to seduce you but not quite. He said he wants to barter me to you for weapons."

"Swine!" The hatred rolled through him like a relentless fire. "Killing is too good for him, but kill him I will." He knew exactly what it would be like to take a knife and feel the give of Muromsky's flesh beneath it.

Maryka saw his eyes ice over, then heat. She had been so certain that some weird fluke of fate had brought him here. Now she was suddenly no longer quite so sure, and apprehension stole through her.

"Theo." His name sounded strange on her tongue and she had to swallow before she could continue. "There are things I have to tell you."

He looked at Maryka. Saw the fear in her eyes. Fear and something else he could not identify. He did not want her to be frightened. It wasn't her fault, he thought. None of this was her fault.

It took all his willpower, but he managed a smile. Slowly he lifted his hands to cup her face.

"There is nothing you have to tell me unless you want to." Leaning forward, he pressed his lips to her forehead.

His lips felt dry and impersonal as they brushed briefly against her skin. Not quite understanding why, Maryka felt an acute sense of embarrassment that had her face heating.

When she shifted away from him, his hands fell away. Thinking that he understood what moved her, he met her clear blue eyes and held them.

"I'm sorry. I know you have suffered. I did not want to frighten you with my touch."

"You didn't frighten me." Her long golden earrings jangled when she shook her head. "I will not deny that I have suffered, Theo, but not the way you think." Because she sensed that he, too, had suffered, that he still suffered, she felt the need to reassure him.

"He took me for his own so that no one would touch me, but his body betrayed him every time he tried to take me. I was his slave, but never his mistress."

"Thank God you were spared that, at least." Relief had him closing his eyes as he remembered the horrible visions that had tormented him for so long.

"Theo, how—how did you happen to come here?"

He looked at her for a long, silent moment before he answered. "I didn't *happen* to come here, Maryka."

"Are you saying you came here, to Gurzuf, on purpose?" She pressed her hands against the sinking feeling in her stomach. "That you knew I would be here?"

"No, I didn't know you were here. I came to Sevastopol less than a week ago." He took a step back from her and turned away to stare at the colored prisms that the sunlight formed in the misty curtain of water that surrounded the fountain. "I looked for him and hoped that he would lead me to you.

"I didn't have much to go on—the uniform of a Russian colonel and the monstrous face. I hired people to find out who he was, where he was. As soon as I was able, I came here." He shrugged. "That's the story in a nutshell."

"You did that for me?" There was pride in her voice and the flattered vanity of a simple-hearted woman. But even stronger was the sudden panic that raced through her. How could she tell him about Janos now? How could she say that she loved another? How could she hurt him so when he had moved heaven and earth to find her?

He looked at her. She was staring at him, a stunned, incredulous look on her face, and in that moment the truth struck him. He had *not* done it for her. The sense of duty, of obligation, was real perhaps, but when you came right down to it, he had done it for himself and himself alone. To feed the need for revenge, which was like a ravening beast within him. To cleanse himself of the humiliation of failure with the other man's blood.

Because the guilt rose again to torment him, he reached for her. "Maryka, my little flower." He spoke the old endearment, wanting to build a bridge to a past that seemed to belong to someone else.

Again she shifted away from his touch with a nervous laugh. "Not so little anymore." She drew her hand down from shoulder to hip, the tips of her fingers tracing her lush curves. "Like dough set to rise."

Then she remembered. Remembered that soon she would grow even rounder. Remembered the child growing inside her. The child of her and Janos's love. The child for whom they had decided to risk the escape. She laughed again to hide the threatening tears.

But all of a sudden the understanding that her life had gone hopelessly awry was so clear that any defense she had had against the tears was torn away. Her eyes filled and filled until the tears overflowed to course down her cheeks.

Theo saw the tears and reached out to touch her. "Don't cry, Maryka. It's going to be all right now." His breath caught at the enormity of his lie. "We will be together and it will be all right."

She gulped in air, wanting, needing to give him a word of
assent, of thanks, but she could not. Her eyes met his for a
brief moment and she silently begged him for forgiveness.
Then she turned and ran.

Long after she had disappeared, Theo still stared after
her.

Lucia was not the only observer of the scene in the garden.

General Muromsky watched Maryka glide up to van Dam
and put her hand on his arm. She had cried and begged, but
she was doing as he had told her. So he wouldn't have oc-
casion to use the silk whip on her after all. He felt a moment of regret that she had been so quick to obey him.

What a stupidly careless fool, he thought when he saw van
Dam frame her face with his hands. When he pressed a
chaste kiss to her brow, Muromsky's eyes narrowed in surprise. As he watched them, a vague impression, a faraway
memory tickled the back of his mind, but no matter how he
scrabbled to grasp it, it remained out of reach.

Stubbornly, systematically, like a dog rooting for a bone,
he dug into his memory.

At the other end of the garden, in the shelter of a latticework bower overgrown with wild roses, a third pair of eyes
monitored the scene, his initial sadness turned to fury.

How could she do that? Janos asked himself. His wide-
palmed, strong hands closed over the wood, unmindful of
the thorns that dug into his skin. He'd seen the way the
stranger had looked at Maryka. And he had felt how she
had tensed and trembled at his side.

He had endured the four-year-long captivity only because of her. He had borne the beatings, the humiliation,
the shame of a life too base for a man of honor. But he had
borne them, at first because he had wanted to protect Ma-

ryka. Later because he had fallen in love with her. And now she went to a stranger and allowed him to put his hands on her.

The hot Hungarian blood that he had bridled so viciously for so long reached the boiling point. As Maryka ran past, his arm snaked out and pulled her inside the bower.

"Just what do you think you're doing?" Janos snarled, and dragged her closer, almost lifting her off the ground. Only then did he see that her face was wet with tears.

Lucia stood at the same window where she had stood two days ago and looked down into the downpour. The rain that had kept them inside since yesterday was so heavy that it seemed to curtain the house in a gray veil. Nevertheless, she had no trouble recognizing the tall figure pacing behind the latticework screen of the veranda that ran around the ground floor on all three sides of the house.

What was she going to do? She fisted her hands and butted them against each other hard enough to hurt. She should have known better than to believe him when he had told her that he loved the *signora*. All men were bastards. Every single last one of them. It would serve him right if she told Signora Giulia that her husband was cheating on her. Lucia squeezed her eyes shut. She didn't want to hurt the *signora*. Perhaps it would be better when they left here. But then there would be another place, another woman.

Sighing, she opened her eyes. He had stopped pacing, she saw. She saw, too, that a figure wearing gauzy oriental trousers had joined him. Not bothering to look more closely, she let loose a stream of curses, slipping seamlessly into the Venetian street jargon she had spoken all her life.

Unable to rest, Theo prowled the veranda. The air, humid enough to touch, was oppressive and brought no relief.

His nerves had grown edgy during the past two days, waiting for the weather to clear. Waiting for an opportunity to steal away from the villa and hire a boat. For the hundredth time he cursed his inability to make himself understood in this barbaric country. Once the rain had stopped, he would have to ask for Julie's help—again. Since the Russian fleet lay before Sevastopol, this stretch of coast was only carelessly guarded. Here was their best chance to escape, as Julie's parents had done so many years before.

"*Uram.* Sir."

The hoarse whisper in Hungarian had Theo starting out of his reverie. He turned to see the dark-haired man he had seen at Maryka's side at their arrival slink around the corner onto the veranda.

"Who are you?" he replied in the same language.

"My name is Janos. I, too, was enslaved in '49."

"You?" Theo's eyes narrowed.

A muscle twitched in his swarthy cheek, but he thrust out his chin. "You will say that I am a man dishonored, but I had my reasons to bear this captivity."

Something about the quiet dignity of the man's demeanor touched him and Theo laid a hand on his shoulder. "I am not one who has the right to cast the first stone when it comes to dishonor, my friend."

Janos shook his head. "Maryka told me everything. You are an honorable man, *uram.* She also told me that you are a kind man. Because of this I dare to come to you."

Theo motioned to him to continue.

"When I was taken I would have escaped or died trying if it had not been for Maryka. At first I stayed to protect her, or at least to comfort her, as best I could. Later I stayed because I loved her."

"You loved Maryka?" The words came out slowly, punctuated by long pauses.

"I know you love her, *uram.* She told me how you searched for her." The words tumbled out and he grabbed

Theo's arm, afraid that he would leave before he heard him out. "But if you love her, you will set her free. You see, she, too, has come to love me."

The enormity of the relief Theo felt was staggering and yet the feeling of betrayal that wound through him seemed to cancel it out. So it had been for naught. Theo stared at Janos, as speechless as if he had been struck dumb.

"If you had not come, we would have escaped. This night a boat waits for us in a cove." He shook Theo's arm. "Will you let us go with your blessing? She will not go otherwise."

Theo gave his head a shake to free it of the daze that seemed to have occupied it. "What did you say? A boat?" His heart began to pound. Julie. This was how he could keep Julie safe. Now it was he who gripped Janos's shoulders. "Did you say a boat?"

"Yes. A boat."

"Large enough to take two more people?"

Janos nodded. *"Igen."*

"The woman who is here as my wife and her maid. You will take them with you?"

"Yes, of course. But what of you?"

"I have something to do first." Theo's eyes turned as hard and cold as gunmetal. "If I can I will go with you. If not, then ..."

"Janos!" Maryka skidded around the corner on her soleless leather slippers. "What are you doing?"

"Shh." Janos clapped a hand over her mouth. "It's all right," he whispered. His eyes veered over to Theo. "Isn't it?"

"Yes." Theo's eyes softened as he looked at Maryka. "Go with God."

"How touching." The mellowness of Muromsky's voice only emphasized the venomous tone. "May I inquire what the meaning of this little scene is?"

The three stilled as if they had turned to stone.

"I did not realize you were fluent in Hungarian, Monsieur van Dam? Perhaps you would care to translate the conversation for me?"

Theo fought off the numbness that seemed to have paralyzed both his limbs and his vocal chords. "I am hardly fluent, General, and our conversation, as you call it, was nothing but an exchange of a few meaningless words."

"I see." His mouth twisted into his terrible smile. "Arik." The cruel-faced Tartar who had been standing in the shadows moved forward. "Take these two away." He pointed to Maryka and Janos with the corded silk whip he held. "See how prettily these two little birds will sing."

Even as Arik moved forward, sounds of a commotion in front of the house arose. Doors opened and were slammed shut, shouts rang out, boot heels clacked on the marble tiles.

A man, rainwater streaming from his uniform, appeared, followed by the general's personal guards.

"What is it?" Muromsky, irritated at the interruption, slapped the leather handle of the whip repeatedly into the palm of one hand. "What's going on, damn it?"

"The British and the French landed in Yevpatoria yesterday, your grace. Prince Menshikov's troops are marching to meet them." He stopped to pull in a lungful of air. "And the British fleet is steaming toward Yalta."

Under the cover of the tumult, Theo heard Janos's quick whisper. "An hour before midnight, a cove exactly half a mile east of the port of Gurzuf."

"We return to Sevastopol immediately." Muromsky turned toward his men, who had poured into the house, and began to give orders, his voice clipped and competent.

When the men had hurried off to their tasks, he turned back to the small group. "Lock these two up, Arik, until we are ready to go, and make sure all the others ready themselves for the journey."

"And the questioning, master?"

"Later." Dismissing them with a wave of the whip, he turned toward Theo, his eyes narrowed to slits. "I suggest you and your wife ready yourselves for the journey." His grimace of a smile appeared. "We, too, will converse later."

If only she could have gone outside, it would be easier, Julie mused. She could have gone down to the shore and watched the water of the bay. Or she would have found an excuse to go exploring and get a closer look at the house just up the slope that had once belonged to her mother. As it was, she could only pace their apartment and wait.

And what did she have to look forward to? Only the end of the charade she had agreed upon with Theo so many weeks ago. And then what? What would be there for her then? She dug deep inside herself for the strength she knew she would need.

More because she wanted to have something to do than because she wanted the air, she opened the window. The air was thick with moisture and with something menacing she couldn't quite define. When over the sound of rain she heard the beat of galloping hooves, the high-strung whinny of a horse and loud, frantic voices, she knew, without knowing what had happened, that they would soon have a new danger to face.

"Lucia!"

Julie looked into the dressing room, but the girl was no-where to be seen. Moving on into the bedroom, she saw Lucia standing at the window, heard and understood enough, despite the Venetian dialect, to know what she was saying.

"Is something wrong, Lucia?"

The girl jolted and whirled around, stumbling away from the window. "No—yes," she stammered, then pressed both hands against her mouth and helplessly shook her head.

Worried, her own cares forgotten, Julie closed the distance between them and rubbed her hands over the girl's shoulders. "What's wrong? Has someone hurt you?"

Lucia shook her head. When she looked away from Julie's questioning gaze, Julie gently took the girl's chin and tilted her head until their eyes met again.

As she looked into the *signora*'s kind eyes, Lucia felt her anger turn into sorrow and her eyes filled and overflowed. With an inarticulate cry, she threw herself against Julie. When she felt the *signora*'s arms go around her to hold her tightly, Lucia felt the sobs locked inside her chest break free.

Julie held the girl as she cried, wondering what had brought the tears on.

When Theo burst through the bedroom door, she felt Lucia stiffen. Before the question could form in her mind, his agitated voice pushed all thoughts aside.

"News has just come that the Allies landed in Yevpatoria yesterday." He was already reaching to touch Julie when he saw her take a tiny step back. Swallowing the hurt, he continued, "Muromsky has ordered us to prepare to return to Sevastopol."

Automatically Julie's hand rubbed Lucia's shoulder, but her attention was trained on Theo. She saw the turbulence in his eyes, she felt his agitation and knew that there was more.

"Julie, will you do something for me?"

Julie gave Lucia a last squeeze and let her go. She moved toward Theo, but kept a careful distance.

"What is it?"

"There is a Hungarian here, also a prisoner. He and Maryka were planning to escape. A boat waits for them tonight." Unable to resist touching her any longer, he reached out and took her hands in his as the words tumbled out, quick and urgent. "I don't want you to return to Sevastopol. It's too dangerous now that the Allies are about to attack. I want you to take this boat to freedom."

"He promised us safe-conduct."

Theo's eyebrows angled upward in a cynical curve. "Do you really believe him?"

Julie shook her head. "You want me to go with Maryka and this man?"

"Not with them. Muromsky ordered them locked up because he caught them speaking to me. Perhaps he will take them back to Sevastopol. I don't know."

She saw something flicker in his eyes, but it was gone too quickly for her to recognize it. "And you? You return to Sevastopol." It was not a question.

"I must." He linked his fingers with hers. "Julie, I know this scheme has its own dangers. But you will be safer on that boat than with me." He raised their joined hands to his mouth. "I need to know you safe."

He searched her eyes and saw the refusal but not the love. "You're not going to do it, are you?"

"Theo, we began this journey together and it would seem we still have a ways to travel."

"Should I remind you that you told me that we've already said goodbye?"

Her mouth curved into a smile that did not brighten her eyes. "There's more than one kind of goodbye, Theo."

Theo opened his mouth to tell her. Tell her what Janos had told him. Tell her that Maryka did not want him. Tell her that he was free. But he knew that if he spoke, he would entrap her. That and his wounded pride kept him silent.

"Why, Julie? Tell me why you will not go."

The words of love bubbled up inside her, but she battled them down. "Because I, too, need to know you safe."

The joy meshed with the guilt and he accepted her words with a nod. Perhaps, he thought. Perhaps they had a chance after all.

Together they began to make ready for the journey.

Chapter Twenty-Four

Dusk was just slipping into evening as the small steamer ship chugged into the harbor of Sevastopol.

The docks where the ship was moored were strangely still and deserted. Even on the deck the soldiers and Muromsky's servants, who stood jammed together around the section of the railing that would be removed as soon as the gangplank had been laid, had fallen silent. The only sounds were an occasional call from one of the sailors as they worked and the lapping of the water against the wooden pilings.

Theo swept his gaze over the deck and then down to the pier below. The eeriness of the quiet sent a shiver crawling up his back because he remembered too well. Remembered that tense moment of quiet before everything explodes into noise and movement. The memory was so clear that for a moment he could almost smell the sun-baked dust, the sweat, the horseflesh on that last battlefield.

The detonation broke through the quiet, its deafening roar throwing Julie against Theo. A moment of dead silence followed before it, too, was broken by a single, long scream from one of the women. Then around them all hell broke loose as shrieks and cries rose. Within moments the clamor on deck was drowned by a second explosion.

Theo tasted panic as he pressed Julie against him, trying as best he could to protect her with his body. When he saw flames shoot up from two of the warships across the harbor, he relaxed marginally, seeing that they were at least not in direct danger. At the third detonation, he understood what the Russians were doing. Within minutes the row of seven warships that had been strung across the mouth of the harbor had been ignited. By the time the last ship exploded into a ball of flame, the first one already lay on its side, ready to slip into a watery grave.

As he watched the string of blazing fires, Theo understood that they were trapped.

"What's happening?" Julie's voice was muffled against his chest. "Are the Allies attacking already?"

"No. The Russians are sinking their own warships to block the harbor for the enemy."

Julie was silent for a moment. "And that means that no one can leave the harbor, either," she murmured.

"Yes." As he spoke, Theo looked up to where Muromsky stood on a narrow metal staircase, surveying the people on deck the way a despot surveys his slaves. Muromsky was watching them, he saw, his eyes yellowish and gleaming like those of a feral animal who has spotted his prey. Their eyes met and Muromsky's mouth twisted into a smile. And Theo understood that he had made the connection between him and Maryka.

Julie felt both the accelerated thump of Theo's heart against her ear and the tension that had suddenly tightened his muscles.

"What is it?" She raised her head to look at him, but he immediately cupped the back of her head and pressed her face against his chest again.

"Nothing." He stared back at Muromsky, the look in his eyes giving warning that he was picking up the challenge.

Julie knew that he was lying, but she would pretend to believe him, she thought as she closed her eyes. She would pretend just for another moment so that she could feel his warmth, hear the pulse of his heart.

The clang of wood against metal roused her from her moment of fantasy. Shifting away from him, she took Lucia's hand and moved toward the gangplank.

At a clipped order from Muromsky, the soldiers scattered to their posts as soon as they reached the governor's palace. The cluster of women in their oriental clothing who huddled closely in the coldly elegant foyer were just as quickly dispatched to be herded off by the majordomo.

Muromsky thrust his chin at Maryka and Janos. "Take them downstairs, Arik. I'll be down in a little while, but perhaps you'll have them singing before then." His casual tone was belied by the cruel gleam in his eyes.

"You need not question them," Theo said softly. "I will tell you everything you want to know."

Beside Theo, Julie stiffened and started to speak, but he squeezed her hand to silence her.

"Go upstairs." He sent Fritz a look. "Accompany *madame*."

"Theo—"

His grip on her arm tightened. "Please." He looked down at her.

Julie saw the anxiety in his eyes but not the love. She nodded her agreement, which she had no intention of keeping, and, motioning to Lucia to follow her, moved slowly toward the stairs. Only once did she look back to see the door of the library close behind the two men. Now she knew where to look for them. Grabbing Lucia's hand, she dashed up the staircase.

* * *

"Your game is up, Monsieur van Dam, or whatever your name is."

Even though he felt the fear for Julie slither up his spine, Theo's nerves eased. Now that the moment to settle old debts had come, he felt a calm descend on him, cooling his blood, slowing his pulse. Even the hatred that he had kept burning brightly during the past weeks seemed to have become a banked fire.

A tiny movement reassured him that his slim, efficient dagger was strapped to his calf. Lifting his eyebrows slightly, he held Muromsky's eyes and said nothing as he waited for the man to continue.

"Who are you?"

"I thought you knew."

Muromsky slammed a fist into the palm of his hand. "Oh, I know. When I realized that you must have known Maryka back in her own country, I knew quickly enough. You must have been that half-dead worm who got my boot in his ribs." His fist slapped again into his hand. "I want to know your name. What is your name?" As his voice rose, little flecks of spittle flew from his mouth.

"I would say that point is irrelevant, but if it aids your peace of mind—" He sketched a bow. "Count Theodore Berg, at your service." Theo kept his voice provocatively soft, his tone ironic.

Muromsky's eyes narrowed. "There was a Berg among the leaders of the rebellion. He escaped, if I remember correctly."

"My brother."

"It's truly a pity I didn't know that at the time." His marred mouth curled in a snarl. "We might have made good use of you to bait a trap."

"I don't doubt it." Theo felt the flames of hatred lick a little higher and tamped down on them mercilessly, aware that he could not afford emotion clouding his judgment.

"Who is Maryka? Your wife? Your mistress?" Muromsky demanded. "And who, then, is the woman who came here with you?" He saw the gleam of temper in the other man's eyes and his own jolt of rage had him baring his teeth. "Do you forget that you promised to tell me everything?" Suddenly he smiled. "Never mind. Arik is skilled. Once he squeezes the answers out of those two, I may let him work on you."

"All right." Using his gesture of surrender as a shield, Theo shifted behind a chair. He would need that bit of cover to get to his dagger unnoticed. "Maryka was my mistress. The woman who travels with me is simply that." He shrugged, hoping to deflect Muromsky's attention from Julie. "Just window dressing to make my own disguise more credible."

"And you expect me to believe that?" Muromsky gave a bark of a laugh. "The two of you give off sparks whenever you're close. Who is she?" He strode up to Theo and grabbed the lapel of his jacket. "And why does she look at me like that with those witchy yellow eyes of hers?"

"I don't know what you're talking about."

"She looks at me," Muromsky whispered, his eyes going blank. The hand that had gripped Theo's lapel slackened until it lay limply against Theo's chest. "She reminds me of..."

Before his mind could ramble on and perhaps latch on to the truth, Theo grabbed his arm. "Listen to me. I will offer you a deal. You let the two Hungarians go and the woman calling herself my wife. Then it remains between the two of us."

Muromsky's eyes focused and he stared silently at Theo for a long moment. Then he began to laugh, the hiccuping treble edging toward hysteria. "Are you serious? Do you really think I would agree to a deal like that?"

"If you have any honor at all, you will agree to it."

"Honor?" His voice rose to a squeak. "You dare speak to me of honor when you weasel your way into my house with a false name and a pocketful of lies?"

"I repeat my offer. I will not offer it to you again."

"Offer?" Muromsky squawked. "What do you mean, offer? You can't do anything. You're one miserable man and I've got enough men who follow my orders to make mincemeat out of you. Do you hear that? Mincemeat!" As he began to scream, bubbles of foam appeared at the corners of his mouth. "They'll cut you up so fine, the pieces won't be fit for fish bait!"

Muromsky's eyes seemed to pop out of his head as they darted wildly from side to side. Even as the thought that there was madness there struck Theo, the door opened to admit the young lieutenant who had escorted them to Sevastopol so many weeks ago.

"Your excellency—" the lieutenant breathed harshly as if he had been running "—a battle has been fought on the river Alma and lost. Thousands of wounded are pouring into the city. Thousands."

Amazed, Theo watched all signs of derangement disappear from Muromsky's eyes as if by magic. Watched him question Naumov and give instructions. When he turned to face Theo again, neither man heard the sound at the door.

In their apartment Julie tarried only long enough to root out the small mother-of-pearl-handled gun that Theo had purchased for her after her misadventure in Venice. She was stuffing extra ammunition into the pockets of her gown when Lucia gripped her arm with all the strength her panic lent her.

"What are you going to do, Signora Giulia?"

"He needs my help."

"No, please, *signora*. Don't put yourself in danger. He's not worth it."

"Don't say that."

The *signora* had never looked at her like that before. Lucia flinched at the cold look in her eyes, but did not relinquish her arm. "But..."

"Do you hear me? Don't ever say that again." She shook off Lucia's arm and went back to putting ammunition into her pockets.

"I'm sorry," Lucia babbled. "I didn't mean... It's just that I saw him in the garden with—" She paused for a moment before the rest of the words tumbled out in a torrent. "With the woman, the one who was tied together with the black-haired man just now. He kissed her. And that after he told me he loved you."

Julie's hands stopped in the middle of a movement. "What? What did you say?"

"I saw him—"

"No!" A bullet clattered to the floor as she grabbed Lucia's shoulders. "At the end. What did you say at the end?"

"He told me he loved you. The first night we came here. He said he loved you but he could never tell you because you loved another man."

A mad burst of joy raced through her before it skidded to a stop in front of the realization that what Lucia had told her only meant they both would be unhappy. Theo's honor demanded that he offer his hand to Maryka and that's what he would do. Bravely she blinked back the threatening tears. There would be time for tears later. Now she had work to do.

"Come now." Motioning to Fritz to follow her, Julie pulled Lucia out of the room. "Stay as close to me as you can."

Downstairs servants were scurrying back and forth like panicked animals who have lost their heads.

"Where did the Tartar take the Hungarians?" Julie put the question to one servant after another, earning nothing but blank, terrified looks. When she ran into one of the women in oriental dress who had come with them from Gurzuf, she breathed a sigh of relief. But the woman, too, could only shake her head.

"Think!" Julie insisted. "He said to take them downstairs. Is there a cellar here? A dungeon?"

"There is an iron door in the cellar. No one is allowed past it."

"Show me!"

Within minutes they stood in front of the dark, studded door. Julie tested it with a small tug and it began to swing open silently on its well-oiled hinges.

"Wait here for me." She mouthed the words at Lucia and Fritz.

"I will not let you go alone," Fritz whispered. "The count would kill me and rightly so."

Julie nodded and opened the door far enough for them to slip into the dim corridor on the other side.

An occasional oil lamp gave off just enough light so that they could see the row of iron doors, each with a small, barred window at eye level. At the end of the corridor one door stood open, a square of light spilling out onto the damp stone floor. Slowly, Julie moved forward.

Her footsteps, the rustle of her gown, even her heartbeat echoed so loudly in her ears that any moment she expected the Tartar to come storming out of the cell to confront her. Her hand turned slick with sweat and, shifting the gun to her left hand, she wiped her palm against her skirt.

She could hear stirring inside the cell—footsteps, the clink of something against the stone floor, but no moans, no cries. At least the Tartar had not begun the torture. The thought had barely formed in her mind when she heard a sound—half scream, half gurgle. All caution forgotten, she rushed forward.

As she stumbled to a stop in the door of the cell, a body, arm raised to strike, came hurtling at her.

Fritz leaped past her, his head lowered, and slammed his head into the man's stomach. Only when he sprawled backward on the floor with a grunt did they see that the man had been Janos.

Julie looked past him and saw that the Tartar lay on the floor of the cell like a huge mound of fat, the bright red blood pooling beneath him as it ran from the vicinity of his throat. When she saw the scarlet line that stretched from ear to ear, Julie felt her stomach rise up into her throat.

As she battled back the nausea, she watched Janos spring up and run to where Maryka stood against the wall, one hand fastened to an iron ring high above her head. With the still-bloody razor, he cut the cord that held her and gathered her close as she collapsed against him.

She saw him press his mouth against her temple as his hand stroked her back in comforting circles. She heard him whisper to her in his own tongue. She didn't understand the Hungarian words, but when Maryka opened her eyes and looked at the man who held her, Julie understood that they were lovers.

Joy surged within her anew—and hope. Because she knew she still had dangerous obstacles to breach and little time to breach them, she ran forward and gripped Janos's arm.

"*Venez*. Come. You must come quickly." When he looked at her with a slight, puzzled shake of his head, she realized that he did not understand French. "*Po russki*? Russian? Do you speak Russian?" At his affirmative nod she spoke quickly.

"You have to get out of here as soon as possible. Everything is in chaos upstairs. I don't know why. You can probably escape unobserved."

"And you?"

"I have to get to Theo. He's in the library with Muromsky." She gave his arm a squeeze. "Godspeed." Whirling around, she made for the door of the cell.

"Wait!"

Already in the dim corridor, she turned to see Janos coming after her, half dragging, half carrying Maryka along with him.

"Wait. We will go with you."

"Are you sure? It will not be easy." She looked at Maryka and their eyes met and held.

The blond woman straightened underneath her gaze and nodded once. "We owe him. *I* owe him."

Julie returned the nod and, without looking behind her, sprinted down the corridor.

They retraced their steps, moving as cautiously and unobtrusively as possible, although no one seemed the least bit inclined to pay any attention to them. They had almost reached the library when the door flew open. Julie flattened herself against the wall and motioned to the others to do the same.

When she saw that it was young Lieutenant Naumov who was rushing out of the library, she decided to take a chance.

"Lieutenant, please tell me what's going on." Running after him, she laid a light hand on his arm. "No one will tell me anything." Her mouth made a charming moue.

"We have lost a battle against the Allies. Thousands of wounded are being brought into the city." His eyes were dark with the misery he had witnessed. "The Allied armies are in pursuit and everything is in complete chaos. Please—" he extricated his arm "—I beg you to excuse me."

Julie returned to the others and leaned back against the wall. If that was the situation, then perhaps they would have a chance if they all made it out of the governor's palace alive. Spurred by hope, her mind began to race. If they made it out of here, surely they would be able to escape from the city. And if the Allied troops were near, then perhaps help was close at hand.

Gesturing to the others to stay back, she cautiously pressed down the handle and pushed the heavy door open just far enough to hear what was being said.

"Now we will go to see how Arik is faring."

Julie heard her uncle's voice.

"But first I will have this counterfeit wife of yours brought here. I would have her accompany us downstairs."

"No! You will *not* have her brought here. I forbid it."

"Do you think to frighten me with that dagger of yours? You wouldn't have the courage to use it."

Dagger! Julie felt the world go dim around her. She had to get inside! She had to prevent Theo from killing him. Not because he was her uncle. Not because he did not deserve it. But because if Theo killed him, the blood of a cold-blooded revenge would be on his hands. And that would always be between them.

Her uncle's demonic laughter jolted her out of her desperate thoughts and her blood chilled. She heard footsteps inside the room and the faraway tinkle of bells somewhere in the servants' quarters.

"Janos," she whispered, "when somebody comes, send them away."

"What shall I tell them?"

"Anything. Tell them he wants a stuffed peacock for supper."

Janos gave her a quick grin and nodded.

"Wish me luck."

"*V dobryi tchas, barynia.* Good luck. We are here if you need help."

Julie put her hand into a pocket of her gown and closed her fingers around the small gun. Taking one last deep breath, she pushed open the door.

Incredulous, horrified, Theo looked from Muromsky's retreating back to the dagger in his hand. He had been waiting for years for this moment, and now that it was here, he was powerless. He had stood not an arm's length away from Muromsky and had been as incapable of striking as if someone had bodily held back his arm.

"Don't do it," he said as Muromsky rounded the desk. "Leave her out of it. She has nothing to do with this." Already he could feel the sweat rolling down his back.

"Turn around." Theo could hear the desperation in his own voice as Muromsky reached for the bellpull. "Turn around, damn you, and fight me."

Muromsky threw him a glance over his shoulder. "You'd like that, wouldn't you," he snarled, and gave the bellpull two quick tugs. "Now, *mon cher monsieur,* I will reunite your little collection of sluts and find out just what is going on."

"How rude of you, General, to speak so ungallantly of those present."

Both men whirled around to face Julie.

"Welcome." Muromsky rubbed the heels of his hands together.

"Julie, damn it, get out of here." The stark terror was like an iron knot in Theo's belly. "He just rang the bell. Someone is going to be here in a minute."

"Yes." Julie sent Theo a quick, reassuring glance before she turned to her uncle to meet his eyes. "And he will be told at the door what the general wishes to have for supper today." She paused. "By Janos."

"What?" Muromsky's voice was a whisper.

"I'm afraid your Arik met with an accident." She kept her eyes on his. "A fatal accident."

"No!" The single word tore out of Muromsky's throat like a scream of pain. "What have you done to him?" The panic exploded in his head. What was he going to do if they had killed Arik? Arik was the only one he could really trust. The only one who was really loyal to him.

Turning back toward Muromsky, Theo saw that the frenzy was suddenly back in his eyes. And they were trained on Julie! Tightening his fingers around the hilt of the dagger, Theo moved forward, placing himself between them.

The second that Theo took a step, Julie sprang forward. "No." She swung out her arm in front of him, pressing it back against his body.

Not allowing her eyes to swerve from Muromsky, Julie spoke quickly, urgently. "Please, Theo, don't do it. He's not worth it, and killing him won't give you back the years."

She took a half step forward. "I ask you to let us go." Her voice rose as she addressed her uncle, but it did not beg. "Haven't you done enough harm already?"

"Let you go?" Muromsky shrilled. "I'll see you all in hell first!"

"Yes, hell," cried Theo. "But it's only you who will be there." He could do it now, he thought. Now, with Julie beside him. Julie, who was so precious. Julie, whom he needed to protect at all costs. Pushing her arm away, he made for Muromsky.

He was going to do it! Her heartbeat pounding in her ears, she moved after him, even though she knew she would not be able to stop him.

"Please, Theo, don't do it." Then, desperate, she spoke the words she had thought to save for a more tender, more intimate moment. "I love you." She whispered the words like a magic incantation—once and then again.

Theo stopped so suddenly that he almost lost his balance. In that one moment everything but Julie was forgotten. He no longer remembered the dagger in his hand. He no longer remembered the madman who threatened them all.

"What did you say?"

Julie knew that she did not dare take her eyes off her uncle, but she needed to look at Theo. She needed it so badly. And so did he.

Giving in to the need, she shifted her gaze to lock with Theo's. "I love you."

Neither one of them heard the rasp of a drawer being pulled out.

"How touching." Muromsky laughed, his voice rising until it broke on a high, hysterical giggle as he watched them turn back to him. Watched their eyes widen at the sight of the pistol in his hand. "Now you will follow orders. My orders," he shouted, and brandished the weapon.

"You!" He pointed the pistol at Theo. "Drop the dagger." He saw Theo's hesitation. Saw the intention in his eyes. Guiding the pistol with both hands, he shifted it so that it was aimed at Julie's heart.

"Go ahead. Let your dagger fly," he taunted. "She will be dead before it pierces my chest."

Theo measured the distance to where Julie stood, thinking to push her aside. Hopelessness spread through him as he saw that he would not be able to reach her quickly enough. He lowered his hand and let the dagger fall to the floor.

"You," he barked at Julie. "I want you here next to me."

"No!" His heart in his throat, Theo moved to cover Julie with his body.

"Aside!" Muromsky roared. As he gestured wildly with the pistol, a shot went off, the bullet digging into the wall behind Theo. "Be silent!"

Julie moved forward, her hand edging toward the pocket where the gun waited.

"It will be all right," she murmured as she passed Theo, but, this time, her eyes remained on Muromsky's.

She was beyond fear as she reached the desk. Even when he reached out and grabbed a handful of her cloak to pull her closer, she felt no fear. He had just pulled her against his side when the door swung open and revealed Janos and Fritz, the two women behind them.

"Stop!" Muromsky felt the light dim around him as he saw the four figures storm into the room. "Stop! You are all devils come to hound me. Devils!" His voice broke on a shriek. "What did you say to him?" He pushed the muzzle of the gun into Julie's neck. "What?"

"I told him that it will be all right."

"All right?" He laughed. "Yes, it will be all right. When I have killed you all, it will finally be all right and I will be at peace."

"No." Her voice, her hand steady, Julie slid her hand into her pocket and gripped the gun. "It will be all right because I am the daughter of your brother, Alexei."

Muromsky jerked his hand away from her as if he had been burned. "Alexei?" He stared at her in horror, unaware that the two men were moving closer and closer.

"Alexei?" he repeated. "Of course. How could I not have seen it?" he whispered. "It was your eyes! From the very first they made my skin crawl. I knew from the beginning that you had come to torment me." His breathing grew ragged. "I'm going to kill you. Then your eyes will be closed and you cannot harm me."

He was mad, Julie thought. The evil he had wrought all his life had distorted his mind and brought him madness. Still she felt a bizarre flood of compassion. "No." She laid her hand on his arm. "You will not kill me. I am your flesh and blood and you will not kill me."

With an inarticulate cry he spun away from her, his mutilated face convulsed in a bout of madness. "He has won," he screamed. "Alexei has won." He began to sob.

Thinking only to protect Julie, Theo leaped toward her, shielding her with his body. When he looked back over his shoulder he saw Muromsky raise the pistol, press it against his own temple and pull the trigger.

Julie jolted at the shot. Even before Theo cupped her head to hold her fast, she knew what had happened. Now, with Theo's arms tight around her, she began to tremble.

"I thought he was going to kill me." Her voice shook with the violent shudders of her body. "I thought he was going to kill us both."

"It's all right now, love." Theo stroked a hand down her back. "He can't harm us anymore."

"*Uram.*" Janos gripped Theo's arm. "We have to get out of here before one of his flunkies comes. They'll blame us for sure."

Theo nodded and led Julie to the door. At the door she stopped. Theo's arm around her shoulders tightened, but she resisted the pressure and turned around. Grateful that she could not see her uncle's body, she whispered, "May God forgive you."

Theo gathered the small group close and together they crossed the foyer toward the doors.

Chapter Twenty-Five

Only one man stood guard at the main door, but he blocked their way with his weapon.

"*Kuda?* Where are you going?" The man's tone was insolent.

Julie stepped away from Theo's protective embrace with an imperious gesture. "*Propustite.* Let us through. Don't you know that thousands of wounded men are being brought into the city?"

"So?" He sounded slightly less sure of himself.

"Don't be an idiot, man!" She pushed at his arm. "They need every pair of hands to help them."

"Do you have permission? Has the general given you his permission?" The guard stepped closer.

"Good God, man." Julie grabbed his arm and shook him. "Are you a Russian? Do you want other Russians to suffer longer than they have to because you're full of idiotic questions?" She straightened to her full height. "Let us through. I command you."

Too used to taking orders not to react to Julie's assertiveness, the man stepped back, but his gaze flicked nervously toward the foyer.

At the bottom of the marble steps, Julie stopped.

"Keep going." Theo gave her a little push. "We have to get out of sight of the governor's palace."

Half-running, they moved down the street, turned one corner and then another and another.

"Now is our only chance to get out of the city, while the gates are open for the wagons carrying the wounded." Theo leaned against a wall, his breathing ragged. "If we can get to either the English or French camp, we'll be safe." He lifted a hand to Julie's cheek. "Do you think you can bluff us past the guards?"

Julie, too, leaned against the wall, trying to catch her breath. "I have to." She pressed a hand against her middle where their child slept.

They had to be on their way. She knew it. And yet the need to ask, to know, was too strong. She closed her eyes for a moment to gather courage. "Theo, is it true what Lucia—"

"What are you doing here?"

At the sound of the gruffly spoken words, Julie whirled to the side, flattening her hands against the wall. Her heart sank as she saw a pair of policemen, their weapons held at the ready.

"Get back to your houses! The army command has ordered all civilians off the streets."

"Thank God, officers." Even as she moved toward them, she said a quick prayer that this was the right thing to do. "Oh, please help me."

"What is it?" the older of the two policemen asked, his voice kind. "Are these people molesting you?"

"Oh, no. They are my servants. Can you show me how to reach the gate where they are bringing in the wounded?"

"No civilians are allowed there unless they are medical personnel," the younger policeman snapped.

"But I must get through. Both my husband and my brother were among the troops who met the enemy." She gripped the older policeman's arm. "You must help me. Please."

"We have our orders, Valya," the younger man grumbled when he saw that his colleague was vacillating.

"Oh, come on, Misha." The older policeman cuffed his friend on the shoulder. "What harm would it do?"

"Softhearted fool," the young man muttered, but he turned and gestured to the small group to follow him.

At the gate, utter chaos reigned. The road was clogged with wagons and carts of all kinds, piled high with wounded. Cries, screams, moans filled the air, which was heavy with the smell of blood and death.

Oh God, Julie thought as she looked around with horror. So many men who needed help. She remembered her words to the guard at the door of the governor's palace and her heart began to bleed. For once in her life she could have done something for Russia. But she thought of the life growing within her and knew that her responsibilities lay elsewhere.

By the time they had fought their way to the gate, she needed no artifice to summon up tears.

"Let me through!" She threw herself at one of the guards. "My husband and my brother are out there somewhere."

"There's no way I can let you through. I could be shot."

For long minutes she haggled with the guards. Then, in desperation, she tugged off the amethyst necklace and thrust it at one of them.

"My servants and I are going through," she shouted. "Shoot me in the back if you will."

Ignoring the shouts behind them, she pushed everyone through the gate. Gripping Theo's hand, she moved forward, forward, ever forward.

And still the wagons with their human cargo kept coming.

Finally, Theo steered them away from the road, unable to watch Julie's suffering.

Exhausted, they stopped at the edge of a brook, grateful that even though they had no food, they at least had water. The terrible sounds from the road were muffled but still audible. But exhaustion pushed them into an uneasy sleep.

The next morning they awoke to a world filled only with the sounds of the forest. When they returned to the road, it was as if the nightmare of the day before had never been.

"You can't go on like this, Julie." Theo's stomach plummeted as he looked at the dark shadows under her eyes. "We were lucky to find water last night, but we have no food. Nothing. I will look for help with Janos and you will stay here with the women and Fritz." He brushed her hair back from her face. "There must be farms here, people," he added desperately.

"No, Theo. We will go together. What if you run into a Russian patrol? What if you hurt yourself? If we are separated, I could not stand it." Just the thought overwhelmed her and she covered her face with her hands for a moment. "We will go together," she repeated.

They walked. Slowly. Painfully. It was midmorning when they found themselves at the edge of an apple orchard. A handcart half-full of early green apples told them that help was near and, for the first time since they had left the city, Julie burst into tears.

The old Tartar couple fed them as opulently as if they were dear and welcome guests and asked no questions. Not even when Julie asked them to bring them farther north in their donkey cart.

They could see the smoke from the fires in the camp when they disembarked from the small cart.

It was a bedraggled group that wandered down into the plain. When they found themselves surrounded by soldiers in English uniforms, Theo could have wept with relief.

They had been given a tent of their own. Julie leaned against Theo, more than half-asleep with exhaustion, and yet she could feel the pain that was slicing through him.

"You hurt, Theo," she whispered. "Will you let me help you?"

"You're too tired, Julie. I cannot risk it."

She struggled to sit up. "Let me try."

"Julie—"

"Shh, love." Her exhaustion suddenly gone, she shifted to kneel behind him. Focusing her mind entirely on Theo, she put her hands on his back. Almost immediately, her palms began to tingle with the power.

Even as Theo felt that first marginal easing of the pain, he remembered all too well how fraught with danger her gift was. Ignoring the new streak of pain, he twisted his upper body so that he could look at her.

"Julie, be careful."

Her golden eyes were fixed on him, but they seemed veiled, and her expression gave no hint that she was truly seeing him. And she gave him no answer.

"Do you hear me, Julie?" His voice rose. "Take care of yourself."

She gave a small jolt and her eyes cleared. "I'll be all right this time," she whispered, and gave herself up again to the power that was flowing through her like a river of golden light.

Later, when she again lay against him, she brushed her fingers over his hand, which, relaxed now, was possessively splayed against her middle.

"It was the morning after I had gone down into the water for Lucia," she murmured. "I knew that love for you was but a step away. I looked into your eyes and took the step."

"Why didn't you tell me then?" he chided gently. "Think of the time we've lost."

Julie tipped back her head to look at him. "Would you have believed me? And if you had, you would have suffered because you had sworn to marry Maryka." She smiled. "Besides, why should I be better than you? All I know about your feelings is secondhand information."

"If I tell you my feelings, I will bind you." Theo's face darkened. "How can I bind you to a man who will never be more than half whole? An exile with few prospects?"

"Theo." She shook her head at his foolishness, then smiled. "Then perhaps you should consider binding me to the father of my child."

"What?" Theo stared at her unable to speak.

"It's true. I don't know yet." She smiled. "But I *know*."

Theo looked into her golden eyes and saw all the answers in the gleaming depths.

"I love you, Julie." He traced his fingers over her beloved face. "I love you more than I ever thought it possible to love."

"And I love you." Her mouth curved. "Theo. My love."

He touched his forehead to hers and surrendered his heart into her waiting hands. The tapestry of dreams had become reality.

* * * * *

Harlequin® Historical

WOMEN OF THE WEST

Exciting stories of the old West and the women whose dreams
and passions shaped a new land!

Join Harlequin Historicals every month as we bring you
these unforgettable tales.

May 1995 #270—**JUSTIN'S BRIDE**
Susan Macias w/a Susan Mallery

June 1995 #273—**SADDLE THE WIND**
Pat Tracy

July 1995 #277—**ADDIE'S LAMENT**
DeLoras Scott

August 1995 #279—**TRUSTING SARAH**
Cassandra Austin

September 1995 #286—**CECILIA AND THE STRANGER**
Liz Ireland

October 1995 #288—**SAINT OR SINNER**
Cheryl St.John

November 1995 #294—**LYDIA**
Elizabeth Lane

Don't miss any of our **Women of the West!**

FLYAWAY VACATION SWEEPSTAKES!

This month's destination:

Glamorous LAS VEGAS!

Are you the lucky person who will win a free trip to Las Vegas? Think how much fun it would be to visit world-famous casinos... to see star-studded shows...to enjoy round-the-clock action in the city that never sleeps!

The facing page contains two Official Entry Coupons, as does each of the other books you received this shipment. Complete and return all the entry coupons— **the more times you enter, the better your chances of winning!**

Then keep your fingers crossed, because you'll find out by August 15, 1995 if you're the winner! If you are, here's what you'll get:

- Round-trip airfare for two to exciting Las Vegas!
- 4 days/3 nights at a fabulous first-class hotel!
- $500.00 pocket money for meals and entertainment!

Remember: The more times you enter, the better your chances of winning!*

*NO PURCHASE OR OBLIGATION TO CONTINUE BEING A SUBSCRIBER NECESSARY TO ENTER. SEE REVERSE SIDE OF ANY ENTRY COUPON FOR ALTERNATIVE MEANS OF ENTRY.

VLV KAL